Love Finds You

in

Holiday
Florida

Love Finds You

in

Holiday

Florida

BY SANDRA D. BRICKER

summerside
PRESS

Summerside Press, Inc.
Minneapolis 55438
www.summersidepress.com
Love Finds You in Holiday, Florida
© 2009 by Sandra D. Bricker

ISBN 978-1-935416-25-8

Scripture references are from the following source:
The New King James Version (NKJV). Copyright © 1982
by Thomas Nelson, Inc. Used by permission.

The town depicted in this book is a real place, but all characters
are fictional. Any resemblances to actual people or events are
purely coincidental.

Cover and interior design by Müllerhaus Publishing Group
www.mullerhaus.net.

Back cover photo of Holiday, Florida, taken by Jim Beck.

Fall in love with Summerside.

Printed in USA.

Acknowledgments

....

Love and gratitude to the folks at The Joy FM in Central Florida
for always providing the soundtrack to my creativity
and the encouragement to my spirit.

Special blessings to
the folks at Lost Angels Animal Rescue
for bringing a real-life clown named Sophie into my life—
and for the work you do on behalf of dogs like her
every day of the year.

Dedication

....

Marian:
I meant to make you laugh, not cry.
But thank you for always thinking I'm brilliant.

Special thanks to
David, Debby, Jemelle, Loree, and Debra (my #1 fan)
for feeding my confidence along the way.

Nestled near the bigger town of New Port Richey and the Greek tourist haven of Tarpon Springs, Holiday, Florida, is winding boulevards lined with tall palm trees reaching toward vivid blue skies and cotton-ball clouds; it is wildlife at its strangest, from snakes and frogs to flawless (albeit quite bold) white birds called egrets; and it is sleepy canals punctuated by lonely wooden docks. I live in Tampa, Florida, just half an hour away from Holiday, and while I was there soaking up the atmosphere, I saw things that really tickled my funny bone (a good break since I was writing a comedy!). Three elderly women power walked down the middle of the street in front of my car, all of them wearing neon spandex and sporting visors and fanny packs. I saw mailboxes fashioned out of fish faces, alligator jaws, and tree trunks; I encountered manicured gardens decorated with neon-pink flamingos; and one very talkative resident put the icing on the cake of my inspiration. In the ten years since I've moved here, I couldn't count the times that I've compared Florida residency to life on another planet! I'm pretty sure Holiday proves that the comparison isn't far off.

Sandra D. Bricker

Prologue

....

Cassie rounded the curve of the street and pulled into the driveway, and there they were! Those horrible, neon-pink flamingos, grinning at her from beneath the palm tree in the front yard. Just that morning, she'd deposited them in the trash receptacle, hoping that would be the end of them. Though something told her she would never be rid of them.

Oh, what a thought!

As she climbed out of the car and stalked toward them, the horror of it buzzed around her like a swarm of gnats. The picture was a vivid one: sitting on the back deck in her old age, sipping one of those terrible Southern beverages Zan was always experimenting with, her silver hair standing on end and frizzy from the Florida humidity. And poking out from beneath the dock…or peering at her from around the side of the house…or possibly standing tall in one of the large flowering plants…those eyes. Those gawking black eyes, just staring back at her, mocking her with their presence.

Cassie yanked the first one out of the ground, where its hard plastic spike anchored it to the front yard, and she tossed it on the grass behind her. Just as she wrapped both hands around the beak of the second one, Zan's laughter taunted her from across the street.

She turned her head slowly toward him, narrowed her eyes, and stared him down, the distance between them bridged by a look her husband had come to know all too well.

11

"Hi, baby," he called out to her, grinning as maniacally as those flamingos he loved so much. "Want some help carrying in the groceries?"

Lounging on the front step of Millicent's porch with his faithful dog, Sophie, at his side, Zan could surely be spotted from the space shuttle in that colorful Hawaiian-print shirt. He waved his arms at her, and the old woman in the rocking chair began to wave as well.

"Hello, Cassie!"

Cassie planted both feet and faced him, with her hands on her hips. "Alexander Constantine, I won't have these horrible things displayed in the front yard. What will the neighbors think of us?"

"Ah, come on, Mac. They'll think we're kitschy. Don't you want to be known as kitschy?"

"I certainly do not."

And with that, she turned her back on him and pulled hard on the beak of the second flamingo—so hard, in fact, that she fell right on her fanny when the bird's spike broke free of the ground.

Zan jogged across the street, laughing the whole way, with Sophie trotting at his heels and pitching out happy little fragmented barks as if they were playing a wonderful new game.

Zan reached her in the next minute. "Come on, Mac. Have a heart. When in Holiday, do as the Holidaens do."

Cassie leaned back into the grass on both elbows and looked up at him, taking in that horrible shirt, the shorts to his knees, and the unmistakable bright blue rubber flip-flops.

"I think you're Holidaen enough for the both of us," she remarked. "What were you conspiring with Millicent about?"

"You know she's my favorite girl after you, Deb, and Sophie."

"Yes, I do, and I'm not sure about the order we place, either," she said, glancing at the orange-and-golden-haired collie standing over her. Sophie wiggled her big ears that flopped over at the tips and wagged her large plumed tail at some hilarity only dogs and her husband could sense. "So what were you charming out of Millicent this time, Zan? A recipe for a kiwi mint julep? Pink lemonade with pineapple chunks?"

Zan grinned as he stood over her, and he reached out for her hands. He planted a kiss on each one and then pulled her to her feet.

"Please let me toss the birds in the trash, Zan."

"If you must."

"Really?"

"Toss away, Mac."

Cassie narrowed her eyes and stared him down. It was almost too easy. But she wasn't going to pass up a golden opportunity if, by some miracle, he was feeling charitable about her animosity for those horrible pink flamingos-on-a-stick.

"Thank you," she said.

As she bent over to pick them up, Zan smacked her on the tush.

"Sophie and I will unload the car," he told her, before waving his arms over his head at Millicent. "Catch you later, Millie!"

"Not if I see you first," she teased.

Happy 25th Anniversary to my Cassie. From your Zan.

Chapter One

. . . .

4 ACROSS: Neat; tidy; organized

"I know you, Mom, and I wanted to talk to you before you started the whole house decorating thing."

Cassie tapped the handset and turned serious. "What whole house decorating thing? Debra, I find it laughable that you think I'm so predictable."

"Oh, come on." Debra chuckled from the other end of the phone line. "Tell me you haven't already gone up into the attic and pulled out the boxes of ornaments and garland, or that you haven't been sitting at the kitchen table making your list for Christmas Eve dinner."

Cassie set her coffee cup on the table with a *thump* and brushed aside the spiral notebook in front of her.

"I'm sorry, Mom. Zach is one of the wise men in the church play, and Jake is going to his seventh-grade dance with that little blond girl he's had a crush on since the third grade. I just can't make them miss any of it. Why don't you come here for Christmas instead? You could see the play, and we could go shopping at the new outlet mall."

Cassie smiled. "I've been wondering about doing something different this year anyway. Like maybe going down to the house in Holiday."

Debra cackled. "Are you serious?"

"Yes. Why?"

"Well, Daddy talked about going down there for Christmas every year since I can remember, and you wouldn't hear of spending the holiday in 80-degree weather."

"Well, he loved to wear those horrible shorts when he went down to Florida," Cassie explained, tucking her hair behind her ear. "I couldn't spend the Christmas holiday with your father walking around in those plaid Bermuda shorts."

"I can still hear him trying to talk you into it." Debra chuckled. In her gravelly Zan impersonation, she added, "'Come on, Mac. Just one Christmas out of all the others that we'll spend in Boston.'"

Debra's laughter was lyrical, and Cassie's hand floated to her heart as a mist of tears glazed her eyes. With a sniff, she fought them back. Zan had called her *Mac* since the time they first met. She was Cassie MacLean then, but the only time he ever called her by her given name was on the morning they'd recited their wedding vows and then once each year on their anniversary. The rest of their lives, she was just *Mac*. She'd almost forgotten, but Debra's casual reference to the nickname brought Zan flooding back to her.

"I've been thinking about selling the Florida house anyway. This will give me time to get it ready."

"Selling it? Really?"

"Debra Constantine Rudolph, don't you give me that weepy reaction to selling the Holiday house after all the years that have passed since you've been there."

"I know, I just…" She trailed off, and Cassie smiled.

"*I just*, too. But it's not practical. None of us ever go down there, honey, and the upkeep on a three-bedroom house in Florida that we never use anymore is just ridiculous. Your father was the one who really loved it anyway. I never shared his vision of walking the golf course on Christmas Eve or of draping colored twinkle lights on those awful plastic flamingos he put in the yard."

"He was a character," Debra commented.

"Yes, he was."

"So you aren't too heartbroken that we won't be coming for Christmas, then?"

"Don't be silly. You have your own family now, honey. You'll make your own traditions. It's the circle of life."

"*Hakuna matata?*" Debra laughed. "That's very *Lion King* of you, Mom."

"Besides, I've hardly given any thought to the holidays yet."

"Thanks, Mom. I love you."

"I love you, too."

Cassie set the handset on the table and leaned back against the metal scrollwork of the dinette chair. Sophie pattered across the kitchen floor with a section of silver Christmas tree garland in her mouth, dragging about three feet of it behind her. When she reached Cassie, she dropped the garland and sighed as she planted her chin on Cassie's knee.

"Thanks for understanding, Soph."

With another sigh, Cassie glanced down the hall at the traffic jam of cardboard boxes overflowing with Christmas decorations. She'd been in the process of sorting tree lights from outdoor strands when Debra had called.

I'm absolutely humdrum, she thought, snagging a quick glimpse of the notebook with an inward groan. *I'm just as predictable as they come!* She looked down at the list.

Roasted turkey—at least twenty pounds
Chestnut stuffing—leave out the celery for Jake
Candied yams—get marshmallows for Zach
Green bean and mushroom casserole—will the kids eat pearl onions now?

She hadn't had time to complete it before Debra had called and accused her of making it. Cassie drew a large *X* across the page and turned the notebook facedown on the table.

As she tucked the lights and garland back into their boxes and sealed the flaps, Cassie counted down the days until Christmas on an invisible calendar before her. With almost three weeks stretched out between lunch with Rachel that afternoon and a lonely Christmas dinner, Cassie began to devise a plan.

A bold and *unpredictable* plan. *Unpredictable* was going to be the name of the game now. No more humdrum for this woman!

By the time Cassie met up with her best friend, Rachel, at the restaurant two hours later, she'd already made plane reservations, reserved a rental car, and made an appointment with Tameka, the lovely real estate agent she and Zan had gotten to know in Holiday. She'd sold them the house, and they'd had dinner a few times with Tameka and her husband, James.

"Are you ser–i–ous?" Rachel enunciated.

Cassie emptied a packet of sweetener into her coffee and stirred it with an ornate silver spoon as she grinned at her friend across the table.

"I'm serious."

"You're going to Florida for Christmas."

"Well," she said, tapping the spoon against the side of the cup and placing it on the saucer, "I'm going to Holiday to get the house ready to go on the market. That shouldn't take more than a couple of weeks. I should finish just in time to spend one Christmas there like Zan always wanted to, say good-bye to the house and all its memories, and come back to Boston just after the new year."

"You're serious."

"Yes!" Cassie exclaimed, nodding her head at Rachel. "I'm serious, already."

"I'm sorry, I just—" Rachel pushed her halo of ash blond curls back from her face and blinked her turquoise blue eyes at Cassie. "Do you think you're ready for this, Cass?"

Cassie reached across the table and took her friend's hand between her own. "He's been gone over a year now, Rach. I think I'd better be ready, don't you?"

"There's no clock timing you on this. You'll be ready when you're ready."

Cassie wanted to reassure her friend. She wanted to declare that the time had indeed come, that she was more than…

Well, there was something to be said for stepping out in faith and *pretending* she was ready, wasn't there? Letting go of Zan and their life together, and moving forward with this new phase, was just not something she could plan out like the rest of the details she was so adept at organizing. And Cassie was a little out of her element there since she felt she could always depend on a good plan when nothing else in life was certain.

"Oh!" she exclaimed, remembering the folded sheet of paper in her purse. "Look what I found."

She dug into her bag, pulled out the paper, smoothed the creases, and laid the page flat on the table between them.

"It's the crossword puzzle Zan gave me on our anniversary, just before he…" Their eyes met, and Rachel cocked her head slightly and tried to smile at her. "You know."

"He was so good at that," Rachel commented. "I'll bet he made as much money selling his crossword puzzles as he did at teaching English lit."

"Not quite," Cassie replied. "But he sure did love to dream them up. Crossword puzzles, word jumbles, searches…Zan just loved words."

"I always thought it was so romantic the way he would give them to you every year on your anniversary," Rachel said on a sigh. "And they'd always describe the wonderful things he saw in you. Hey, let's do it together. Do you want to?"

"I thought I'd take it down to Florida with me and work it there. But we could start it." She looked over the clue list and landed on one. "What's a seven-letter word for neat, tidy, and organized?"

Rachel paused and then grinned. "Cassie?"

"That's six letters."

Just once, she would have loved to come across a clue for a different type of Cassie.

Dangerous.

Rebellious.

Spitfire!

"Orderly," Rachel blurted. "The seven-letter word for *neat* and *organized*. It's orderly."

Orderly. Well, that figures.

Cassie's spirits deflated. She folded up the puzzle and placed it back into the front pocket of her purse.

"I was Christmas shopping on my lunch hour the other day," she said. "I came across the neatest little gift that I thought about getting for Debra, and now I find myself wishing I'd gotten it for myself."

"What was it?"

"It's called a 'Surprise Yourself' box. Have you heard of it?"

"I don't think so."

"It's a beautiful little cut-crystal box with a hinged lid," she explained. "Inside are 365 cards, one for each day of the year. On the front is a scripture verse. And on the back is an instruction for that day. I think it's about applying the Word to your everyday life because it will say something like, 'Visit someone who's sick' or 'Look for an undiscovered talent in yourself.'"

"What a great idea!" Rachel exclaimed.

"I'm sitting here thinking I should have that box. I'd like to do something to surprise myself—or to surprise others, for that matter. Rachel, I'm so predictable."

"This from the woman who just made last-minute reservations to fly to Florida for Christmas."

"The first unexpected thing I've done in twenty years."

"Cass."

"I know! Let's do something crazy now," she suggested. "How about a slice of pie?"

"Want to split?"

"Nope. I want my own. And I'm having…pumpkin!"

"Whoa," Rachel teased. "Let's not go completely crazy too fast. At least forego the whipped cream."

"Nope. I'm having pumpkin, and I want whipped cream."

"All righty then."

"Fasten your seat belt, Rach, because I'm having a cappuccino with it."

The waiter stepped up beside them, and Rachel smiled at him. "You might want to call security. I don't even know this woman. She's absolutely…zany."

Ooh, ZANY. There's a word I wish Zan would have used in one of his Cassie puzzles.

Boston was dusted with snow, with temperature in the upper twenties, when Cassie got on the plane bound for Tampa International Airport. She'd had a hard time finding clothes to pack for a 50-degree difference in weather, but she figured she could pick up a few things once she arrived. And there was always the array of clothes still hanging in her Florida closet. If only she could remember what was there.

After collecting one suitcase and one dog at baggage claim, Cassie took care of her car rental and was on her way. Sophie claimed her spot in the back seat and lay down, her little front paws crossed in front of her, swiping Cassie's hand with one affectionate lick as she belted her in. Sophie appeared just as prim and ladylike as a dog with floppy pointed ears could be, in that moment anyway. Never mind the laps she'd taken around the backyard that morning, figure eights at 150 miles per hour, with her new plush reindeer toy hanging out the side of her mouth. Not so ladylike then. More like a commercial for doggie NASCAR.

At last Cassie climbed in behind the wheel and was on her way. She took a wrong turn from the airport somehow and ended up driving miles out of the way and across a bridge above the deep green Gulf, eventually stopping in St. Petersburg on the other side. A gas station attendant pointed her back again, in the direction of Tampa and across what he called the Howard Frankland Bridge, and he sold her a map that would lead her to Holiday from there. She hadn't been to Florida in such a long time, and Zan had always been the driver back then, so not much of anything looked more than marginally familiar all the way out to New Port Richey.

All that changed, however, when she rounded the curve of the road and finally saw the disfigured little sign that announced with no pomp or circumstance at all the entrance to Holiday, Florida. Around the battered golf course, past the neighbor's very memorable mailbox shaped like a large trout…then two bumps and a pothole later, she pulled into her driveway and turned off the ignition.

Oh, there they are, she thought, dropping her head back against the headrest with a laugh. *Those ugly plastic flamingos, leaning sideways in the garden.*

Zan had picked them up at a local grocery store and they'd argued all the way home about displaying them, finally agreeing to leave them in the backseat of the car until they could come to some understanding. The next morning, however, Cassie had taken her coffee out on the deck—and there they were, poking out of the enormous planters on either side of the wooden dock leading out to the Anclote River.

After that, the flamingos had become pawns in an ongoing game. Cassie had tossed them into the trash can at the side of the house one morning, and that afternoon they'd turned up on the front lawn. Once she'd hidden them in the shrubs at the back of the house, but the following morning at first light, there they were again, peeking through the bedroom window. On their last visit to Holiday, Cassie had noticed the horrible things poking out of the tall flowers in the garden as she and Zan pulled out of the drive and headed for the airport, just where the birds were still.

She'd pumped the door handle and her feet hadn't even flattened against terra firma when she heard it.

"Cas–sie? Hun–ny bunny? Is that you?"

Millicent headed across the street toward her, toddling at a speed that defied her seventy years, reflecting the sun with her neon-pink bike shorts and matching visor and the fanny pack around her waist plop-plop-plopping against her hip with each eager step.

"Hi, Millicent."

"Oh, hunny bunny!" the woman exclaimed. "It's been such a long time."

Cinching her arms around Cassie's waist, Millicent rocked her from side to side to side. Squirming her way out of the embrace reminded Cassie of peeling out of a tight, wet bathing suit.

"We were all so sorry to hear about Zan," she said as Cassie popped open the trunk.

"Thank you."

"Are you all right? Doing okay? I stopped Frank Mitchell a few weeks ago when he was over here doing the yard work for you, but he said he didn't have any idea what your plans were or when you'd be coming back. We were all so worried, hunny. It was such a loss, wasn't it? He was such a prankster, your Zan. I'll just never forget him."

"Thank you," Cassie managed, reaching into the back seat and releasing Sophie from the belt.

"Sophie!" Millicent sang as the dog leaped out of the car. Sophie excitedly circled the old woman twice and then ran for a patch of grass. Once she'd done her business, Sophie kicked up some sand from the grass and started to run. As usual, she looped around the palm tree and back again, mapping out one large figure eight across the lawn. What was it about that dog and the number eight?

"Sophie's very excited to be back," Millicent observed as they watched her.

"I think the dog is a little loopy, if you want to know the truth."

Millicent chuckled as Sophie tore off across the yard again, pausing at the top of her 8-curve to fly into the air and twist around for no apparent reason, as if catching some invisible Frisbee.

Yanking the suitcases from the trunk and snapping up the

handles, Cassie said, "It was a long trip, Millicent. Could we catch up tomorrow?"

"Oh, of course we can. Of course. I'm on my way to meet the girls for miniature golf, but can I bring you over some supper a little later? Something you can just heat up? You won't feel like going out to the market."

"That's so sweet of you, but I thought I'd just order a pizza."

"Oh, you know they don't make pizza down here like they do up North," Millicent objected, wrinkling up her nose and shaking her head. "You don't want a local pizza."

"I really do," Cassie said and laughed. "Call me crazy, but I've actually been looking forward to it."

"Well, if you're sure. Are you sure, bunny?"

"I'm sure. But thank you, Millicent. It's nice to see you again."

The woman didn't move a muscle to leave, so Cassie pulled the suitcases along behind her and headed for the front door.

"We can give you a ride to church on Sunday, if you'd like," Millicent called after her. "There's a scrambled egg breakfast in the rec hall after."

Cassie nodded. She'd almost forgotten the sweet little church on the border of town. She and Zan always looked forward to visiting. The pastor was young and enthusiastic, and he had a hand in providing his congregation with a more active social life than an A-list Hollywood crowd, minus the drugs and alcohol, of course. But Cassie hadn't been too interested in attending church in the last year. Something about walking in alone and sitting there with that big scarlet *W* on her chest.

Widow. The strangest word in the English language.

Cassie turned the key in the lock and then waved at Millicent. Sophie flew past her as she tugged the luggage inside, and the collie had sniffed her way through every room in the house before Cassie even closed the door behind them.

Frank had promised to stop by that morning to air out the house. A lovely cross-breeze between the large window in the living room and the open, screened-in glass doors leading out to the deck told her he'd kept his word. Cassie sighed as she stood in front of the screen and looked out toward the river beyond the wooden dock. She felt a bit like she was standing in the middle of a spot she'd only dreamed about once upon a time. Her home in Boston, her administrative job at the law firm, learning to manage on her own: these had become the things her life was made of. The Holiday house was foreign to her now and yet strangely familiar and comforting at the same time.

A brown anole lizard glided across the deck and stopped at the other side of the screen door, the reddish sack beneath its little reptilian throat pumping. She took an instinctive step back from the screen and then chuckled. Cassie recalled when she'd come to Florida and seen one of the creatures for the first time. She'd screeched when it sped across the patio floor near her foot, and the ruckus drew out several of the neighbors. She'd been mortified when they explained to her that an anole was as common in this setting as a lightning bug would be up North.

"It's part of the fabric of Southern living," Zan had assured her. "Nothing to be afraid of."

That might have been comforting if the news that evening hadn't highlighted another aspect of Southern living with a story about a three-foot lizard of some kind standing guard on a local's patio. Cassie recalled that she hadn't been able to sleep all night.

When the lizard on the other side of the screen door suddenly sprinted into action, Cassie jumped, her distant memories shattering as she backed away from the door. Even reminding herself that she was fifty-five years old—*not five*—and she probably looked like Godzilla to the tiny thing, she still couldn't shake off the shiver that ran up her spine and tingled the top of her head. Little lizards running around wherever they wanted to go, well, that was just wrong somehow. Like so many other things about Holiday, Florida, it made the place seem like a primitive foreign country to her, and Cassie was quite certain she would never adjust to it.

She grabbed the handle on her suitcase and tugged it behind her down the hall and into the master bedroom. The moment she stepped through the doorway, the past was there to meet her once again, engulfing her like a torrential wind and carrying the whisper of Zan's laughter around her into a spun shell of memories. Cassie folded in half and collapsed to the edge of the bed, still gripping the pull handle extended from her luggage.

Sophie hopped up on the bed beside her.

"No, Soph. Get down."

The dog reluctantly jumped to the floor but cozied up to Cassie's leg and planted her chin on her knee. The way she looked up at Cassie, those big golden brown eyes wide and glassy, it sort of seemed like Zan's dog was missing him at that moment, too.

She pulled Sophie's favorite toys from the zippered pocket of her suitcase and tossed them toward the large round doggie bed in the corner. Sophie chased them and moved from one to the other. She couldn't seem to decide between the reindeer, the squeaky ball, and the floppy dog.

Cassie shook the nostalgia from her head, nudged the suitcase toward the closet, and popped to her feet. "Dinner," she said out loud.

Sophie grabbed the ball with the corner of her long, pointy collie mouth and then tucked the reindeer into the other side, squeaking them both incessantly as she hurried down the hallway and into the kitchen in pursuit of Cassie. Cassie was scanning the business cards anchored to the freezer door with funny little ceramic magnets. She plucked off the brightly colored mermaid Zan had bought at the Weeki Wache Springs mermaid show, a bizarre little roadside attraction that drew curious patrons from far and wide, and she took down the card it anchored.

A Pizza Holiday was a little hole-in-the-wall at one of the strip malls on the edge of the small town—a place she never would have considered frequenting in Boston—but Zan had insisted on it the afternoon they closed on the Holiday house. At the local establishment, they'd discovered an unexpected chef specialty called "The Popeye," a concoction of spinach, feta cheese, mushrooms, and sausage that had them coming back for more every time they returned to Florida.

"A Pizza Holiday, where every meal with us is like an Italian holiday. How can I help you?"

"That's a mouthful to have to say when you answer the phone," Cassie commented.

"Yeah, my dad owns the place. It's not like I have a choice," the girl returned grimly.

"Vanessa?"

"Yes? And who's this?"

"This is Cassie Constantine, Vanessa. The last time I saw you, you were folding napkins at the counter and your feet didn't even touch the floor. How old are you now?"

"I'm sixteen," she replied. "Are you guys down for the Christmas break? You haven't been in for a long time."

You guys. Cassie's heart pinched.

"Well, I am. My husband passed away."

"He did? I'm so sorry. I didn't know."

"Thank you," she replied. "I think I'd like to get a pizza delivered."

"The Popeye?"

"Yes."

"Large with extra sausage?"

"Oh, no. Small, please. With extra spinach."

"And would you like—"

"Vanessa, hang on, please."

The earsplitting grinding of metal against wood, not to mention Sophie's insistent barking, forced Cassie to the screen door, where she peered outside just in time to see a large pontoon boat take off the end of her dock.

"I'm sorry," she said into the phone. "I'll have to call you back."

Cassie closed her phone and set it on the table behind her before rushing outside and jogging halfway down the dock, her barking dog at her heels. Cassie had forgotten how *colorful* everything was in Holiday, including the residents. But her immediate reminder stood at the edge of the boat in the person of Georgette Hootz, with her shocking orange hair and lipstick to match, shielding her eyes with a fuschia golf-gloved hand as she waved at Cassie with unusual vigor.

"Cassie? Is that you? George, look, it's Cassie Constantine."

"Who?"

"Zan's wife."

"Eh?"

"Oh, you old coot."

Georgette hoisted herself over the side and scaled the broken dock before taking off at a full waddling run toward her. Sophie met her at the end of the dock and sniffed at her knees the whole way up the platform.

"Hi, little Sophie. How have you been?" As Georgette headed for Cassie, full steam ahead, she exclaimed, "So sorry about your dock! George has to have cataract surgery next month, and he just can't see like he used to."

"Is anyone hurt?" Cassie asked her.

"Oh, we're dandy. It's just the dock that needs a medic."

Cassie swallowed a gulp of unspoken retort just as Georgette reached her and hugged her so tightly that her air pushed up past her ribs and forced out a groan.

"We were so sorry to hear about Zan," she cried, as she shook Cassie from side to side. "He was such a good man. I asked George, 'Whatever is Cassie going to do without him?' Are you doing all right, dear? Have you got things in order for yourself?"

"I'm working on it."

Over Georgette's shoulder, Cassie watched as a lean but muscular man with sun-kissed chestnut hair—definitely *not* George Hootz!—stepped up from the pontoon over the broken edge of the dock. He was wearing knee-length khaki linen shorts and a bright blue knit shirt, tan deck shoes, and dark, rectangular sunglasses. After a moment, he turned back to the boat and offered a hand, pulling George up to the dock alongside him.

Cassie lost her breath again, but not because Georgette had squeezed it out of her.

"Who's that with George?" she asked as the man leaned over and tickled Sophie on top of her head.

Georgette released Cassie and turned around with a smile. "That's Richard," she said. Then she cranked up that frantic wave of hers. "He bought the Kleinbeck place a few blocks over from us a couple of years ago. Widower, addicted to chasing those tiny white balls around on the golf course. Naturally. I suppose no man comes to Florida without golf on his mind. Oh, and he's a ballroom dancer like you wouldn't believe."

Ballroom—

"Sorry about your dock," George offered, scratching his silver head as he approached with Richard. "Seems a little farther out into the canal than I remembered."

"George Hootz, that dock did not move since the last time we were out here," Georgette chastised him. "You old coot."

"Hen," he returned, and Georgette waved him off with a sour grimace.

"Richard Dillon, meet Cassie Constantine."

He lowered his glasses to reveal blue eyes that actually sparkled. His chiseled features narrowed at the jawline, and he had those charming Dennis Quaid sort of parentheses on either side of his grin, making it seem like his entire face smiled right along with his lips. Cassie thought it odd that those simple parentheses made her heart beat a little faster.

"Pleased to meet you."

"Is everyone all right?" she asked as she shook his hand.

"Well, my bursitis has been acting up this week," George replied. "Usually means we're looking for some rain in the forecast."

"That's not what she's asking, George. She means from the collision with the dock."

Richard caught Cassie's eye, grinned, and then replaced his sunglasses.

"Oh, that," George answered back. "It was just a little tap. That dock hadda be pretty rotten to crumble the way it did."

A strange sucking sound drew their attention just then, and they all turned back toward the canal. Just about the time Cassie realized that the boat seemed lower, it rocked back and forth and then moved lower still.

"What in the world—?"

Sophie raced to the edge of the dock and let out a few concerned barks, but before any of the humans could say another word, the pontoon boat with the bright yellow striped awning disappeared beneath the water with a belch.

Chapter Two

....

11 DOWN: One who can be trusted to advise

"Pass your bowl for succotash, dear."

Cassie reluctantly obeyed, and Georgette dipped a large spoon into the Crock-Pot and poured a heaping serving of meat and vegetables into the bowl over a scoop of limp egg noodles.

Georgette closed her eyes and put a hand on each of their shoulders. "Lord, bless the food, bless the guests; bless our homes and bless our rest. Amen."

"Poetic," Richard commented, and Cassie grinned.

"The Crock-Pot is the greatest invention of our time," Georgette informed them as she reached for Richard's bowl. "There's no messing it up, no matter what it is. You just toss it into the pot, leave for the whole day, and come home to a hot and hearty meal. It's amazing, really. Do you have a Crock-Pot, Cassie?"

"I think I do. I don't really use it much—"

"Oh, you should. You must. I have a cookbook…."

Georgette toddled into the kitchen and rummaged around.

"Georgette has a cookbook for everything," Richard said on half a whisper. "For my birthday, I got *Putt-Putt Meals*. Meals that make themselves while the chef is on the golf course."

Cassie snickered but reeled it back just as Georgette returned to the table.

"Here it is," she said, displaying a book for them as she read from the cover. "*From Artichokes to Zucchini.* One hundred healthy Crock-Pot meals for vegetarians and carnivores alike."

Cassie's eyebrows arched over widened eyes, and she nodded in slow motion. "Carnivores. That's...really...*interesting.*"

"Here, you can borrow it," Georgette insisted, handing her the book.

"Well, actually, my Crock-Pot is at my house in Boston. I don't think I'll be—"

"Then you take it home with you when you go. You can always mail it back to me. Oooh, or better yet, we could make a trip down to Bealls first thing tomorrow and get you one for use right here in Holiday!"

"Oh, Georgette, that's so nice of you, but—"

"Supper's on, George," the woman called out to her husband, who was already asleep in the living room recliner. Turning back to Richard and Cassie, she said, "You two dig in. I'll go wake the old coot."

Cassie tried to serve up a bite from her bowl, but the egg noodles slipped right through the tines of her fork.

"I'm thinking a spoon," Richard suggested, waving his own utensil at her.

He demonstrated, digging down into the bowl and bringing a heaping bite to his lips, his spoon overflowing. A noodle dangled over the side, so he stuck out his tongue beneath it and then clumsily dropped the contents into his open mouth.

"Oh, good," she said on a nod, and Cassie dipped her own spoon into the bowl with better results.

Once she had an overflowing bite at the ready, she glanced at Richard. His blue eyes were narrowed in response to that first taste he'd taken, and actually…they'd gone a bit gray. His nose and mouth were crumpled, and he shook his head at her emphatically.

"No?"

"Uh-uh. No."

While Georgette clomped toward the table, she created a quick tunnel through the succotash with the back of her spoon and pasted a smile on her face as she looked up.

"How is it? Delish, right?" Georgette asked them, slipping into the chair across from Richard.

"Mmm." Cassie nodded.

Georgette filled George's bowl and placed it before him as he joined them at the table.

"What is it?" he asked, staring down into his dinner. "Looks like slop."

"I told you. Hearty beef succotash over a bed of noodles." Cassie imagined that's just the way they'd described it in the *Hearty Crock-Pot Meals for You and Your Old Coot* cookbook.

George looked up at Cassie and squinted. "The wife loves her Crock-Pot. She tell ya about the joys of Crock-Pot cooking yet?"

Cassie nodded.

"Yeah. The greatest invention of our time—she tell ya that?"

"Oh, hush up and eat your supper," Georgette reprimanded him. "There's rainbow sherbet for dessert."

"Mm, none for me," Richard said after wiping his mouth with a napkin and then draping his nearly full bowl with it. "Thank you so much for the wonderful dinner, but I've got to be heading home." Looking at Cassie, he added, "Thank you for the ride over here."

"Don't be silly," she exclaimed, jumping up to her feet. "I'll give you a lift before I head home myself."

"Are you sure? I don't mind walking, but if you're sure…"

"Of course."

"Neither of you wants rainbow sherbet?" Georgette asked them, as if they'd lost their ever-lovin' minds.

"Oughta serve sherbet first," George said, pushing the concoction around in the bowl in front of him. "Coats the stomach."

"Hush."

"Thank you for dinner," Cassie said, giving Georgette a hug. "I couldn't eat another bite."

The woman's eyes darted toward the full bowl in front of Cassie, and she frowned.

"I had a really late lunch," she lied.

"Sorry about the dock," George interjected between surprisingly enthusiastic spoonfuls of succotash. "I'll get somebody out there in the morning to pull up the pontoon."

How about someone to repair my dock? she thought, knowing full well that he had no intention of going that far.

"Ready?" Richard asked her.

"Ready."

Georgette walked them out the door and down the driveway, bidding them good night the whole way. She stood there, with the streetlight turning her bright orange hair into a sort of neon sign and her arm becoming somewhat spastic, as she waved good-bye.

Cassie stopped at the corner and asked, "Which way? And hurry, before she realizes I left the cookbook behind and takes off after us."

"Left. Unless you're still as hungry as I am. Then take a right, and we can make a run for sustenance."

Cassie yanked the wheel to the right and hit the gas. "That sounds fantastic. Have you ever eaten at A Pizza Holiday? I was in the middle of ordering from them when my dock jumped out into the canal and hit George's boat."

"Ha!"

"I have such a taste for their pizza. I've been thinking about it for days."

"Sounds fine. I can't remember the last time I had pizza."

Just a few minutes later, they pulled into the empty parking lot and noticed that the tiny restaurant was dark. A sign on the door announced that they closed at 9 p.m. on weeknights and 11 p.m. on Fridays and Saturdays.

"It's after nine o'clock?" Cassie asked.

Richard tapped his watch. "It's not even seven thirty."

They both stared straight ahead in silence for several seconds before Cassie said, "How about Benny's?"

"Really?" he asked with a bit of a scowl before shrugging. "All right. I'll try that."

"You've never eaten there before?"

"I don't really experiment much with the local cuisine. I like to prepare my own food whenever I can. That way I know what's in it."

Cassie resisted the urge to inquire further but turned the car toward Benny's Coffee Shoppe. Once inside, she started to get the idea that Richard Dillon wasn't exaggerating about his aversion to the local restaurants—or to other people preparing his food. She watched, fascinated, as he ran a napkin around the rim of his water glass and then used it to wipe down his flatware.

"So," he said, breathing on the butter knife in his hand and then polishing it with his napkin, "what's your story? How long have you lived here in Holiday?"

For a moment she remained silent, enrapt as he set down the knife and continued his mission to rid the world of water spots, this time focusing on his fork.

"Um, I don't really live here. When my husband was alive, we bought a winter home in Holiday. We spent a few weeks a year down here until he passed away. Now I'm just back to get it ready for the real estate market."

"It's not exactly a seller's market these days," he observed, as he pressed a second napkin meticulously flat against the edge of the table and then placed it on his lap.

"I'm in no real hurry," she replied. "The place needs some work, so I'll concentrate on that while I'm here. Afterward, I guess it will sell when it sells."

"You mentioned earlier that you're from Boston."

"Yep. Born and raised."

"What a great town!" he exclaimed. "I know the place pretty well."

"Really! Did you grow up in the area?"

"I suppose I did, but not in the sense you mean." She could see that he was teasing, but Cassie didn't quite get the joke. "I actually went to school—"

"Are you ready to order?" the waitress asked, plucking the pencil from behind her ear and tapping the eraser on the edge of the table.

"Club sandwich," Cassie replied. "Light on the mayo. Fries. And iced tea, no lemon."

"And for you?" the woman asked Richard.

"Egg white omelet," he answered. "Spinach, mushrooms, onion. What kind of cheese do you have?"

"American and cheddar."

"That's it?"

"That's it."

"Cheddar, I guess."

"Toast?"

"Rye."

"We've got white or wheat."

Richard frowned. "Wheat."

"To drink?"

"Coffee?" he asked hopefully.

"Of course."

"Decaf."

"Decaf it is." She stuck the pencil back over her ear and sauntered away.

The left side of Cassie's mouth twitched, but she forced the smile back into hiding as Richard glanced at her.

"What about you?" she managed. "What brought you to Holiday?"

"Early retirement," he answered. "My wife and I planned for it from the time we were first married. Everything we did was about where we would retire and how early we could do it. We'd hoped for the wine country in northern California for a while, but we could cut off eight years if we came to Florida instead. The cost of living in California has really skyrocketed, over the last decade in particular."

"So your wife moved here with you?"

"No."

She waited for an explanation. Just about the time she decided she wasn't going to get one, Richard clicked his tongue and sighed.

"Half of the house was packed up for our move down here, and the Realtor had a buyer for the place in Philadelphia. But just three days after I retired from the firm, Caroline passed away."

"Oh, I'm so sorry."

"She'd dropped her purse when we were leaving my retirement party. When she bent down to get it, she smacked her head on the corner of the car door. She said she was fine, and we never connected the dots when she had a headache the next day."

Cassie's heart lurched. *How horrible!*

"Two days later, she was gone."

What did a person say at a moment like this? Cassie's mind was blank.

"All those plans we made. For almost thirty years, we saved and planned and scheduled for one specific day. But before the day could even arrive…"

He didn't finish the thought, but he didn't need to. Cassie understood everything he wasn't able to say.

"I am so sorry," she told him with sincerity.

"We were just a breath away from having everything we'd planned for. It rocks your faith, you know?" he said.

"I do know." *Better than I could tell you.* "I lost my husband suddenly, too," she admitted. "One morning you just wake up and look around you and realize, *I'm fifty-five years old, and I am completely alone.* I never thought I'd be alone at this age."

The silence that crept up on them was broken as the waitress plunked their plates on the table between them. As she filled Richard's coffee cup, he asked for more creamer, and it came out as a raspy whisper that he had to repeat so that she could hear him.

"Sorry," he said. "More cream, please?"

"Sure thing."

Richard waved good-bye to Cassie and slipped his key into the lock on the front door. Once inside, he dropped his keychain into the large ceramic bowl on the buffet, paused to sprinkle some food into the tropical fish tank, and then sat down at the upright piano in the corner of the living room. He began to play somewhat mindlessly, and it turned into Chopin without any forethought at all.

Cassie Constantine dogged his thoughts with her smooth brown hair, apple-cheeked smile, and very *northern* porcelain skin. She'd revealed her age with the same unabashed confidence with which she'd ordered a club sandwich and fries after 7 p.m. Not that she probably had to worry much about calories on her small frame. But didn't all women worry about calories?

Richard stopped playing and pulled at both knobs to unfold the varnished keyboard cover before heading in for a shower. He'd hoped his thoughts of Cassie would stay behind in the living room, but they followed him like a boisterous puppy nipping at his heels.

The woman was a dichotomy of straight-laced and...*and what? Carefree*, he decided.

She was so different from the other women he'd met since moving to Florida. Most of them were over sixty and somewhat leathered by the southern sun. One of them had shown particular interest in him, but despite his propensity for judging a book by its contents rather than its cover, he just couldn't seem to get past the fact that she had the undeniable and somewhat repulsive face of a barn owl.

God, forgive me. But Maureen Heaton is not easy to look at.

Cassie Constantine, on the other hand, was a deep breath of crisp air. She was very *Bostonian* in her appearance and refined demeanor, seeming to watch him with the discriminating eye of a teacher sizing up an unruly student, and yet there was something disarming about her, too.

Richard couldn't decide whether she was really interesting or just a little bit off-putting, but he was leaning toward the latter. He hadn't noticed, at first, the way she scrutinized him when he cleaned up his silverware, not until he laid his napkin across his lap and caught her trying to conceal a smile that was ever so slightly flavored with superiority. Just the very fact that she'd chosen a place like Benny's for a meal should have told him right up front that she wasn't someone he wanted to spend much time with anyway.

So why was he still sitting there thinking about her?

Perhaps it was because she'd come off so genuine and concerned when he'd talked about losing Caroline. Richard didn't even know why he'd felt compelled to tell her all that, but her response was thoughtful and empathetic, and she hadn't made him feel the least bit self-conscious about getting choked up the way he had.

Not until now, anyway.

His throat tightened as he replayed it in his mind. He'd never been comfortable with revealing vulnerability, particularly to someone he didn't know well. He wondered what Cassie's perception of him had been tonight. In fact, he couldn't seem to stop speculating about that, and he rewound portions of their conversation again and again throughout the night. Thoughts of Cassie lingered in a tangled knot in his chest until he finally drifted off to sleep sometime after 3 a.m., and the weight of it was still there when he opened his eyes again at sunrise.

I'm either going to marry her, he thought as he propelled himself across the surface of the pool with lap after lap, *or I'm going to have to take measures to keep her as far away from my life as possible.*

Since he had no intention of marrying Cassie Constantine— or anyone else for that matter—Richard's choice was simple.

Until after breakfast, anyway.

When he phoned the Hootzes and learned that they were on their way to Cassie's house to meet the salvage crew, Richard jumped into his car and sped over to join them.

"I wasn't expecting to see you this morning," Cassie said after he rounded her house and walked across the lawn toward them.

"I thought George might need some backup," he said. He smacked the older man on the shoulder with a smile. "How are they doing with bringing up the pontoon?"

George grumbled something indiscernible and then slipped away from Richard's greeting and stalked closer to the edge of the dock to watch the action.

"I don't know why we're bothering to bring the thing up," Georgette piped up. "It's not like it's going to be in any condition to use again."

"Well, we can't just leave it there under the water with the end of my dock," Cassie offered. "That can't be the thing to do." Then she looked to Richard with a hopeful expression. "Right?"

"Well…I guess—uh—" He was coming up with nothing, so he just shrugged and followed George to the end of the dock.

The salvage men were tossing around terms like "ballast weight" and "flotation bags," but Richard didn't understand them. He just stood next to George, trying to look as if he did. He wondered if Cassie had figured out that he didn't have a nautical bone in his entire body, which caused him to stick out in Central Florida like a thumb that had been tapped by a weighty anvil.

Ask me about golf, he thought. *You want to excavate a ball from a sand trap? I'm your guy. Have a craving for useless golf trivia? Just say the word. Who holds the record for the most Ryder Cup appearances? Nick Faldo. Who has the most PGA tour wins? Sam Snead! Second to Sam? Jack Nicklaus.*

"How about you, Richard?"

"What? Beg your pardon?"

"Lemonade," Cassie said. "Would you like some?"

She looked really attractive with her hair piled up on top of her head like that. Richard noticed the loose wisps as the breeze caught them and brushed them against her china-doll face. Her bare shoulders were stained pink from the sun, and when she turned her head, he noticed that the straps of her sundress were going to leave a line if she stood outside much longer. Hadn't anyone educated this woman on the necessity of sunscreen?

"To drink?" she enunciated. "Thir–sty? Some *lem–o–nade*? Yes? No?"

Richard almost gasped, but he caught it before his cool was entirely blown. At least he hoped he had. "No. I mean, yeah, that would be great."

"I'll help you," Georgette chimed in, and she toddled off behind Cassie and followed her to the house.

The dog awaited their arrival from behind the glass door, wagging her plumed tail with such vigor that she looked as if she might fall over.

Richard clamped his eyes shut and cringed as the two women burst into laughter on the other side of the sliding door.

"What's so funny?" George asked him, glancing back toward the house.

"Who knows," Richard commented. "Women."

Chapter Three
....

21 ACROSS: Insightful; pervasive; thorough

"I think you make him nervous," Georgette said as she filled the glasses with ice cubes.

"Oh, I don't think so," Cassie replied. "I think he's just...odd."

"Ooh, a crossword puzzle!" Georgette exclaimed. Cassie turned toward the woman just in time to see her swoop in on Zan's puzzle. Cassie had been working on it earlier that morning. "I love crossword puzzles. Oh, but this isn't from a magazine, is it? Did you make this up yourself?"

"Zan liked to create them. He gave me that one on our anniversary."

"That's a strange anniversary gift, isn't it? And you said *Richard* is odd!"

Cassie shared a laugh with her. "They usually came with flowers or a beautiful dinner or a very thoughtful gift. He'd make one every year, using all the words he thought described me. It was just a thing between Zan and me."

Cassie was glad for the interruption when the doorbell rang, and Sophie chimed in an accompanying announcement. "That's going to be my Realtor!" she shouted over the ruckus. "Would you mind taking the drinks to the men while I meet with her?"

Tameka Plummer was even lovelier and more exotic than Cassie remembered, and she gave the woman an embrace as the Realtor walked through the door. "It's so good to see you!" Cassie said. Turning toward her barking dog, with a stern clip to her voice, she snapped, "Sophie! Quiet."

"This was sitting on your front step," Tameka said, handing her a small cardboard box from Rachel Capshaw in Boston, addressed to her in very familiar, round handwriting. "Cass, James and I were so sorry to hear about Zan. You know how much we loved him."

"Thank you so much."

Pushing her mass of loose, copper-tinted curls away from her radiant dark face, Tameka's chocolate eyes narrowed with sadness. "Are you doing all right, girl?"

"I have more good days than bad now," she replied. "I still miss him, of course. But I'm getting on with things."

"James sends his love to you. He says there's a four-course soul-food dinner at our place with your name on it while you're here."

"Oh, I'm there," Cassie answered with a chuckle.

Tameka linked her arm with Cassie's as they walked into the house.

"Tameka Plummer, meet Georgette Hootz," Cassie said as Georgette headed for the sliding doors with glasses in her hands.

"*Tuh–mee–kah*," Georgette pronounced. "What a beautiful and unusual name. It's a pleasure to meet you, sweetheart."

"You, too," she replied while Cassie pulled the door open for Georgette.

"Thanks, darlin'."

"So you want to put the place on the market?" Tameka asked as Cassie tugged the door shut again.

"Not quite yet, but I'm hoping we can do that around the first of the year. Right now I'd really like it if you would help me decide what improvements to make so I can get top dollar."

"I can do that. Grab a pad of paper to make some notes, and we'll do a walk-through. And try to remember that we're going to concentrate on things that will give you the greatest return on your dollar when you go to sell the place."

Appliances outdated
Consider new kitchen tile (counters okay)
Master bath—overhaul
Speak to Frank—"curb appeal"
Rethink lighting in kitchen and dining room
Paint throughout
Glass sliders—change to French doors?

As Cassie took note of the last suggestion, Tameka watched the excavation efforts on the other side of the glass doors.

"What on earth happened out there?" she asked.

"Oh!" Cassie added *Fix dock* to the list. "My dock apparently grew like Pinocchio's nose, just as the Hootzes were floating by on their pontoon boat."

Tameka's face cracked with laughter.

"Ten minutes later we stood there and watched the thing sink."

"Oh, goodness! That's just…well, *hilarious* is what it is. I'm sorry. But as long as no one was hurt, that is funny!"

"We'll be holding a memorial service for my dock sometime next week, but everyone else escaped unscathed."

"Are they going to fix it?"

Cassie glanced up from her notepad and angled her head. "This is George Hootz we're talking about. I think he's waiting for me to offer to repair his boat. My dock is just what jumped out into the waterway before he could steer out of its path."

Tameka laughed merrily then suddenly squinted into the sunlight and pressed her lips together. "Is that Richard Dillon out there?"

"Yes. Do you know him?"

"I sold him his house. Terrible thing about his wife. What was her name…? Caroline, that's right. Girl, they were the sweetest couple when they came down to Florida and started looking around. And then she had an accident right before they moved in. It was awful." Tameka ran her hand down the front of her dress and then shook her head, leaving her curls dancing for a second afterward. "Hey, before I forget, do you want me to speak to James about helping you with your updates? Business is a little slow right now, so he's available."

"Oh!" Cassie remembered that Tameka's husband was a contractor. "That would be great."

"I'll have him give you a call later today."

"Thank you so much."

Richard poked at the door with his elbow and, when she noticed, Tameka rushed toward it and finished the job. His hands were loaded down with three empty drinking glasses as he stepped inside. "Tameka?" he questioned. He set the glasses down on the counter and turned toward her.

"Richard, how are you?"

"Not too bad," he said, pulling her into a quick embrace. "How about you and James?"

"Busy as ants in a bread box."

"That's a good thing. Are you Cassie's Realtor?"

"Yep. I was just walking through to suggest some improvements to get the place ready for launch."

"Not too much work, I hope," he said, glancing at Cassie.

"About what I expected," Cassie replied.

"Will James do the work?" he asked.

"Some of it, I hope."

"Well, listen, I'd better get on the road or I'll be late for my next appointment," Tameka told them. "Cassie, lunch later in the week?"

"I'd love that."

Tameka blew them both a kiss and floated out the front door.

"I'll take these into the kitchen," Richard said. He picked up the glasses he'd left on the counter and rounded the corner.

"You don't have to do—" Before she could complete the thought, he already had water running into the sink and was washing the glasses. "—that. Well. Okay."

Cassie shrugged and picked up her cell phone and then scrolled through her address book in search of Frank Mitchell's number.

"Hi, Frank. It's Cassie Constantine. I'm going to the nursery this week to pick up some flowers to make the front of the house a little more appealing. I wondered if you could suggest something to green up the grass a little. I was thinking of installing an irrigation system of some kind. Well, give me a call when you get this message so we can discuss it. Thanks. Talk to you later."

"It looks like Bermuda grass."

"I'm sorry…what?"

"Your lawn," Richard said from the other side of the counter, as he dried the last glass. "It looks like Bermuda grass. It's still warm enough that you could probably get away with some overseeding with rye grass. That would keep it looking a little healthier through the winter and shape it up nicely in spring and summer."

Cassie cocked her head and narrowed her eyes. "Are you into landscaping?"

"Golf."

"Golf?"

"I'm into golf. That's what they do with a lot of Southern golf courses because of the challenges of the weather. You'll want to be aware of the water restrictions, too, because they're pretty stringent down here right now."

"Water restrictions?"

"Florida is in a drought. Has been for years, but it's gotten serious enough that they're doling out tickets if you're caught watering your lawn on an off day. A lot of people have given up on the idea of a lush lawn in deference to the new laws about water usage."

"Are you serious?" Cassie had never heard of such a thing! Not allowed to use her own water?

"Your landscaper—that was your landscaper on the phone, right?"

"My lawn guy, yes."

"He'll know about all of this. If you put in a sprinkler system, you can get one that can be programmed to water only on a certain day at a specific time."

Speaking of time, she thought, *you certainly seem to have a lot of it on your hands.*

Georgette opened the slider and poked her head inside. "Shuffleboard tourney at the senior center later today. Want to come along?"

"Thanks, Georgette, I appreciate that. But I've got a lot to take care of here at the house."

"All righty. Have a good one!"

She waved as she and her husband passed the glass door and headed around the side of the house. Cassie noticed that the salvage men were sailing away down the canal, a waterlogged pontoon with a torn yellow awning in tow.

"Oh, good," she commented. "They're finished. Now I just have to worry about who to call to fix the dock. I don't suppose you have any golf-related dock-repair tips for me."

"Sorry. I don't see many docks out on the links."

"A shame."

"Do you play?"

"Play what?"

"Golf," he clarified with a chuckle.

"Oh, no. My husband loved the game, but I've just never been able to figure out the attraction."

"I'll pretend I didn't hear that," he replied, shooting her one of those parenthetical grins that set her heart to pounding. *Ratta-tat-tat-tat*—her heartbeat sounded like an unexpected spray of automatic bullets. "So it looks like you have quite a laundry list of things to do here," Richard continued.

Cassie wondered if he always hopped from topic to topic like that, or if she was just slowed down by that smile of his.

"Yes, it's a little overwhelming. But I'm going to take this afternoon to get organized and make some lists to get a handle on things."

"That's your thing," he observed.

"What?"

"Lists." He pointed to the pad of paper.

"I'm an administrator. I can't do anything without making a to-do list. What was your profession before you retired, Richard?"

"Well, I'm a list-maker, too. I was an attorney."

Cassie chuckled. "I manage a law partnership in Boston."

"No kidding," he replied. "Which one?"

"Denton, Kendrick & Associates."

"I went to law school with Michael Kendrick."

Cassie's hand floated to her mouth in astonishment. "You did, really?" And then came the clarity. "You went to Harvard Law School?"

"Yes, I did."

Well, that explains a lot. Michael Kendrick's propensity for OCD-seasoned perfection was evident in Richard Dillon, as well. *The two of you could have been separated at birth!*

"What a small world," she said instead.

"Indeed."

Cassie chewed on her bottom lip as she ran her finger down the list she'd made. "I'm thinking the painting should come first. So maybe we start with the kitchen and the bathroom…and then replace the chandelier in the dining room?"

"Okay."

"I went to the home improvement store in New Port Richey and bought some things."

James followed her into the dining room and waited, tickling Sophie behind the ear as Cassie rifled through large plastic bags.

"I thought a copper backsplash would be nice in the kitchen, so I got these tiles. I think I'd like to try installing them myself, and I can help with the painting, as well. I ordered a new refrigerator, a new gas range with this *very* Tuscan copper hood, and a dishwasher—this one has no power at all—and they'll come to install everything on Friday."

Cassie caught up with herself, realizing that she was talking a mile a minute, and she smiled at James and sighed. "I'm sorry. I'm on a whole other wavelength with all these details."

"No problem," he replied, but she knew he was probably hoping she would just get to the part that involved him. He was too sweet to say so, though, so he just stood there, attentive and quiet.

Tameka's husband was a really handsome man, over six feet tall, muscular, with dark cinnamon skin, a completely bald head, and a great, confident smile. The two of them made a gorgeous couple, in fact. They looked like a commercial for the middle-class African-American lifestyle.

"They loaded the tiles for the kitchen and bathroom floors into the trunk of my car," she told him. "I got large alabaster ceramic tiles for the kitchen; they kind of look like natural stone. The ones for the master bath are glazed porcelain with a mosaic pattern. If you could carry those in for me, along with the cans of paint, we can go over everything and decide where to start."

James took her car keys and headed through the kitchen door to the garage while Cassie unpacked the copper scrollwork chandelier from its box.

"That's really nice," James commented, as he rolled in a utility dolly loaded with boxes of tiles. "These go in the bathroom, right?"

Cassie looked into the top box and nodded, admiring the deep blue, wine, and gray hues of the oversized mosaic tiles. "Oh, I like them even more now."

James smiled and pushed the dolly forward and down the hall. "The wall sconces and the faucets," he said over his shoulder, "they're for the bathroom, too?"

"Yes," she called back before following him.

Sophie marched behind James, first one direction and then the other, like an obedient soldier. Once those tiles were unloaded and lined up against the bedroom wall outside the master bath, James did the same with the boxes of kitchen tiles, piling them underneath the dividing counter on the dining room side, with Sophie still at his heels.

"Cans of paint," he announced. "Terra Cotta Glaze goes in the kitchen?"

"Yes."

"Café au Lait?"

"Dining room."

"Seafoam Blue."

At once they both replied, "Bathroom."

James was an amiable workmate. He had everything in its proper corner of the house in less than thirty minutes and then began sorting out the supplies for painting and grout.

"Where should we start?" she asked him from the dining room floor, surrounded by the hammered copper tiles with the gun-metal glaze for the backsplash in the kitchen.

"Looks to me like you have your heart set on starting with the kitchen," he answered, his hand on his hip as he looked down at her.

Cassie giggled. "Zan was Greek, and he liked those very clean lines, pale blues and greens, and lots of *white*. I've always wanted a Tuscan kitchen with those rich, bold colors. Now I get to do that."

"For someone else," he said, laughing.

"For me, until someone else buys the place," she returned.

"That's a lot of work for just a few weeks of enjoyment."

"I didn't say it was logical. So if you're going to try to make *sense* to me, you can just go home right now, buddy."

James chuckled, offered his hand, and pulled her up to her feet.

"Let's get started then."

It was nearly 6 p.m., with James rinsing out the paintbrushes in the sink, when Cassie finally stepped back to admire their work.

The terra cotta walls complemented the light wood of the cabinets, and the small, square copper tiles on the backsplash added interest and texture to the room.

"I'll get an early start on the floor tomorrow," James told her. He gulped back several swigs of water from a glass nearby. "We should have it ready for the appliances by Friday."

"James, thank you so much for all your hard work today."

"Glad to do it," he told her. "But I have a feeling about this house."

"What do you mean?"

"I expect you're going to fix it up so nice that you won't want to move out."

"Oh no," she assured him. "That won't happen. By the time this is all finished, I'll be happy to turn it over to someone else and get back to my life in Boston."

"If you say so."

Once James was gone, Cassie threw together some red seedless grapes and sliced oranges on a plate, warmed up some Brie, and pulled out the whole-grain crackers she'd bought at the store that morning. It seemed like a fitting supper to match her emerging Tuscan kitchen. As she ate, Sophie stretched out on her side and took a nap while Cassie pulled out her crossword puzzle with the thought of chipping away at the clues.

21 Across. Insightful, persuasive, and thorough.

It sounded as if Zan was describing an attorney or a Boy Scout rather than his wife. Frustrated, Cassie folded up the crossword again, and she made a promise to herself to make some plans the very next day to do something unexpected.

But what? she asked herself. Not that it really mattered, as long as it wasn't something *insightful* or *thorough!*

Cassie glanced at the tiles stacked under the counter and then did a double take. She'd forgotten all about the box from Rachel that Tameka had carried in when she'd arrived at the house the previous day. She tossed a grape into her mouth and then lugged the box over to the table, tearing into it. She pulled away the crumpled Christmas wrap that doubled as packing material. Just as she suspected, the box was filled with holiday gifts. On the top was a small envelope with Cassie's name scrolled across it in large round letters.

She paused to spread some cheese on a cracker and pop it into her mouth before opening the card.

I know I'm not Jewish, but there is something to be said for the whole eight-days-of-gifts thing. So you can call yourself Esther and open one each day, or you can save them all for Christmas morning. Either way you go, open the small gold one with the red velvet ribbon today. Right away!

This is the first Christmas that we've been apart in too many years to count. I love you, and I hope you find your bliss this season. Blessings, Rachel.

With all of the activity since her arrival in Florida, Cassie had just about forgotten that Christmas was upon her. She'd been shopping all year for Debra and her family, and it had cost her nearly fifty dollars to mail the gifts before she left Boston. Then she'd given Rachel a gift certificate to their favorite day spa and left all thoughts of Christmas cheer behind her when she boarded the flight to Florida.

She plucked the small gold box with the red velvet ribbon out of its cardboard home and set it down in front of her. After just a few seconds, she picked it up and shook it, first with gentle enthusiasm, and then harder, while holding it up to her ear. Cassie had always possessed a freakish talent for guessing the contents of Christmas packages, but this one wasn't giving any hints at all.

She ate two more grapes and then untied the bow and peeled away the tape. She didn't recognize the significance of the gift at first, but when she opened the box and produced a small crystal box with a hinged lid, a slow smile emerged in crooked little jerks.

It's a "Surprise Yourself" box.

Cassie remembered telling Rachel about wanting one. She eased open the lid, and it creaked slightly. She produced a small, glossy card from inside.

"'God sets the solitary in families,'" she read aloud. "Psalm 68, verse 6."

She turned over the card and read the back of it to herself.

Be a companion to someone who feels alone.

Cassie read the instruction several times and then placed the card back into the crystal box at the very back.

After she finished eating, she kicked off her shoes and padded down the hallway toward her bedroom. She stripped out of her clothes and left them lying on the bed, and then she soaked for nearly an hour in the garden bathtub in the master bath, dreaming wide-awake about the end result of the efforts to transform her surroundings.

One thing's for sure, she thought as she closed her eyes, sank deeper into the hot water, and leaned her head back against the edge of the tub. *Whoever ends up living in this house is going to be one lucky son-of-a-gun!*

Chapter Four

....

3 DOWN: Having keen discernment; ingenious

Cassie had intended to start painting the dining room while
James worked on the kitchen floor that morning, but her interest
waned about forty-five minutes after she'd started the longest wall.
Humming along with the throbbing hip-hop spilling from his iPod,
James matched the rhythm only he could hear with every *tap-tap-
crunch* of old tile removal. So Cassie rinsed out her paintbrush
and opted instead to lace up the Reebok wannabes that had been
in her bedroom closet for an undetermined amount of years. She
tucked the earbuds of her generic MP3 player into place and clipped
Sophie's leash to her collar, and the two of them headed out the
front door.

Cassie hadn't been listening to as much contemporary Christian
music recently as she once did, so she found herself surprised at
that old soaring feeling, an instant connection in her heart, at the
resurgence of a selection that used to be one of her favorites but had
been consistently skipped over in recent months.

She started humming along with Steven Curtis Chapman, and
she'd no sooner put foot to pavement at the end of the driveway
than her plans for taking a run were thwarted by a fast-moving
fanny pack wearing a gray-haired woman.

"Hunny bunny!" Millicent called out to her. Cassie considered pretending she hadn't heard. But reluctant conviction got the better of her, not to mention the tug Sophie was giving the leash as the dog attempted to greet the woman.

Cassie stopped in her tracks and paused the sound track in her ears. "Morning, Millicent."

"How are you settling in? I've seen a lot of activity over there these last couple of days. I don't think I've had that much company in a year's worth of Saturdays."

"Oh, I decided to do a little renovating to get the house ready to sell."

"Sell?" Millicent's round pomegranate face fell faster than a skydiver without a parachute. "You're selling?"

Cassie stroked the woman's arm and then nodded. "Zan was really the one who wanted a place down here. And when Debra was young, we used to love bringing her down. But she's got a family of her own now, and Zan's gone. The upkeep just isn't worth it for a house that's never used."

"Sure," she said. "I understand. I guess I just thought eventually you all might retire and move down here year-round."

"I'm sure my husband had that in mind," Cassie replied with a smile. "But I can't see that happening now."

"You never know, though, do you? You might stick around a week or so and fall in love with the place. It takes a good couple of weeks for Holiday to settle in on you." She gave Cassie a desolate little smile, hopeful in its depth, and then varnished by a clear sense of reality. "That's a shame," she surrendered. "Such a shame."

"Thank you, Millicent. It means a lot to me that you'll miss me when I go."

"You're here now, though, hunny bunny," she brightened. "How about keeping me company over at the church this afternoon? We're having a dance lesson!"

"A dance lesson," Cassie repeated. "Millicent, you don't know how funny that is. I was born with two left feet."

"Oh, you don't have to be any good," she told her. "Just be my other half so I can take the lesson."

"I'm sorry. I have so much to do here."

And there it went again. Her round face deflated and then bunched up like a fist.

"Sure. I understand. I'll see you another day."

Millicent turned away and headed back up her driveway without so much as a glance behind her, and it did something to Cassie as she watched the rigid form move away from her that way.

Right out of nowhere, straight up from the pit of her stomach, the words churned: *Be a companion to someone who feels alone.*

The very first card in her "Surprise Yourself" box. She'd forgotten all about it in the light of day.

"Hey, Millicent," she called out, against her better judgment. "What time is that dance lesson?"

One might have thought the sun had forgotten to shine that morning and that, with those few innocent words, Cassie had provided the reminder.

"One o'clock."

"Want to grab some lunch first?"

"I have some chicken chowder simmering right this minute," the woman exclaimed, shuffling back down the driveway toward Cassie.

"You save that for your dinner," she said. "What do you say we go have a pizza?"

"Oooh, cheese," Millicent lamented. "Dairy's not so good to me."

Cassie wondered if she was ever going to get that spinach pizza she'd been thinking about since before leaving Boston.

"Chicken chowder it is, then!" she declared. Millicent looked as if she was going to burst into happy tears at any minute. "I'll come by around noon. Can I bring anything?" Cassie asked.

"Just your dancing shoes," the older woman cried, and then she was on her way up the drive again, this time with a spring in her step and intermittent chuckles tossed over her shoulder as she hurried.

A couple of hours later, they shared a bowl of chicken chowder at the table in Millicent's glass-enclosed Florida room.

"This is delicious!" she exclaimed. "I've never had anything like it."

"It was my grandmother's recipe," Millicent told her. "We had it once a week when I was growing up because it was so inexpensive to make. I've fattened it up over the years by adding asparagus and sweet peas, but it's pretty much the same."

"I'm very happy we didn't opt for the pizza," Cassie told her. "Let me load the dishwasher for you, and then we'll take off for the church."

A smile passed over Millicent's lined face. "I'm so glad you decided to come with me."

"I am, too. I needed a little fun."

Cassie knew that part was no lie; she couldn't remember the last time she had a really good time. But the truth of the matter was that she didn't expect today to be that day. She had agreed to go along with Millicent for one reason and one reason only: because Millicent bore the sudden and striking expression of a lonely person in need of a companion.

"Hurry, hunny. Hurry!" Millicent cried as she climbed out of the passenger side of Cassie's car and scurried up the church sidewalk. "It's fox-trot day."

Cassie picked up the pace, reaching the door to the recreation hall just in time to open it for Millicent. She followed the woman down the long linoleum-tiled corridor, strains of "I've Got You Under My Skin" growing louder with each step forward.

"I'm sorry. I'm sorry we're late," Millicent whispered as they stepped into the group gathered around the center of the massive room.

"Oh, good, you've got a partner!" one of the ladies said to Millicent, and then the woman reached out and squeezed Cassie's wrist.

"This is my friend, Maureen Heaton," Millicent told her. "Mo, this is Cassie Constantine. She lives across the street from me."

Maureen had a very odd birdlike quality to her features, with big overlapping eyelids and a thick nose that pointed downward at the very tip.

"Nice to meet you," the woman practically hooted.

Not every couple there, to Cassie's surprise, was comprised of male and female counterparts. Several other dance teams were made up of two women. Apparently the dance was the thing above all else. Cassie grinned as she glanced around at the other couples.

Metal chairs dotted the circumference of the room, and Cassie was stunned to realize that Richard Dillon was the male half of the duo floating across the floor in front of them. As the music faded to a close, the onlookers erupted in applause.

"She's so beautiful," Maureen said to Cassie. "And he's just magnificent."

Magnificent? Richard Dillon?

"The fox-trot is a very smooth dance. There should be no jerkiness. It's called 'the Rolls-Royce of dances' because of the smoothness of the steps." Taking the hand of the woman dancing with him, Richard demonstrated. "It should be like this. Slow, slow, quick-quick. Slow, slow, quick-quick. And there are a couple of distinctive moves of the fox-trot. Anyone want to wager a guess?"

"Those quick forward steps," someone called out.

"Excellent," he replied. "Those are always done on the toes, like this."

As cheesy as the whole situation was, Cassie couldn't take her eyes off of him. He moved like a professional dancer, and she found her heart tapping out the beat of his weaving steps as he crossed the floor.

"And then the slow steps," he told them, "are on the heel. Like so."

"Who's the woman dancing with him?" Cassie whispered to Millicent.

"That's Laura, Faye's daughter. She's a schoolteacher over in Ruskin."

"His girlfriend?"

"Just his dance partner sometimes, I think."

How ridiculous is it that I'm relieved to hear that?

"Now, the feather step goes like this," he showed them. "It's when the man steps away from the woman. Let's all try it."

"Do you want to be the man or the woman, hunny bunny?" Millicent asked her as she grabbed her by the hand.

"Cassie should be the woman," Richard said as he walked behind them, "and you lead her, Millicent. You're the taller of the two of you, by a hair."

"Okay, follow me, then, Cassie-dear."

Laura started the music from the beginning, and Cassie stepped on her partner's toes twice before the first bar was complete.

"Maybe you should lead," Millicent suggested. "I have a corn on that foot."

"I'm so sorry." Cassie winced. "Millicent, I'm just so *bad* at this."

"Slow, slow, quick-quick," Richard instructed from the other side of the room. On the final "slow," Cassie rolled right over Millicent's corn for the third time.

"Oh, no! Millicent, I'm sorry."

"Laura, why don't you lead for Millicent?" Richard said as he crossed the floor and reached for Cassie's hand. "Let me show you."

"Oh, really, that's okay, I—" And with that, she tromped right on Richard's well-meaning foot. Recoiling from his arms, Cassie cringed. "I'm so very sorry."

"Let's try again," he offered.

"Really?" she exclaimed. Planting her hands on her hips, she grimaced again. "Are you some sort of glutton for punishment?"

"Not in the least," he said, and he pressed her hand into his and commenced the dance one more time. "You can do this," he promised just before taking the first step. "Slow, slow, quick-quick, slow."

When she managed just those few steps without landing on any of his toes, a smile broke out across Cassie's face as fast and furious as a just-popped champagne cork. But her joy was short-lived because, with the very next step, Richard cried out and so did she.

"Have you ever danced before in your life?" he asked her, his expression contorted with pain.

"Of course I have," she replied. Then, with a shrug, she looked at his clenched face and added, "I can *twist*…and I used to do a better-than-average *pony*…ooh, and I can *hustle*!"

Richard stared at her for a long, uncomfortable, and excruciating moment. Then, without a word, he spun around and headed off across the room away from her. He said something to Laura in a hushed voice, which the lovely blond questioned before finally turning toward a stack of albums on the table and picking through them. When she found what she was looking for, she removed the vinyl from its cover and placed it on the turntable before nodding at Richard.

"Ladies and gentlemen," he announced. "There's been a change of plans. Today…we are going to learn the hustle."

The familiar *oooooh ooh ooh ooh ooh* started to play, and Richard grinned at Cassie, making her heart do a mad flutter—not because of the delightful smile trapped between those attractive parentheses, but because she knew the song well enough to know what was coming next.

Doot doot doot da doo da doot doot.

"Ms. Constantine, let's show them how it's done."

Cassie's doubts flew away on silent wings, along with the 30-plus years between now and the time she last danced to this song. She vaulted toward Richard, eager to move up beside him.

Three steps back—bump! Three steps forward—bump!

By the first overhead clap, Richard had stepped into line beside her, and they danced side by side in perfect sync.

After the rolling arms came the signature Travolta move, and all of the onlookers began to applaud. Before she knew it, every one of them had hurried to form lines on either side of her and Richard. Maureen Heaton nearly knocked a couple of people down trying to take the spot next to Richard. And then, as the rhythm of the music built, more than a dozen Floridians over fifty—*many of them pushing seventy in fact!*—were disco-dancing as if there was a glitter ball hanging overhead.

"I can't believe this!" Cassie shouted to Richard over the music on a rolling fit of laughter. "You are insane."

He pulled a contorted face and spun into the Travolta move just then, pointing at the ceiling and then at the floor. Cassie could hardly contain herself.

"You're hysterical!" she exclaimed.

Richard Dillon, hysterical. Who knew?

Cassie and Millicent stopped at a roadside stand on the way home from the church, and Cassie bought three bags of produce for less than twenty dollars. Oranges, carrots, and bib lettuce; leeks, bell peppers, and zucchinis; tangelos and a small bag of the most luscious tomatoes she'd seen since summer.

"These are the last of the tangelos this year," the young woman said as she rang up the purchase. "They're still looking good." And then she punctuated the announcement with the snap of her gum.

Cassie dropped off Millicent at the bottom of her driveway, and then she turned into her own and pressed the button to open the garage. She noticed that the lawn had been mowed and some new flowers planted in the garden along the front of the house, a telltale sign that Frank Mitchell had been by.

James's truck was nowhere to be seen, and she felt a twinge of disappointment when she glanced at the clock on the dash.

Barely four o'clock, and he's already quit for the day.

She wondered, as she gathered the bags from the backseat, how long it was going to take to finish the upgrades at this rate. But when she pushed open the kitchen door and rounded the corner, Cassie's jaw fell open and hung there like a barn door off its hinge.

The kitchen floor was completely laid, and brand-new appliances stood where the old ones had been just that morning. A sticky note adhered to the front of the refrigerator announced, *"They delivered a day early. Floor's done. See you tomorrow to finish the dining room."*

Cassie leaned against the arched opening to the kitchen and sighed. The copper hood over the stove was a perfect match to the backsplash, and the paint color on the walls was rich and beautiful.

The appliances, the exquisite alabaster stone floors, all of it, every aspect…in two days' time, it had become the kitchen she'd always dreamed about.

The realization that she would be giving it away to a complete stranger one day very soon draped over her like a wet woolen cloak for a moment. Perhaps with the money she would make on the sale of the house, she could recreate the masterpiece in her own home in Boston. That thought lifted her spirits somewhat, and she set about putting away the fruits and vegetables.

Just as she let the last tomato tumble into a large Mexican-style ceramic bowl on the counter, the doorbell rang. Cassie quickly put the plastic bags into the recycle sack hanging on the pantry door before pushing past her barking dog to answer it.

Richard Dillon stood facing her, smiling. "Afternoon."

"Did I leave something behind?"

"Not unless you count me."

Her brows furrowed, and she pressed her lips together. "I don't think I forgot you, exactly."

"Can I come in?"

Cassie shrugged and then pulled the door all the way open with a nod.

"I didn't mean to embarrass you today," he told her as he passed through.

"Yes, you did." Cassie closed the door. "You loved every minute of that."

"You looked like you were having a pretty good time with it, too," he pointed out.

She tilted one shoulder. "I have to admit, I haven't had so much fun in a long while."

"Well, that's kind of why I'm here. The seniors have asked if we can include disco in the weekly dance lessons."

"Disco!" she exclaimed as they entered the dining room. "Are you joking? The waltz, the rumba, and...*the hustle*?"

"That was my reaction at first," he told her. "But then I realized there a lot of dances we can teach them that are line dances and not dependent upon a partner."

"We?"

"I was hoping—"

"Sorry. But *you* could teach them. Oooh, like the *bump*! But a gentle version so no one breaks a hip."

"Right. All they really need is a little exercise," Richard remarked. "They were sure getting that today—and having a lot of fun while they were at it."

"That's so great," she beamed. "Millicent won't have a partner once I go back to Boston, so the line dances will work out really well for her."

"When do you leave?"

"Just after the new year, I think. It's sort of dependent on how fast the work around here goes."

"And how's that proceeding?"

"See for yourself." She invited him, rolling her arm toward the kitchen.

Richard's reaction was much the same as hers had been when she came in through the garage just a short while ago. "Is this the same room?"

"Isn't it fantastic?" she exclaimed. "I'm so proud of what's been accomplished in just two short days!"

"These are some pretty dramatic changes just to get the place ready for the real-estate market."

"Yeah," she said, standing back and observing the overall picture. "But it's so beautiful. I guess I was just...inspired."

"It sort of makes you want to cook a meal, doesn't it?"

"You know, it does."

"How about we do that then?"

"Today?"

"Sure. Do you have plans?"

"Well, not really. Aside from some painting I'd hoped to do." She nodded toward the partially painted dining room wall, and Richard smiled.

"Why don't we work on that first and then have dinner a little later. Deal?"

"You're going to help me paint," she stated in a flat, suspicious tone.

"Why not? You don't think I can hold a paintbrush?"

"Oh, I'm sure you can *hold* one."

"All right, you snippy little thing. You're on. Let me show you how to paint a room."

"Well, you can't wear that," she said, giving his impeccable navy blue linen shorts and light heather-gray shirt a quick once-over.

"A fashion critic, too?" he asked her.

"I mean, you'll get paint all over you."

"You just worry about yourself, young lady," he challenged. "I'll worry about me."

Cassie excused herself and changed into gray sweat pants and a gray T-shirt with a large pink flower screened across the front. She stopped in the bathroom just long enough to pull up her hair into a high ponytail, and by the time she returned, Richard had already spread a drop cloth over the dining room table and chairs, taped a plastic tarp to the floorboards to cover the carpet, and poured paint into the tray. And he was dipping a roller for the second time.

"Cute," he commented when he saw her, before quickly turning away. "We need music."

Cassie flipped on the stereo in the living room. It was already tuned to The Joy FM, an exceptional local contemporary Christian station that she and Zan had discovered years back. The selection of music and the radio personalities were so unique, in fact, that they'd been supporting the station from up in Boston.

She and Richard hummed along with Mark Schultz as they tackled the task at hand. A little over an hour later, they set down their rollers and admired their surroundings. Cassie's back and arms ached, and she toggled her neck from side to side until it cracked.

"It looks great."

"I love it," Cassie agreed, pressing both hands against her lower back and stretching. "But you know what it needs in here?" she said.

"A chair rail?"

Cassie turned her head slowly toward him and gawked. "Yyyes. How did you know I was going to say that?"

"Because it needs a chair rail. But you're just fixing up the place enough to get it sold, right? You don't want to sink too much cash into it."

Cassie nodded her head and then suddenly noticed something very strange. Turning toward Richard, she stared him down.

"What?"

She sighed. "Look at me."

"Okay."

"What do you see?"

"A Café au Lait–dipped Cassie."

"Right. I've got paint on my face and hands," she said, extending them toward him. "It's even in my hair."

"You might want to grab a shower before dinner."

"But you don't have a drop on you."

Richard glanced down at himself and then shrugged.

"How did you do that?" she demanded. "How did you not get a drop or splatter of paint on you? You're wearing navy blue, for crying out loud. And you're perfectly clean. Except for that dog hair, of course."

Richard rubbed off the offending orange fluff, rolled it into a ball between his palms, and pushed it into one of the empty plastic bags tucked into the sack hanging on the back of the pantry door.

"I just think it's strange, that's all."

"Would you feel better if I had a spatter or two on me?"

"Kind of, yes."

"All right," he said, heading toward the paint tray, determination driving him.

"No!" she exclaimed. She rushed toward him and tugged him away from it by the arm, laughing. "Don't! Richard, don't!"

"Thank heaven," he said. "I was worried you were actually going to let me do it."

"You mean you would have?" she giggled.

"The truth?"

She nodded. "Of course."

"No way!"

Chapter Five

....

2 ACROSS: Vital; stimulating

Richard's head was not in the task. He'd washed a selection of the vegetables he found in the refrigerator and begun chopping them, but his thoughts were like a plume of smoke floating toward an air vent.

It wasn't the fact that Cassie was in the shower just a few yards away from him that had his brain humming; it was more to the point that she was undoubtedly going to emerge with her hair smelling like cookies. He'd caught a whiff of it when they were in the car that first night on the way to Benny's and then again that very day when she'd tromped all over him during the fox-trot. The vanilla shampoo she used should probably be outlawed.

He wasn't able to find parchment paper anywhere in the pantry, so he used aluminum foil to create a sack around the vegetables and then gingerly added a beautiful salmon filet overtop of them. Adding some chicken broth and a few slices of orange, he then sealed the packet and placed it in the baking dish.

Twenty minutes. That would give him time to touch up those edges Cassie had missed around the baseboards before cleaning the brushes and tapping the lid into place on the paint can. Since fresh paint fumes didn't mesh well with *Poached Salmon a la Richard*, he decided to set the table outside on the deck. The collie followed him to inspect the choice.

"Good grief," Cassie exclaimed when she emerged a half hour later and joined him on the deck, freshly showered and—naturally!—smelling like sugar cookies fresh from the oven. "You really know how to get things done."

Her bangs feathered across her brow, and that beautiful silky hair looked slightly damp where it skimmed the slope of her freckled shoulders. He noticed perfect little cinnamon-frosted toes peeking out from the straps of simple leather sandals, and he tried not to stare at the silver ankle bracelet just an inch or two beneath the billowing hem of her colorful sundress, despite the fact that he wanted a closer look. He found himself brimming with curiosity about the charm dangling from it.

"I thought we'd have dinner on the deck to escape the fumes, if that's all right with you."

"Fine," she nodded. "You found the filet?"

"I did. And you were right, it looks great."

"Poaching it?"

"As we speak."

"Water, iced tea, or pink lemonade?"

"Water, please," he replied.

A gentle breeze wafted from the canal as the orange sun began to settle for the day. A boat floated down the river, and the hull was draped in bright Christmas lights. An enormous lighted wreath was displayed on the back.

"I have to get this recipe from you," Cassie swooned. "This is just about the best salmon I've ever had. And I'm a big fan of salmon."

"Mm, me too. All fish, really."

"I also love a good shrimp cocktail," she exclaimed. "Very cold, with a light horseradish sauce. It's not an appetizer in my life; I can make a meal out of that."

"We can pick some up at the fresh market," he suggested. "Maybe next week."

He thought she hesitated for a moment, and his stomach churned at the realization that he'd assumed too much. But then she smiled and nodded.

"Sounds good," she said, and then she sipped from her glass of pink lemonade.

Richard looked away from her, focusing on the dog curled into a large sleeping ball at one end of the deck.

"What's your dog's name?"

"Sophie."

She lifted her head at the mention, blinked twice, and then resumed her nap.

"She's a nice dog."

"She can be," Cassie said with a chuckle. "And she can also be a terror."

Richard glanced at the dog again. *Hard to picture.*

"Zan was on a golf day one Saturday in Tampa with some friends. They stopped afterward for lunch at this little hole-in-the-wall place they liked to go to, in one of those shopping centers. Also in that center was a Petco. Out front, a dog rescue group had about a dozen dogs that were up for adoption."

"I see a surprise coming your way," Richard commented.

"Oh yeah!" she replied, and her little nose wrinkled at the memory. "So he comes home and the dog beats him into the house, starts tearing through the place like she owned it. Which of course, right away, she did."

Richard laughed. "All's well that ends well, though, right?"

"Well, the road to the happy ending is littered with dog hair and nonstop barking. But the real happy ending is that she has a home after a pretty rough start in life, thanks to this local group called Lost Angels Animal Rescue. I really don't know how those people do it."

"I've heard of them," he recalled. "My buddies and I have played in their golf tournament fund-raiser for the last couple of years. They seem to do good work."

"It's heartbreaking work," she told him. "There are so many stray dogs and cats with terrible histories. That group is just dedicated to them. I don't know if I could take it, but Zan and Debra would have enlisted in a heartbeat if we'd lived down here year-round."

Richard nodded. "Your husband seems to have been a kind man," he observed. "Having a heart for the downtrodden."

"My husband was a big Greek marshmallow. Funny and charming. And his charm wasn't lost on any female, even the canine ones. Sophie adored him. And he had Millicent across the street completely wrapped around his little finger. She and every geriatric woman, and every dog from Boston to Holiday, for that matter, grieved when he died."

Richard let out a laugh. "My wife was like that with cats. Wherever she went, cats…kittens…they just gravitated toward her. It was a little creepy, actually, except that she was so great with—"

He noticed the mist in her eyes just an instant before she turned away and looked out at the water, and Richard leaned forward and touched the top of Cassie's hand.

"Can I ask you something personal?" he said, deciding to nudge the subject away from their lost partners.

"I'm not sure," she replied with a sniff. "Give it a try."

"What's the charm on your ankle bracelet?"

Cassie smiled and then crossed one leg over the other, gathering the skirt in her hands just enough to display her ankle to him. Richard leaned in for a closer look at the black-and-white enamel crossword puzzle charm with a silver-tipped pencil stretched across it.

"Zan had a thing for words."

Well, that didn't really change the subject at all.

"He created puzzles and jumbles and word searches. Every year on our anniversary, he would make a crossword puzzle just for me, and one year he gave this to me along with it."

"I'm a bit of a crossword puzzle geek myself," Richard admitted.

Cassie nodded her head, serious for a moment. "I can picture that," she told him, and then she grinned. "I can see you on a Sunday morning with your coffee and the paper and a very sharp pencil, laboring over the crossword. Or do you do your puzzles in ink just to be"—she shook both hands over her head—"a little crazy?"

He laughed, and then suddenly Richard could visualize those Sunday mornings, too. But in his portrayal, Cassie was there as well, sipping coffee and looking over his shoulder and shouting out the answer before he ever had the chance to come up with it.

He shook the image from his mind and then sank back against the chair. Just about the time he thought he might recover, Cassie stood up, leaned across the table, and stacked the plates, leaving an aromatic trace of sugar cookies lingering when she carried them inside.

"So what do you think of your new kitchen?" James asked her, standing in the doorway. He took a sip of coffee from a silver travel mug.

"It's fantastic, isn't it?" she exclaimed. "I really love it."

She didn't mention that it had already been christened by Richard when he made them the lovely salmon dinner the night before, but the recollection made her smile.

"I see you were feeling energetic," he observed, nodding toward the fresh paint on the dining room walls.

"Oh. Yes. A friend came over last night, and we ended up finishing it."

"I'll hang the new lighting today, and you'll have one more room complete."

"Well, not exactly complete." She treaded with care. "I was thinking, if it wouldn't be too much trouble, that a chair rail might be nice."

James focused on the wall behind her, and she saw the light dawn in his dark eyes. "That would probably look pretty good."

"Oh, good! If you'll measure for me, I'll go pick it up today."

James produced a metal tape measure from his toolbox and, while he took the measurements, Cassie went to the desk for something to write on.

Her eye was drawn to the crystal "Surprise Yourself" box that was angled into the corner of the desktop, and she smiled.

Yesterday's surprise had resulted in a wonderful day. She'd danced the hustle, spent time with Millicent, and enjoyed a fabulous salmon dinner with Richard Dillon—and all of it had started with an effort to "surprise" herself and be a companion to someone who was feeling lonely. She wondered what might be in store next, and she creaked open the lid and pulled out the front card.

"Trust in the LORD with all your heart and lean not on your own understanding" Proverbs 3:5.

She flipped the card over.

Do something today that you said you would never do!

Cassie shrugged and placed the card into the box, at the very back. She felt certain that she hadn't actually *said* she would never buy a chair rail, but that was her plan for the day just the same. Once James provided the measurements, she tore off the sheet of paper on which she'd written them down and headed out the door.

Just as she was backing down the driveway, Cassie's cell phone rang. She put the car into PARK and flipped open the phone.

"Mom?"

"Debra! How are you, sweetheart?"

"Really good, Mom. I have some news."

Cassie's heart thumped hard several times. "What is it?"

"We're going to have another baby!"

Tears sprang to Cassie's eyes as her hand flew to cover her mouth. "My baby's having another baby," she crooned. "That is such wonderful news, honey. But I thought you guys decided not to have any more kids."

"I guess God had other plans," Debra said on a chuckle. "It was a complete surprise."

"How far along are you?"

"About four months, can you believe that? I thought I just needed to cut back on the ice cream treats."

"That's so great. Hey…do you think you might have a girl this time?"

Debra laughed. "I don't know. They didn't tell me that."

"Well, think pink, will you, sweetheart? I'd love a little granddaughter to round things out."

"Okay," she promised. "I'm on my way to pick up Jake from school. He's got a sore throat, but I'm thinking pink right now, Mom."

"Good! Give all your fellas my love."

"I will, Mom. Talk to you soon."

Cassie closed up her phone and tossed it on the seat beside her. With both hands on the steering wheel, she clamped her eyes shut and sent a prayer of thanks upward. When she opened her eyes, drops of tears cascaded down her face.

She reached for a tissue from the package under the dash. As she dabbed her face, her eyes landed on the two large plastic flamingos in the garden. She'd always despised those things so much, from the very first day Zan had insisted they bring them home. One of them, the one balancing on just one leg, was cocked sideways, as if it was a little bit drunk.

"Come on, Mac. We'll hang Christmas lights on the palm tree in the front yard, and these pink guys can stand underneath it, like presents under the tree."

"We are not hanging Christmas lights on the palm tree, Zan."

"Why not?"

"Well, for one thing, because we're spending Christmas in Boston with Debra and her family. We're going to have a traditional blue spruce tree, a turkey with chestnut stuffing, and snow on the ground, if we're lucky."

"Debra won't care if we have a tropical Christmas instead! In fact, she'd be just the girl to love the idea."

"No, Zan."

"Think about it?"

"Okay, I thought about it. And we're having a traditional Christmas at home."

"Can the flamingos come to visit?"

"Alexander Constantine, I can promise you one thing. Those horrible flamingos will never be a part of our holiday celebration."

"Never?"

"Not ever."

"Well, now you've hurt their feelings."

"Don't be ridiculous."

"Mutt will get over it, you're right. But check him out, Mac. Doesn't Jeff look sad?"

Cassie's tears started again, and this time they were coming in streams. Wiping her face with the back of her hand, she reversed out into the street and drove straight to the home improvement store. Along with five sections of carved cherry chair rail molding, she also purchased two boxes of gaudy, colorful outdoor Christmas lights, three boxes of simple white twinkling ones, and a 25-foot extension cord.

While James unloaded the molding strips from her car and set about cutting and placing them, Cassie gathered her boxes of lights and the crisply rolled extension cord, and she headed straight for the front yard.

Do something today that you said you would never do! she was reminded. And what could be more *never-never* than draping Christmas lights on the five-foot-tall palm tree in front of the house?

Once she figured out how to conceal the extension cord in the low shrubs that outlined the front walk, Cassie plugged the cord into the outlet and flipped the switch. She clapped her hands when the palm illuminated with bright red and green lights, and she jumped from one foot to the other. If anyone saw her, she knew for certain they would send the men with the little white coats, but she didn't care. She was thrilled. And Sophie was certainly entertained by her glee. The dog stood in front of her with her ears happily pinned back, panting in a way that made her look like she was laughing.

There was something exhilarating—in fact, *liberating!*—about what she'd just done. She couldn't wait to call Rachel and tell her that she'd managed to "surprise" herself two days in a row now, thanks to that thoughtful Christmas gift. But the call would have to wait, she decided. First, there were a couple of pink flamingos that needed a new home under that palm!

Cassie plucked the drunken flamingo from the garden and dragged it by the beak across the sidewalk, through the shrubs, and over the lawn toward the palm tree. As she planted it into place, she glanced across the street and spotted Millicent sitting in the rocker on her front porch.

"Hey there, dance partner!" she called, before giving her neighbor a wave.

The older woman returned it, and it seemed to Cassie that it was a bit halfhearted. She was quick to drag the second flamingo from the garden, and once it was secure in its spot beside the other, she dusted off her hands and set out across the street.

"Afternoon, Millicent," she said as she meandered up the sidewalk with Sophie on her heels. "How are you today?"

"Just dandy," the woman replied, but her attempt at a smile didn't quite make it to her eyes. "I see you're getting into the holiday spirit over there."

"Florida style," Cassie admitted. "What about you? Is your tree up?"

"Oh, I didn't get a tree this year."

"Can I ask why not?"

"No reason, really. I guess I'm just not feeling very jolly."

"Believe me, I hear that," Cassie told her as she sat down on the porch step. "We're nearly finished with the work on the house, with the holiday just a couple of days away, and I just realized that this is the first Christmas I haven't spent with my daughter and her family."

"Oh, that's a shame."

"But there was good news from them today," she beamed. "Debra's expecting a baby. This will be their third child."

"You look far too young to be the grandmother of three," Millicent told her. "I envy you that big family. Bernard and I missed out by not having children. I never thought so until after he was gone and I spent that first Thanksgiving alone."

"Will you be alone on Christmas?" Cassie asked.

"Oh, yes. I usually am."

"Would you be willing to come over and have Christmas dinner with me?"

The woman tilted her head away for a moment, and when she looked back again, her eyes were smoky and red. "I appreciate the thought, I really do. But—"

"Please say yes, Millicent," Cassie interrupted. "I just hate the idea of being alone."

"You…you do?"

"It would be so much fun to have that to plan for," she went on, trying to interject as much enthusiasm as she could muster for Millicent's sake. "I could make a turkey and all the trimmings for us. And maybe after dinner we could put one of those sappy Christmas movies into the DVD and watch it with our pie. What do you think?"

"Well…," the woman said, and then she chuckled. "It does sound enticing."

"And we've just finished the renovations on my kitchen and dining room, so you'll be able to see what I've been doing over there! What do you say? Will you come keep me company on Christmas?"

Millicent looked very much like she was about to cry, but Cassie pretended not to notice. When she agreed, Cassie jumped to her feet and hurried over to her, wrapping her in an eager embrace, as if the woman had just done her the greatest favor of her life.

"Thank you so much!" she exclaimed. "I'm so excited for the holiday now."

"I might just get excited, too," Millicent offered. "Thank you, Cassie."

"Well, I need to go over and check on James. He's putting up the chair rail in my dining room, and then we're going to hang the new chandelier."

"That sounds just fine, dear."

"We'll decide later on a time for dinner," Cassie said as she headed down the sidewalk. "Oh! What's your pleasure for pie? Pumpkin or apple?"

"Either one will be delicious. How about I make the cranberry sauce? I have my mama's recipe somewhere inside," Millicent said. She pushed herself out of the rocker and wobbled to her feet. "I'm going to look for it right now."

"Ooh, I love cranberries!" Cassie called back to her. "Talk to you later."

Cassie's heart soared as she and Sophie jogged across the street and up the driveway. If she hadn't decided to light that dumb palm tree, she might never have seen Millicent sitting there…or uncovered those holiday blues the older woman wore like a woolen scarf.

She noticed that she had a much lighter step at the idea of spending Christmas with someone who really needed her. No one had needed Cassie for a very long time, and she'd forgotten how much she enjoyed the feeling.

Wondering if Richard Dillon had anyone to spend the holiday with, Cassie walked into the house and then stopped in her tracks with a gasp.

The copper grapevine chandelier illuminated the dining room with amber light, and James had moved the long rectangular dining table into place beneath it, with the eight chairs neatly hugging its edges. He'd placed the cherry molding at the perfect level, about one-third of the way up the wall. Aside from screaming out for appropriate accessories, Cassie's dining room had been transformed into her original vision.

James came around the corner from the hallway and smiled at her. "What do you think?"

Cassie placed her hand over her heart and just sighed.

"I think that's good?"

"Yes," she confirmed. "It's very good. It looks amazing, doesn't it?"

"Well, I'm a chrome-and-glass kind of guy myself," he teased. "But I think the place is beautiful, and it really does suit you."

"Thank you so much, James. You've done such a lot of work."

"Come and see the light fixtures in the master bath."

"You've already hung them?"

"Yeah. Now I'm working on pulling up the floor. Do you need anything out of there before I get too far?"

"Probably. Let me move some things to the guest bath for a couple of days."

James followed her down the hall and stood back as she leaned around the doorway to the bathroom. Simple pewter scrollwork accented the three-light fixture now hanging over the beveled bathroom mirror, and matching sconces stood alone on either side. Seafoam Blue had already been applied to the one wall where the new lighting was placed, and Cassie picked up one of the floor tiles and held it next to the painted wall.

"Ohhh," she sighed softly. "This room is going to be exquisite."

She was already thinking of a shade of deep wine for the towels to accent one of the mosaic colors in the tiles and perhaps including a panel of leaded glass instead of a traditional window treatment so that the light would stream in through the window above the garden tub.

"I'll pull up the rest of the flooring this afternoon," he told her. "And then I think I can get the new floor laid on Monday. I hope it's all right if I take the weekend off."

"Of course," she said. "Any experience I've had with renovations like this has taught me to expect nothing but delays and problems, James. You've been an absolute dream."

"Tell that to my Tammy-girl," he said with a grin. Cassie thought it was sweet to hear him refer to Tameka in such a loving expression.

"Do you and Tameka have plans for Christmas?" she asked him.

"We're going to Tammy's folks' place in Ocala on Christmas Eve."

"And for Christmas Day?"

"I don't really know yet," he replied with a chuckle. "I just go where I'm told."

"Well, if the two of you would like to join me for Christmas dinner, I've invited a neighbor woman, and we'd love to have you with us."

"I'll talk to Tammy and let you know. Thanks, Cassie."

She found herself hoping that they could come. Christmas was shaping up to be quite an unexpected event!

Cassie grabbed her shampoo and conditioner from the cubbyhole over the tub and a few toiletries from the counter. "I'll put these in the guest bath and let you get back to work on the floor," she told James. "Then do you know what I'm going to do? I'm going to hang twinkle lights out on my deck."

"Aren't you in a festive holiday spirit!" he teased.

"You know, all of a sudden, I kind of am."

Chapter Six

. . . .

8 DOWN: Better than all the rest

Cassie looked at herself in the bathroom mirror and laughed right out loud. She remembered Debra coming home from a night out with friends many years prior, covered in multicolored splatters of paint.

"We were painting Jackie's new apartment, Mom, and the next thing we knew, we were having this crazy paint fight!" she'd said. Cassie interrupted her with a scream and a shove to keep her daughter from touching anything.

She hadn't been fighting with anyone, but Cassie certainly looked the part. The gray sweats she'd worn to paint the dining room were covered in dry spatters of Café au Lait, and now she'd added droplets of Seafoam Blue down the leg and smeared it across the sleeve of her T-shirt. A streak of blue highlighted her bangs, and a matching smudge ran down one side of her nose.

The results were worthy of the cost, however, and she stepped out into the bedroom and looked in at her beautiful pale blue master bath. She could hardly wait until Monday after James laid the glazed mosaic floor tiles so she could see the finished product.

"Perfect," she said aloud. "It's perfect."

She stepped back in the bathroom and rinsed the brushes in the bathtub as she made a mental list of added touches that might be nice.

I'll take a drive over to Tarpon to shop around for a lead glass panel for the window.

Don't forget wine-colored guest towels and a mat for the floor.

Ooh, maybe a new towel rack? The shiny silver one that's already there doesn't match the brushed pewter sconces.

A whispering thought tickled the back of Cassie's brain. *You're going to sell the place. It doesn't have to be a showplace.* But she brushed it away by trying to recall the name of the store where she'd seen framed panels of leaded and stained glass like the one she wanted for the bathroom window. Perhaps Millicent would want to go along with her after Sunday services. They could have lunch at one of the Greek restaurants near the sponge docks. Years had passed since she and Zan had visited the area, and she wondered if it had changed much.

Cassie shed her clothes near the closet in the bedroom, careful to fold them so that the wet paint didn't end up on the carpet or wall. She'd awoken before dawn that morning and made the spontaneous decision to paint the master bath. As she glanced at the clock on the night table now, she realized it was still early—barely 9 a.m.

The idea of going to church feathered across her mind, and she debated with herself over it. She could make the ten o'clock Sunday church service if she hurried and then be in Tarpon Springs by noon. It had been such a long time since she'd been to services, but the old-fashioned church with the tall white steeple at the edge of town sort of called to her for some reason, and she wished she had a phone number for Millicent to see if she'd go along with her.

The old blue Volvo was missing from the woman's carport by the time Cassie left her house at 9:45, so she drove to Grace Community on her own. The choir was already singing when she opened the large door at the back of the church and headed up the aisle to find a seat. Millicent was seated a couple of rows ahead of her with several of her lady friends; Cassie recognized them from the dance lesson in the recreation hall.

When the pastor invited the congregation to greet one another, Millicent hurried toward Cassie and took her by the hand. "Come sit with us, why don't you?"

Just as she sat down in the pew beside the women, she noticed Richard two rows up, seated with Laura, his pretty blond dance partner. She watched him, wondering if their eyes would meet, but he never even glanced in her direction.

The pastor's sermon revolved around the story of Jonah. Although he was a wonderful storyteller, Cassie had to push for the extra effort it took to focus on his words. She thought that it bordered on the ridiculous how she kept glancing over at Richard and his beautiful blond companion.

Enough already. Are you sixteen years old? Pay attention!

The pastor told how God had instructed Jonah to go to a city called Nineveh and warn the inhabitants about their rebellious behavior against Him. Jonah didn't want to be the one to admonish them, and so he ran in the opposite direction, boarding a ship headed for Tarshish.

You are not a teenager, and he's not your boyfriend. What do you care if Richard Dillon has an eye for blonds? And if Laura the Dancer finds him mutually attractive, it's her bad luck.

"A great storm came up on the sea," Pastor Sullivan told them. "Isn't that just the way? You're running away from one thing and then you get yourself into more trouble than you ever imagined."

Cassie chuckled along with the parishioners, and Millicent poked her with her elbow. It took all of her strength not to dart one more glance in Richard's direction.

"So the sailors, realizing that Jonah's rebellion from God was the reason for the terrible storm, threw Jonah overboard, and he was swallowed up by a whale. You all know the story. When the whale regurgitated Jonah out on dry land a few days later, he went to Nineveh as he'd been commanded. All that gook and grime inside the belly of the whale could have been avoided if he'd just followed God's leading in the first place."

Cassie wondered how many times she'd made the same mistake as Jonah, avoiding what she was supposed to do and then having to do it anyway. She thought about Zan's many pleadings to spend Christmas at the house in Holiday and how many times she'd refused. And now here she was, but she didn't have Zan to share it with anymore.

After the benediction, Cassie leaned over toward Millicent and asked her if she was interested in joining her for lunch in Tarpon Springs.

"Oh, we're serving at the pancake brunch in the hall. You come and have some pancakes, huh?"

"I have to pass," Cassie told her. "I'm looking for a specific shop in Tarpon near the sponge docks. I haven't been there in years, but I really want to see if it's still there."

"See if what's still there?"

She turned to find Richard standing beside her, and she greeted him with a shaky smile.

He's just a random man, Cassandra. What is your problem?

"Cassie's going fishing," Millicent teased. "She's looking for a store that used to be out in Tarpon Springs near the docks."

"What store is it?" he asked.

"I wish I knew. But they had framed panels of stained glass hanging in their window."

"Oh, I have to run now to serve pancakes," Millicent announced. "You have a good time, Cassie. I'll see you later."

"Would you like some company?" Richard asked her once Millicent and her friends had gone.

"Well, what about Laura?"

"What about her?"

"Aren't you here with her?"

Cassie knew she must have sounded like a jealous girlfriend, and she immediately wished she could grab the words back. She wished it even harder once she caught a glimpse of Richard's smug smile.

"Laura's here with her mom, Faye," he explained. "I just sat with them."

"Oh," she said, trying to sound casual and realizing she was a miserable failure. "Okay. I just wondered."

"Would you care if I had come with her?"

"Don't be ridiculous. I just didn't want to be rude and steal away her date."

"A date…to church?"

"Whatever."

Did I really just say "Whatever"?

"Whatever?" he blurted on a laugh. "You really are jealous. Cassie, you're making my whole day!"

"Hush!" she exclaimed, and then she turned on her heels and headed for the door.

"Cassie," he called. He grabbed her elbow with a firm hold. "Cassie, come on. I was teasing you."

Cassie's heart was pounding, and she was mortified that this man was so adept at bringing out her inner sixteen-year-old girl with the mad crush on the high school quarterback!

"Do you want to go to Tarpon with me or not?" she muttered, pulling her arm out of his grip.

"I would like to, very much," he replied.

She tried not to exit in a huff, but with her head tilted upward and those long strides she was taking, she knew it was one more thing at which she had failed.

"Uh, I can drive," he suggested. "My car's over here."

She made a reluctant change in direction, following his lead through the parking lot. The second he could no longer see her face, Cassie cringed.

I'm such a dope.

When she had behaved in a similar manner at the actual age of sixteen, she recalled her mother asking, "Cassie, how old are you again?"

She suddenly wanted to tell her mother to hush up as well. And she would have, too…if the woman hadn't passed away five years prior.

Cassie and Richard meandered along Dodecanese Boulevard between flocks of tourists of every age and ethnicity. The street was narrow in parts, and it wound its way from the bayou on one end to the aquarium on the other. Edged with large cane-and-lantern streetlights and dotted with shops and restaurants, Tarpon Springs was reminiscent of a Greek seaside village. Along the way, just beyond the marina and various sponge boats docked down the right side of the street, shop owners and restaurateurs alike could be heard speaking to one another in their native language.

A chubby man with no more than twenty greasy strands of hair on his head was wearing a stained apron and called out to his friend in Greek. The man replied, slapping him on the back. Richard cast a glance at Cassie as they passed them.

"I think the cook said that it's a great day," she told him. "And his friend said something about it being as beautiful here as it is in Greece."

"You speak the language then?"

"I float around it," she corrected. "I can figure it out sometimes. I couldn't hold a conversation. Zan used to say I was an honorary Greek twice removed, by default and then by marriage. But I do love the culture."

Cassie pushed her silky brown hair away from her face and then tucked a strand of it behind her ear as they continued down the avenue. Just the simple act made Richard's chest constrict a little.

"I'm not sure about this, but I seem to remember the shop in question being somewhere in this area," she told him. "I hope they still sell what I'm looking for."

Richard noticed a poster for the upcoming Epiphany celebration, and he nodded toward it. "Have you ever attended?"

"I haven't. It's right after the new year, isn't it? We always spent the holiday season in Boston. Have you?"

"A couple of times since I moved south," he replied. "Will you still be here?"

"I don't know. Probably not."

Richard's heart sank a little. "It's worth sticking around for," he told her. "The population of the city doubles in size. Everyone comes out for the party."

"I don't really remember the whole idea of the festivities," she admitted.

"The Greek immigrants depended upon the sea for their livelihood, so the Epiphany was born out of their hopes that God would bless their boats and keep them safe in their work."

"Don't they toss something into the water at the end and all the little kids go in after it?" she asked him, and then she paused to peer into the window of a jewelry store.

"At the end of the ceremony, they throw a large wooden cross into Spring Bayou, and the boys around sixteen or eighteen years old dive in to retrieve it. The one who recovers the cross is supposed to be blessed for the following year."

"Right," she nodded as if it was all coming back to her.

"Afterward, there's music and more food than you can imagine."

"Oh, I don't know," she said, tossing a grin—and her light brown hair—over one shoulder toward him. "I can imagine an awful lot of food."

"You and me both," he replied. "How about we grab some lunch? We're coming up on one of my favorite places in the area."

"All right."

Santorini Mediterranean Grill sat at the waterside. Through their windows, patrons could watch local fishermen while enjoying traditional Greek cuisine. Richard hadn't paid the restaurant a visit for several months, but he was greeted like an old friend when he led Cassie through the front door.

"Do you like spinach?" he asked Cassie once they'd settled in at their table.

"I love it."

"They make a beautiful spanakopita here. Spinach and feta cheese baked inside filo."

Cassie's eyes sparked. "That sounds really good."

"We'll start with that," Richard told the waitress. "And a couple of iced teas?"

She nodded her approval.

"Zan's mother tried to teach me to make spanakopita," she told him. "I just didn't have the knack that she did. I can't work with that thin dough. So I got the brilliant idea of putting it inside a wonton instead."

"Oooh." Richard grimaced.

"Yeah. Not so much the brilliant idea I thought it was. So what's good for lunch?"

"What are you in the mood for?" he asked her.

"I love Greek salads. Is theirs any good?"

"It is. Let's get a Greek salad for two, and we'll have them add chilled shrimp to it."

Cassie picked up her napkin and dabbed the corner of her mouth. "I'm sorry, did I just drool?"

After lunch, they continued their stroll down Dodecanese, stopping here and there to step inside shops and look around. But the boutique that Cassie was seeking wasn't anywhere in sight, and Richard felt her disappointment when he looked into her eyes.

"I guess it's just been too long," she said on their stroll back down the street. "I should have known better, but I had to look."

"Tell me more about what you're looking for."

"It was this large panel of leaded glass, like a stained glass design except without the color. It was about, I don't know, I guess maybe three feet wide and about two feet in height, and it hung from a chain. For some reason I've always remembered it, and I got it in my head that it would be just beautiful hanging in that very high window in my master bath, reflecting the light."

"That would have been nice," he agreed.

"I haven't given up," she said—it sounded almost like a warning. "Don't go using the past tense on me just yet."

Richard didn't imagine Cassie had much experience in the art of surrender. He had visions of her tromping through the desert in the middle of a sandstorm if she heard about a panel of leaded glass somewhere out there on the other side.

A duo with a lute and violin began to play traditional Greek music across the street, and Cassie and Richard stopped for a couple of minutes to listen. Several elderly men emerged from the restaurant behind them, and they interlocked their arms as they stood shoulder to shoulder and began to dance. Richard remembered seeing Anthony Quinn do a similar dance on the beach in *Zorba the Greek*.

"Do you think the seniors at the church would like to learn the Sirtáki?" Cassie asked with a grin.

"Nothing about that group would surprise me after their enthusiasm for the hustle."

Cassie tossed back her head and laughed, and it was melodious in its harmony against the grand, rolling guffaws of the dancing men. They sounded like an underground train making its way toward town, with Cassie as the church bells on the hill above them.

Cassie turned to Richard and slipped him a hopeful smile. "I feel like having something sweet," she said. "Where can we get some baklava?"

"I know just the place."

When they'd almost reached the café he had in mind, Cassie let out a scream that she muffled with both hands over her mouth. She began to hop from one foot to the other, and then she pointed at a long plate of leaded glass hanging by a thick chain in a shop window.

"Is that it?"

"That's it!" she cried, before flying into the store.

By the time Richard stepped up to the counter, she already had the glass in her hands and was telling the clerk the story of how she'd had a piece just like this one in mind. When he saw the price ring up on the register, his gut wrenched.

Well, at least it's mobile, he thought. *She can take it with her when she goes.*

Richard hated that Cassie was spending so much on her home when…well…what he really hated was that he had such an enormous secret to keep from her. But she'd thank him in the long run. He hoped.

"Isn't it just gorgeous, Richard? I can see it hanging in that long, high window in the master bath, reflecting prisms of light. Oh, it's going to be just beautiful!"

Richard had thought many times since meeting Cassie that she reminded him of the actress Sally Field, and, as she gleefully paid for her magnificent find, she looked to him very much like a young surfing Gidget who'd just taken on her first respectable wave.

"Pack it very carefully," she suggested to the clerk, "with lots of cardboard on both sides. If I break it before I get it into my window at home, I'll just cry."

Isn't it just the ultimate, Moondoggie? The utter living end? I swear, if it breaks before I get it home, I'll die. I'll just dii-eeee!

"Richard Dillon! How are you, buddy?"

"Better than fair, Mick. How about you?"

"About to become a grandfather," his old friend told him.

"Connie's having a baby?"

"She sure is. Let me tell you, my friend, nothing ages you faster than that."

Richard laughed and then shifted the phone against his shoulder. He wished he'd planned out this conversation a little better before dialing his old college chum.

"How are things down in Florida?" Mick Kendrick asked him.

"Sunny and warm. Same forecast, different day."

Talking about the weather? It began to set in on him how transparent this phone call actually was.

"The last I heard, you were thinking of buying into a new business down there. Any truth to that rumor?"

"Still thinking," Richard replied. "Hey, listen. I met up with someone who says she knows you."

"Uh-oh. Who is she, so I can start plotting my deniability?"

"Cassie Constantine."

"Cassie! You met Cassie?"

"She owns some property close to mine in Holiday," he revealed. "I was pretty shocked when she told me who she works for."

"Cassie's a peach. Been through a lot in the last year or so."

"So I gather."

"What a small world," Mick remarked. "You meeting Cassie."

"Isn't it though," Richard replied. "So, Mick. What can you tell me about her?"

"What do you mean? What are you looking for?"

"I just think she's interesting," he said. "Hearing that she works for you, I figured you could tell me a little bit about her."

"What're you doing, a background check, Dillon? Or are you interested for some other reason? My administrator hasn't gone and started applying for jobs in Central Florida, has she?"

Out of hand. How did one phone call get so out of hand so fast?

Chapter Seven
....

18 DOWN: Intensely hot; characterized by passion

"What were you thinking? Can you tell me that? Can you just tell me what you were thinking?"

Cassie had asked him the same question at least a dozen different ways, and Richard Dillon still hadn't come up with a satisfying response. In fact, he hadn't given any response at all!

"You called my boss and gave him the impression that I'm down here job hunting, Richard. Please tell me what you were thinking?"

"I didn't mean to give him that impression, Cassie. He came up with that one all on his own."

"How? Can you tell me how!"

"Just calm down," he suggested. "It was an innocent conversation. I just mentioned what a small world it is, that I'd met someone who worked for him."

"Yes, I work for him!" she exclaimed. "He's my boss! And now he thinks you were doing a background check for possible employment."

"He doesn't think that."

"No?"

"He couldn't think that."

"Really."

"What would I be hiring you for? Dance instructor?"

When he followed up the comment with a snicker, Cassie felt her blood pressure rise, and her temples immediately began to pound. It infuriated her to no end that he'd chosen to take the smug way out.

"He mentioned that you've been considering a business venture, unrelated to the law," she seethed, trying with all her might to calm the stormy seas raging inside. "Something about buying a business here in the area."

Richard's face dropped.

"What, not so funny anymore?"

"I really didn't want anyone down here to know about that. It's just something I've been thinking about. There's nothing written in stone."

"And yet you allowed my employer to think you were considering me for a position in this *possible, well, maybe, nothing in stone* new venture? Who does that?"

He sighed and then shook his head. "I'm really sorry about that, Cassie. I can see that I've upset you, and I didn't mean to."

"Why did you call Mr. Kendrick and ask about me, Richard? Why would you do that?"

And there it was again. That vacant, desolate expression, with his face bunched up like rapidly drying fruit.

After almost a full minute of expectation, Cassie groaned and walked away.

"Cassie," he called after her, but she kept on walking.

One foot in front of the other, she thought. *He's just a lunatic with a chiseled face and a nice smile. Keep walking.*

Cassie crossed the well-lit parking lot and headed straight into the sanctuary. Millicent and her friends were already gathered, huddled together like a colorful grape cluster on a vine, and Cassie stalked toward them.

"Merry Christmas Eve, hunny bunny." Millicent greeted her with an enthusiastic hug.

"Same to you," she replied, and then she gave a deep sigh over Millicent's shoulder in an effort to expel all remnants of Richard Dillon.

"Come and sit with us," one of the woman's friends invited, and Cassie nodded thankfully.

The choir had just entered into a lively rendition of "Joy to the World" when Stella Nesbitt joined her favorite cronies in the row in front of Cassie.

"Happy Christmas," she sang, reaching over the back of the pew and squeezing Cassie's hand, and then she brushed the air a foot or two in front of Millicent. "Happy Christmas, Millie."

Pastor Sullivan had just stepped up to the microphone when Stella turned completely around in the pew ahead of her and waved her arms as if she was hailing a taxi. A tall, lean man in a sport jacket and jeans appeared in the aisle, and he gave the woman a hurried embrace. When he started to step into the row beside her, Stella's face crumpled, doughy, like bread left on the counter to rise.

"It's crowded up here," she whispered, and then she wiggled a chunky finger in Cassie's direction. "Sit right here instead."

"Oh." Cassie slid across the varnished pew, and then Millicent followed suit. But as the man pushed into the row beside her, she couldn't help but notice that there was more available space beside Stella and her friends than there was next to her.

"My nephew, Hunter," Stella whispered to Cassie, her mouth forming the words with animated dexterity. Cassie nodded. "Hunter, this is Cassie Constantine. Down from Boston."

Cassie nodded a second time, this one directed at the young man seated beside her.

"Hunter lives up North, too," Stella murmured. "New York City."

"Aunt Stella," he said in a hushed tone, whirling his finger in circles to tell her to turn around.

"Okay, all right," she replied. "We'll talk after."

Cassie and Hunter exchanged uncomfortable smiles, and then both faced the front of the church. It wasn't until Pastor Sullivan reached the part of the story where there was no room at the inn for a pregnant woman and her new husband that Cassie took note of the dozen or so glances Stella and her friends had been making over their shoulders toward her. But it was that goofy grin out of Millicent that finally brought the point home for her

Oh, Lord, am I…? Is this…? Oh, for goodness' sake.

She was being set up!

Hunter Nesbitt wasn't a day over thirty-five. And at twenty years her junior, Cassie could have easily been old enough to be his…

Oh, my.

Sneaking a sideways glance in his direction and then focusing on him for a fraction of a second, Cassie's stomach constricted as she turned to face front again to meet Stella's face full-on. Her head was spun around like a character in a scary movie, her grin so wide that it looked like the corners of her mouth were strung up on invisible wires.

"Aunt Stella!" Hunter reprimanded on an attempt at a whisper.

"O Holy Night" was Cassie's all-time favorite Christmas carol, but she hadn't even noticed the choir singing it until the final bar of the song. And the moment that the congregation was dismissed and wished a very Merry Christmas by Pastor Sullivan, Stella was out of her own row and standing over Hunter at the end of Cassie's.

"Now let's do it right," Stella said, with her hand on Hunter's arm. "Hunter Nesbitt, meet Cassie Constantine."

He stood up and they shook hands, both of them appearing somewhat reluctant. Cassie felt a surge of hot embarrassment rise from her ribs to her throat as a half dozen elderly women watched them while grinning from ear to ear.

"Good to meet you," he muttered.

"Hunter came down at the last minute to spend the holiday with his lonely old aunt," Stella explained.

Lonely? Stella Nesbitt had more going on than the social director on a Carnival cruise!

"I was telling Stella about our plans for Christmas dinner," Millicent chimed in. "I thought perhaps she and Hunter might join us."

"Oh." Cassie felt her heartbeat in the hollow of her throat. "Umm, really?"

"You don't have to do that," Hunter said in quick bursts, like an auctioneer. "I planned on taking Aunt Stella out for Christmas dinner."

"Don't be silly," Millicent interjected. "Christmas is no day to spend at a restaurant. It's a time to be with friends. Isn't that right, Cassie?"

"Umm, yes, I suppose—"

"Please," Hunter said softly, leaning toward Cassie as if sharing a secret. "Don't let them pressure you into something."

"No," she breathed. "Really. The two of you should join us at my house."

"Of course you should," Millicent chimed in.

"Really?" Stella exclaimed, hand over heart, as if she was hearing the idea for the very first time. "Well, we'd just be honored to join you for Christmas. What a lovely invitation."

"Who's invited where?" Richard asked as he popped up out of nowhere.

"Cassie has just invited us to share Christmas dinner with her," Stella replied. "Richard, have you met my nephew, Hunter Nesbitt?"

The two men shook hands, but Richard's eyes were on Cassie.

"Pleasure," he mumbled. Then to Cassie he said, "So you're hosting a Christmas shindig."

Oh no, you don't! You're not getting an invitation out of me, she thought.

She planted a quick peck on Millicent's cheek, shot a "Nice to meet you" in Hunter's direction, spun on her heels, and headed down the aisle.

"See you tomorrow, then," Stella called after her.

Cassie returned an all-inclusive "Merry Christmas" with a wave over her shoulder and made a beeline for the front door.

It struck her on the drive home that Florida was a bit like another planet to her. The weatherman had shown a map of the Eastern Seaboard on the news that morning, and Boston had been blanketed with several inches of fresh snow overnight. Once she'd shaken the last thoughts of Richard Dillon from her head, she rolled down the window of her rental car and let the balmy 75-degree breeze run its fingers through her hair.

Her cell phone jingled from inside her purse just as she pulled into the garage, and Cassie dug for it.

"Hello?"

"Hiiiii, Graaaaaammmaa."

"Oh, stereo greetings," she commented. "How are my two favorite boys?"

"Good," Zach replied. Then Cassie heard a shuffle as he took the phone away from Jake. "I was in the Christmas play tonight, Gramma."

"Oh, that's right, Zachary. How did it go?"

"I was Wise Man number two. I got to wear a long beard and rubber flip-flops."

"Oh, well, that sounds like fun. Did you memorize your lines?"

"Yep, I had four of 'em. And I only flubbed one. Daddy says even Zac Efron has to say his lines again sometimes, so that's pretty good."

"That's *very* good."

"Gimme that," she heard, and then Jake was on the line. "Hey, Gramma."

"Merry Christmas, Jacob."

"What are you doing for Christmas since you're not with us, Gram? Are you lonely?"

"Thank you for worrying about me, Jacob, but I'm not too lonely, no. I went to Christmas Eve services at the church. There was a choir that sang, and there were lots of candles and poinsettia plants. It was very pretty."

"Did you have anything sweet?" he asked. "I remember you and Gramps like your sweets on Christmas Eve."

"Well, your grandfather liked his sweets every day of the week. But no, I haven't had anything sweet yet. What do you suggest?"

"We're having green angel cake."

Cassie softened, melting into a reminiscent smile. Angel food cake cut into layers, filled with mint chocolate chip ice cream, and frosted with whipped cream. It was Debra's favorite, ever since she was a little girl.

"That sounds so good," she told him. "Have an extra bite for me?"

"If Mom'll let me, you know I will."

She and Jake shared a laugh, and then he told her, "Mom wants the phone. Merry Christmas, Gram."

"Merry Christmas to you, too, Jacob."

"Hi, Mom."

"Hi, sweetheart. How are you feeling?"

"Like I've eaten a whole bowl of raw cookie dough. The morning sickness with this baby is suddenly an all-day affair."

"Oh, I'm sorry. A late bloomer, huh?"

"What are you doing tonight, Mom? Are you all alone?"

"No, I'm not all alone," she replied. "I went to Christmas Eve services, and I'm getting home right now."

"And tomorrow?"

"Tomorrow I am having a rather large group for dinner."

"You are? Who?"

"James and Tameka. You remember them?"

"Yes. That's great."

"And Millicent, from across the street."

"How is she?"

"She's well. And one of her friends is coming, with her nephew from up North."

"Wow, Mom. I guess you're making all your traditional dishes."

"You know it."

"Ohh, I'm going to miss your yams with the marshmallows on top."

"You had your chance," Cassie teased. "Now someone else will get them."

"That's mean! So you're not going to miss us in the least!"

"Oh, honey," Cassie said on a sigh, "you know better than that."

"I'm just glad you'll have friends around you. How's the house coming along?"

"Really beautiful," she said as she walked into the kitchen and flipped on the light. "You wouldn't recognize the place. It's just lovely, Debra."

"Maybe you'll like the place so much once the renovations are done, you won't want to leave."

Cassie laughed at that. "Why does everyone keep saying that?"

"It's possible, right?"

"Oh, I wouldn't count on it. I'll be happy to sell this house to someone who can make a home here and then be on my way back home."

"Well, have a nice *holiday in Holiday*, Mom."

"I will, sweetheart. Kiss your fellas for me."

"Will do. Love you."

"I love you, too."

When they'd furnished the Holiday house, Cassie had insisted that Zan was out of his mind for thinking they'd ever need such a large dining room table. But as she stood beneath the arched doorway separating dining and living rooms, she smiled. Any other table might not have accommodated the crowd she was about to feed.

Stella and Millicent were comfortable on the living room sofa, sipping from tumblers of ginger ale with sprigs of fresh mint and cackling about someone's new hair color that turned out to be more blue than silver. Stella's nephew Hunter smiled at Cassie through the pass-through to the kitchen as he basted the turkey and tried not to splash any of the juices on his bright red shirt.

When the doorbell rang, Sophie trotted happily toward it, barking and jingling the bells Millicent had tied around her collar.

"Merry Christmas," Tameka sang as she came through the door carrying two beautiful pumpkin pies.

"Same to you," Cassie returned, giving her a hug and smiling over her shoulder at James.

"I hope you're going to forgive us," Tameka said.

"What for? You brought pumpkin pie, and that's really all that matters, isn't it?"

Tameka chuckled and shook her head. "My husband was out on the golf course this morning."

"You played golf on Christmas morning?" Cassie teased. "Really, James?"

"Hey. Don't judge me."

"And he ran into a mutual friend who said he was spending Christmas Day alone."

"Oh, no. Well, I hope you invited him to join us."

"Good!" Tameka cried. "I was hoping you'd say that, because when James told me he just arbitrarily invited the guy to dinner at your house without ever bothering to ask you if it was all right—"

"Don't be silly. Of course it's all right. But you said a mutual friend. Who is it?"

"Here he is now," James exclaimed, waving at the front door. "Richard Dillon."

Oh, of course it is.

"Richard, come on in, bud," James said, smacking his friend on the back once he was through the door.

"Merry Christmas, Cassie," Richard offered, flashing her one of those smiles of his and then extending a bouquet of a dozen long-stemmed red roses toward her. The petals looked as if they'd been crafted out of velvet. "I hope you like roses."

"I do." *Who doesn't like roses? Of course I like roses.* "Thank you so much. Come on in, everyone. What can I get you to drink?"

Millicent had brought along two gallons of her sweet tea, a gallon of a questionable pineapple concoction, and minted ginger ale. And while she made sure that everyone was introduced to one another, Cassie poured two fresh glasses of tea for the Plummers and made one additional mint ginger ale drink for Richard. All the while, she seethed, and when she dropped the ice into his drink, it was with a little extra thrust behind it.

Cassie had just barely managed to stop thinking about Richard Dillon and the fact that he'd let Mick Kendrick think that she was down here in Florida looking for another job.

"Tell me the truth," Mr. Kendrick had said when he phoned her. "Are you getting ready to turn in your resignation? Dillon's hiring you away, isn't he?"

Why in the world would he have called the man to ask about her, anyway? And now here he was, just minutes away from sitting down across the table for Christmas dinner.

Richard chose that moment to come around the corner into the kitchen, and he seemed to take a slight step backward when his eyes met hers.

"Who soured your cream this morning?" he asked, and then he held up his hand. "No, wait. Don't answer that."

"I think you have some nerve, wrangling an invitation to Christmas dinner at my house after that stunt you pulled," she said, pushing his ginger ale across the counter toward him.

"I was hoping to get a chance to explain, once you'd calmed down a little."

"If you're waiting for these jets to cool, you're at the wrong airport, mister."

Cassie placed the two glasses of sweet tea on a platter and carried them past him.

"The wrong… *What? Cassie.*"

She served the iced tea with a pasted smile on her face for the sake of her other guests, but it withered the moment she rounded the corner and returned to the kitchen.

"Listen, Cassie."

"I don't want to discuss it."

"But—"

"I don't think you heard me. Until you tell me the real reason you called my employer to ask questions about me, I am not going to discuss this with you."

Producing two trays of appetizers from the refrigerator, Cassie pulled back the plastic wrap covering them and began straightening the slippery rolls of ham wrapped around cream cheese and diced scallions.

"That looks delic—" She slapped his hand before he could remove one of the hors d'oeuvres from the platter. "Hey!"

"Don't mess it up before the guests even see it," she warned him. "Go sit down in the living room, and you can serve yourself when everyone else does."

James appeared unexpectedly and joined Cassie and Richard at the counter. "What do you think of the changes in this place?"

"It's becoming quite the showplace," Richard replied.

"You've got to see the tile floor in the master bath. Mac, do you mind if—"

The *Mac* reference startled her, and Cassie looked toward James with a slight jerk.

"I'm sorry, Cassie. I just always remember Zan calling you that, and it kind of stuck. I'm so sorry."

"James, it's fine."

"I was just going to tell Richard about the changes we made in the master bath. Do you mind if I take him off your hands?"

"Please do," she remarked, and then she turned her back to them as she placed miniature teriyaki beef kabobs and quiches into the microwave for ninety seconds.

When she turned around again, Tameka had taken Richard's place, and Cassie jumped.

"Sorry. I didn't mean to startle you."

"Hey, what do you think of the changes in the house, Tameka?"

"I think I wish my husband would do this kind of work at our house." She grinned. "It looks great, especially the kitchen. It's updated and chic. I think you'll be able to recover more than every dollar you put into the place with the sale price."

"I hope you're right."

"I did hear a rumor yesterday that might be both good and bad news for you, though. There's a big corporation in negotiations to take over several properties in this area."

"How would that affect me exactly?"

"Well, we could probably get a good price for your property pretty quickly, but if the rumor is true and their interest is just to tear it all down so they can build a resort of some kind, then the upgrades weren't necessary."

"That would be a shame," Cassie commented. "It's so beautiful. Someone could really be happy here."

"But your interest is just in selling the place and getting back to Boston, right?"

Cassie sighed. "How soon can you put it on the market?"

"I'll try to get more information about this corporation and see if I can't get them to nibble on your place first. How about we talk again on Monday?"

"Works for me. The sooner I unload this place and get back home, the better I'll like it."

Cassie glanced up from the appetizer tray and noticed Millicent standing behind Tameka, her round face deflated and wearing her disappointment like a long string of pearls.

Cassie felt like she might choke on regret. "Millicent, I'm sorry. I didn't mean—"

"I know what you meant," the older woman interrupted. "You have a life to get back to."

Millicent turned around and returned to the living room sofa, the hollow thump of her thick, rubber-soled shoes telling the tale of her letdown.

"Anything I can do to help with dinner?"

Cassie looked up at Richard, standing there all smug and clueless, and she tossed the dish towel in her hand to the counter with a snap.

"What?" he asked, and Tameka pursed her lips and shook her head as if to tell him not to speak. "What did I say now?"

"Oh, just…just…go to the living room," Cassie said. Pulling the plate of warm appetizers out of the microwave, she pushed it toward him. More softly, she added, "And take these with you, please."

Once he was gone, Tameka waited a couple of beats before placing her hand on Cassie's arm and squeezing it. "What's going on, girl?"

"Oh, nothing. It's just Richard Dillon."

"I'm sorry," she whispered. "I thought the two of you were friends. I would never have let James bring him along if—"

"No, no, please," Cassie said, waving her hand and shaking her head. "It's fine that he's here."

"It looks real fine."

"It is."

"There's obviously something not right between the two of you."

"I think it's just a chemical thing," Cassie said on a whisper. "You know how some days you're the windshield and out of nowhere you meet that person who is the bug that splatters all over you on the highway?"

Tameka roared with laughter at that, leaving Cassie to wish she'd been joking.

Chapter Eight
. . . .

7 ACROSS: Unforgettable

"What a wonderful meal," Tameka declared as she pushed her plate forward and leaned back against the chair. There were agreements all around.

"What's the stuff in turkey that supposedly makes you tired?" James asked, patting his stomach with both hands.

"Tryptophan," Hunter replied.

"Well, it's working."

"That's because you consumed more turkey than the rest of us combined," Tameka pointed out. "He'll be down for the count an hour after the pie settles."

"Would anyone like another slice?" Cassie asked them, and James groaned. "Or more coffee?"

"I just put on another pot," Richard called out from the kitchen.

Tameka raised an eyebrow at Cassie and then grinned as she leaned over toward her. "He seems very comfortable in your kitchen."

"No, he just wants to make sure he's the one handling the food," she replied in a whisper.

They shared a giggle, and Cassie's eyes fell on Millicent at the other side of the table. She was a solemn and quiet hive that all the other bees in the room buzzed around. Stella and Hunter, on either side of her, appeared oblivious as they chattered on, Stella including her friend in the conversation, but never quite noticing that she wasn't the least bit involved.

Cassie scraped back her chair and rose to her feet. From behind Millicent, she bent down and wrapped her arms around the woman and planted a kiss on her fleshy cheek.

"Can I talk to you outside?" she whispered.

Millicent stood up without reply, and the two of them stepped out to the deck. White twinkle lights spiraled the wooden railing on three sides, and the half moon did the rest to light the night as it reflected off the glassy water of the canal.

"It's a beautiful evening," Cassie said, offering Millicent a patio chair.

"Very."

"Millicent, I wanted to confide in you about something, if I can."

The woman's eyes lifted, and she looked at Cassie through curiosity mixed with surprise.

"That comment you overheard earlier, about how I wanted to just sell this house and get out of here…well, someone has been driving me a little crazy lately, and in the heat of the moment, I blurted that out."

"I didn't mean to *drive you crazy*, Cassie. I've just been enjoying our friendship. I liked having you around and—"

"Oh, Millicent!" she exclaimed. "It's not *you* that's driving me crazy, silly!"

"It's not?"

"No, of course not. And I'm so sorry that you heard me say it, because if I could take one thing home with me when I leave Holiday, it would be you."

"It would?"

"Yes, it would. In fact, I think you might like Boston, if you're interested," she teased.

Relief flooded her when Millicent found her smile again.

"You are so dear to me," she told the woman.

"Maybe…you don't really…have to go."

The suggestion was childlike, and the hopeful glaze of emotion in Millicent's eyes just about broke Cassie's heart.

"You have so many friends here," Cassie reminded her. "And you have your ceramics classes and dance lessons."

"I'm taking a cooking class with Stella over in New Port Richey starting on the sixteenth."

"See? You have a lot going on. I'm guessing you won't miss having me around as much as you think you might. And we'll keep in touch. We'll have long talks on the phone, and we'll write letters."

"I've got the e-mail now."

"That's great. So we can e-mail each other and chat on IM." When she saw the haze of confusion on Millicent's face, she clarified, "Instant messaging."

"I don't know the messaging just yet."

"Maybe I could show you. I know it's not the same as waving at each other from across the street, but we're friends, Millicent. Boston won't change that."

"Well," the woman said, with a sigh following. She leaned in toward Cassie with a very serious expression. "The truth is…there's somebody kind of driving me crazy lately, too."

"Oh?"

Millicent nodded toward the house and then raised one eyebrow and curled up the corner of her mouth. "Mm-hmm," she hummed.

"Stella?"

The woman nodded once more, with conviction.

"Ohh," Cassie replied. "A little pushy, isn't she?"

"A little?" Millicent answered. "The old broad is an expert on every subject, including the ones that she's not."

James and Tameka were the first to leave, and then Stella walked Millicent home so that they could make another batch of sweet tea to take to the prayer chain meeting at the church the following morning.

Richard looked so ridiculous that he was almost cute with Cassie's lacy "Jesus is the Reason for the Season" apron draped over his pale green shirt as he rinsed the dinner dishes and loaded the dishwasher.

"You look rather adorable in that apron," Hunter mocked as he helped Cassie fill plastic containers with the dinner leftovers.

"Don't I, though?" Richard returned. "Jealous?"

Cassie resisted the urge to tell him that the apron was even too frou-frou for her to wear; she certainly hadn't imagined a man wearing it in her kitchen!

And then she remembered that Zan had bought it for her in hopes that she would agree to spending just one Christmas holiday in the warm Florida sun. Emotion glazed her eyes as she remembered the Fourth of July barbecue out on the deck—Zan brushing his famous sauce over several racks of ribs, wearing that same apron, and looking almost as preposterous as Richard did just now. But then, Zan could always carry off "preposterous" pretty well. And far more naturally than Richard could.

Cassie held back a chuckle as she handed Hunter the last container, and Hunter stacked it inside the refrigerator with the others.

"You'll be eating turkey and the trimmings for days!" he told her. "Hey, want to go walk off some of that pie?"

She hated that her eyes darted so quickly toward Richard before she could stop herself.

"There's a gorgeous half moon out there and it's 73 degrees. I don't see much of that in New York in the month of December, and I know you don't in Boston. Come on. Let's go for a walk."

"Well…"

"You kids go ahead," Richard commented without looking up. "I'll finish things up here."

His indifference seemed almost genuine, and that pinched at Cassie in the hollow place just above her ribs.

"Let's do," she said. "Let me get a leash on Sophie, and I'll grab my jacket in case I need it."

She didn't.

The gentle breeze off the water was mild, so Cassie just folded the jacket over her arm as they followed the sidewalk up the street and around the corner. The sky crowned the neighborhood with a midnight blue awning, the stars twinkling like light breaking through tiny pinholes. The silhouettes of tall palm trees were traced against the landscape in the distance, and the occasional spotlight from the houses they passed illuminated the way.

"You'd think it was an April night, wouldn't you?" Hunter commented, and Cassie nodded in agreement.

"I don't think I've ever been down here at this time of year. I had no idea it was so pleasant."

"So why don't you tell me about yourself, Cassie? What's your life like up in Boston?"

She had the sudden impression that she was on one of those reality dating shows and her bachelor wanted to cram in as much information-gathering as he possibly could while they managed to find some time alone.

"Well, I'm an administrator for a law office there. I started out as a legal secretary about fifteen years ago, and I've been with them ever since."

And fifteen years ago, you were, what, being potty-trained?

"So you enjoy your work?"

"Yes," she answered. "I'm an organizer at heart, so it's a good fit for me. What do you do in New York?"

"I'm a numbers cruncher."

"Accountant?" she tentatively clarified.

"Not exactly, but it's far too boring to tell you about."

"I see." She didn't really, but there was no spark of curiosity that made her want to inquire further. "I've been to New York a few times. It's very...*large.*"

"I went to college there, so by the time I got my degree, I knew some people and liked the town and then got a great job. It wasn't really a conscious choice to stay. It was just a sort of natural progression."

Okay. Well, we've covered the weather and our careers. Where do we go from here?

"Cassie, would you like to have dinner with me while I'm here?"

She stopped herself just short of gasping.

That's where we go from the forecast and job status?

"That's very sweet of you, Hunter."

"I know what you're going to say. You think I'm too young for you." He stopped and put his hand to rest on the fold of her arm, overtop her jacket. "To tell you the truth, when my aunt suggested that we hook up, I was primed to blow her off. But I am really attracted to you, Cassie." He seemed to be rather stunned by his own revelation. "So I'd like you to give the idea a chance."

Cassie sighed. "Thank you, Hunter. Really. But I don't think so."

"Is it so easy for you to just toss something away without even knowing if—"

"I'm sorry. I'm just not interested in a relationship."

"Who said anything about a relationship?" he cackled. "Why don't we just—"

"Thank you, but no."

Now respect your elders and stop pushing me!

Hunter shrugged and shook his head. "If that's the way you feel, I guess... Well, okay."

"It really was a pleasure to meet you, though. I'm happy you could join us today."

He didn't even bother with the courtesy of reciprocating, but he sure did step up the pace back toward her house after that.

"I think I'll check in on my aunt over at Millicent's place," he said. Then he brushed her cheek with a broken kiss and crossed the street. "We'll be over to say good night when she's ready to go."

The soft hum of the dishwasher greeted her when she and Sophie returned to the dimly lit house. The dining room table was cleared and the chairs were in perfect placement around it. The kitchen counters and sinks were wiped clean. Cassie noticed that the glass door and screen leading out to the deck were open, and then she saw Richard seated in a patio chair that he'd pulled out to the edge of the damaged dock.

He didn't so much as flinch as she walked down the dock toward him. She stood behind him in silence, unsure of what to say.

"Have a nice walk?" he asked, still without any movement at all.

"It's a pretty night."

"Yes, it is."

"Do you feel like another cup of coffee?"

She didn't even really know why she'd asked. Richard's presence was a little like a square of sandpaper in her shoe, rubbing against a blister at the back of her heel.

"Nope," he said, and he pushed up to his feet and turned to face her. "Too late for coffee."

Cassie began to wring her hands, and then she stammered slightly as she told him, "I have decaf. Or there's still some of Millicent's sweet tea in the fridge."

Richard stared at her for a long moment and then asked, "What are you doing, Cassie?"

"What do you mean?"

"Earlier, when I arrived, you couldn't even stand to look at me. Now you want to have coffee with me?"

Cassie looked up at him and grimaced. "I just can't get a read on you, Richard."

"What would you like to know?"

Bracing herself, she answered him. "For starters, I'd like to know why you called Mr. Kendrick and asked questions about me."

"I think you can figure that out." He glanced down at the dock and rubbed the toe of his shoe over a splintered board. "You're not that clueless, are you, Cassie?"

"Clueless!"

"I called my old friend to find out more about you," he blurted. When he looked up at her, his eyes were disks of blue fire. "About your life in Boston. About...*you.*"

"But why?"

"You're really going to make me say it?"

"Say what?" she exclaimed.

"That I'm interested in you, Cassie. Very...I'm *very interested* in you."

"Hello–oo–ooo..."

Cassie took an instinctual step backward as Stella poked her head around the glass door and called out to them, but her gaze was frozen solid against Richard's.

"Cassie?"

"Coming."

It almost produced a physical pain as she peeled her eyes away from the choke hold of Richard's, but she managed it and then retreated up the dock and into the house.

"I just wanted to thank you for such a lovely celebration," Stella said, her whole hand wrapped around Cassie's wrist as she shook it from side to side. "It was so nice to be included. Thank you, darlin'."

"You're very welcome."

"Let me just step out and say good-bye to our dance master here," she said, nodding toward Richard. "Hunter's out front. Go and say good night, will you, Cassie? I think he's quite smitten with you."

Before she could reply, Stella was on her way across the deck.

Cassie released a long, laborious sigh, and then she headed toward the front door and opened it. Hunter stood a few feet away on the sidewalk, looking up into the night sky.

"Thank you for coming," she said from the doorway. "It was nice getting to know you, Hunter."

He was motionless for a long moment, and then he turned and looked at her strangely. Without any warning at all, he plodded toward Cassie, hauled her into his arms, and planted his mouth over hers. She heard Sophie growl softly as Cassie yanked herself out of his embrace.

"Ohhh!" she groaned as she pushed him away. "Stop that! What are you doing?"

"Kissing you good night."

"You have a lot to learn about women, Hunter," she exclaimed, both arms poised in front of her in a defensive stance. "You don't just…*do* that!"

"Fine," he grumbled, and then he spun on his heels and stomped down the driveway. "Your loss," he called back.

Sophie barked at him twice as he went.

"Good grief!" Cassie breathed. She wiped her mouth with the back of her hand. "Do I have some sort of"—she blew an unsavory noise out between her pressed lips—"sign on my back or something today?"

"Where's Hunter?" Stella asked as she crossed the living room.

"He left," Cassie growled.

"Oh."

Stella seemed disappointed. But Cassie was somewhat thrilled to have him gone.

"Well, Merry Christmas, Stella. Have a nice night."

What was it Zan used to say? Don't let the barn door hit your donkey from behind.

"All right then. Good night, darlin'."

Cassie closed and locked the front door and then leaned against it for a moment. She took one deep breath and then headed through the darkened dining room to the slider and looked around outside for Richard.

He'd moved the chair back to the deck, and he was gone. Cassie stepped outside and craned her neck in one direction and then the other, but there was no sign of him.

Just as well.

Stella's interruption had been fortuitous, because Cassie had no idea what she would have said to him anyway.

He's interested in me. What is that supposed to mean?

What kind of future could Richard Dillon possibly have imagined for them? Not that she could deny the odd and startling chemistry between them, but chemistry could be disappointing and fleeting. Two people needed more than biology to build upon. They needed something in common, some bond between them. They needed to be cut from the same fabric.

Cassie picked up the cardboard box from Rachel that she had slid underneath the desk in the corner, and she carried it to the living room and dropped it to the floor in front of the wingback chair. She peered into the box by the illumination of the Christmas lights on the palm tree beyond the window.

She pulled out the first of the three gifts wrapped in shiny paper and tied with bouncy spirals of holiday ribbon. She shook the box once and then again, and then she held it up to her ear for a third shake.

"Bath salts," she said. She opened it to confirm her correct guess.

The second present was a no-brainer. She held it before her and stared at it for a moment, and then she shrugged. "A book. Maybe a devotional." *Just what I need to start the new year out right!*

Right again.

The third gift made a *phloosh-phloosh* noise when she shook it. Some sort of jewelry.

Cassie pulled off the ribbon and eased open the metallic green box. Inside were the most horrible neon-green-and-pink plastic palm tree earrings. She plucked them from the box, held them up toward the light from the window, and frowned at them.

Palm tree earrings, Rach?

Beyond the earrings, on the other side of the window, Cassie noticed the two pink flamingos on the lawn…which, of course, reminded her of Zan.

So much for the lofty theory that two people have to be cut from the same cloth to make a lasting relationship.

While Cassie imagined that she had been constructed from a durable, dependable burlap, she was certain that Zan represented something colorful and breathable. He was 100 percent pure cotton.

With a Hawaiian print, no doubt.

Chapter Nine

....

1 DOWN: Energetic; forceful

Cassie broke the yolk on her egg and burned the toast, which didn't really matter because she was out of butter. She used a fork to stuff it all down the disposal and then went looking for the leftover pumpkin pie—only to find a pristine, empty pie shell with no trace of filling inside.

"So–phie," she called with nonchalantly.

Sure enough, the strawberry blond collie trotted around the corner, her tongue hanging off to one side and her needle nose and mouth covered in orange remnants.

"Bad dog," she said, tipping the pie plate into the trash and letting the empty crust fall out. "I hope you don't plan on making me pay for that later."

Cassie decided on a two-day-old turkey sandwich and some cranberry sauce for breakfast and then slipped into one of the dining room chairs.

1 Down. Seven letters, meaning energetic and forceful.

Nothing came to her, so she took another bite of her sandwich and was just about to move on to the next clue when her cell phone rang.

"Cassie? It's Millicent. Do you want to have lunch before we go for our dance lesson?"

Cassie had forgotten all about it.

"It's cha-cha day, hunny bunny. I can hardly wait!"

"I'll have to meet you there today. I have to stop in to see Tameka and sign some papers."

"Oh. All right."

"It starts at one?"

"Sharp."

"I'll be there."

Cassie wondered what had happened to the idea of disco. *Cha-cha day.* She cringed as she folded up the crossword puzzle and returned it to the desk drawer, then popped the last bite of the turkey sandwich into her mouth.

She paused and glared at the "Surprise Yourself" box. It stared back at her with a throbbing pulse for several seconds before she finally groaned and picked it up.

"Train up a child in the way he should go, and when he is old he will not depart from it" Proverbs 22:6.

She turned over the card.

Mentor a child who might benefit from your wisdom.

Cassie laughed out loud as she pushed the card into the back of the box and closed the lid. The chances of coming across a child—*or even anyone under the age of fifty!*—while in Holiday were pretty remote. And finding one that needed mentoring...or could learn anything at all from her? Slimmer still.

She shook her head as she hurried into the bedroom to change into some dancing clothes. She decided on her skinny black jeans, a capped-sleeve black T-shirt with shiny black beads drizzled across the front, and white Keds. As she pulled her hair back into a bouncy ponytail, Cassie fought against the urge to reach for her makeup kit in the pink canvas bag.

Why wear makeup? she asked herself. *Because you're going to see Richard Dillon?*

She turned up her nose at her own reflection and marched straight out of the bathroom. But by the time she reached the hall, she'd surrendered the fight and went back for a little lipstick.

And maybe some foundation and mascara.

A little blusher couldn't hurt either. She was also seeing Tameka, after all. And she always looked so beautiful.

Cassie reached down and flicked on the curling iron.

Just a quick touch-up.

🌴 🌴 🌴

"Tameka? I'm running a little later than expected. Any chance we could meet up around three thirty?"

"That's perfect. I have a couple of stops to make myself."

"How about a late lunch? At A Pizza Holiday? If I don't get some spinach pizza soon, I'm going to cry."

"Well, we don't want that. I'll see you there at three thirty."

Closing her cell phone, Cassie jogged up the ramp of the church and into the recreation hall. A fast instrumental Latin beat greeted her, and she hurried into line beside Millicent as the group watched Richard and Laura move to the music. Millicent squeezed her hand and grinned and then twirled her hips several times to show off her dark red dress with the layers of fringe on the skirt.

"Fancy!" Cassie whispered. "Perfect for dancing."

"I know," Millicent replied with eager enthusiasm.

The dancers were in perfect harmony, and Cassie couldn't help but notice the sleek, straight lines of Richard's body as he moved. Every step and turn was so precise and timed. She feared she wasn't likely to have that kind of balance or rhythm in her lifetime, no matter how hard she practiced.

When the music came to a crescendo and then faded to a close, Cassie joined the others in thunderous applause. She rocked to her tiptoes and clapped her hands with eager appreciation.

"Okay, let's all partner up," Richard told them. Cassie faced Millicent. "The cha-cha is a lively Cuban dance. The dancers should synchronize their movements, working parallel to one another. Let's start with a basic count. You'll dance five steps to four beats, like this. One, two, cha-cha-cha. One, two, cha-cha-cha. Got it?"

They all paired up and began with the most fundamental of steps. Cassie found herself counting aloud as she and Millicent struggled to stay in sync.

"One, two, cha-cha-cha. One, two, cha-cha-cha."

"Let's all stop a minute and watch the Hootzes," Richard called out, and Cassie craned her neck to locate them in the room. "Georgette, start out on your left leg."

As the music began and the Hootzes started to dance, Cassie's hand flew to her mouth. She was astonished!

George Hootz had *moves*!

"You two have done this before!" Richard exclaimed. He and Laura stepped back and let the older couple dominate the floor. While Georgette was clearly the stronger dancer of the two of them, Cassie could hardly believe her eyes when George started with the hip action.

"Three whole beats and two half beats," Richard narrated from the sidelines. "Notice that there are no forward steps on the heel.... Get your footwork correct first and then add the hip action.... That three-step is called a *forward basic.*"

Millicent reached out and tugged Cassie toward her. She was itching to dance, and she and Cassie began taking the steps along with George and Georgette. In just a few seconds' time, several other couples were trying it, too.

"You haven't trampled my corns even once, *cha-cha-cha!*" Millicent exclaimed.

"I was just thinking that myself, *cha-cha-cha.*"

"So, by the way, what happened with Hunter, *cha-cha-cha*?"

"Not worth telling, *cha-cha-cha.*"

"Cassie, excellent!" Richard called out. "Just watch your rhythm."

And with those few words, Cassie promptly lost her balance and crushed Millicent's corn with the ball of her foot.

Cha-cha-cha.

Richard watched as Cassie spoke briefly to Millicent and then turned away and walked right out the door. She didn't so much as give a glance in his direction.

"You were wonderful, Richard."

Maureen Heaton stood before him, abject and timid.

"Thanks, Maureen."

"I'd give anything to dance like that."

"It only takes practice," he reassured her as he gathered his belongings.

"How did you get started?" she asked, peering up at him, hopeful and somewhat tragic. "Have you danced your whole life?"

"No," he answered on a rolling laugh. "My wife insisted that we take dance lessons before our wedding. She didn't want me to humiliate her when it came time to have our first dance as husband and wife. She'd always dreamed of doing a Viennese waltz, and I could no more do a waltz than I could…sew her a wedding dress."

Richard sat down in one of the folding chairs against the wall, and he nodded at the empty one next to him.

"So the two of you waltzed into your new life together," she surmised as she folded into the chair beside him. "How romantic."

"We enjoyed it so much that we kept taking lessons. Then, after a few years, we started to compete."

"I saw some of the photos. You were a handsome couple on the dance floor."

"You did? How?"

Maureen gulped and then admitted, "I Googled you."

Richard smiled at her. The poor woman was nursing quite a crush. As meek as she was, she'd never even tried to conceal her feelings, and he wasn't quite sure how to handle it. He couldn't reject her outright. At the same time, he certainly couldn't let her think there was a future in it.

"I guess I'd better get going," he said, pushing up out of the chair.

"Richard?" He turned and looked down at her, waiting. "Do you think sometime…at one of the lessons…or maybe afterward sometime…do you think we could, just once, dance together?"

Richard weighed her request. "You want to dance with me."

"The truth is," she said as she rose from the chair, "I love dancing more than almost anything else in the world. And it's been a lot of years since I've had a partner to dance with. Well, besides Catherine."

He laughed at that, and Maureen giggled like a schoolgirl.

"You don't have to if it makes you uncomfortable," she said, her head angled downward. "I just thought it would be something I'd remember, you know?"

He wasn't sure why he hadn't seen this sweetness in Maureen Heaton before. Beneath the clumsy, nervous little barn owl, there lurked a tenderhearted and engaging woman.

"What's your pleasure?" he asked her.

"Pardon?"

"Rumba? Salsa?"

"Waltz," she replied. "I would really love to waltz."

Richard went over to the card table in the corner and flicked through the record albums and CDs stacked against the wall. He wanted to take care not to choose a song that was romantic but was determined to make a choice that would lend itself well to the smooth float of the waltz. John Mayer's "Daughters" was perfect.

He stepped up to Maureen and reached for her hand. In that moment, Richard watched a transformation take place that astounded him. Meek little Maureen converted into a strong and confident dance partner. She floated along across that floor, self-assured, graceful, and as light on her feet as anyone with whom Richard had ever danced. In many ways, he was reminded of Caroline.

As the music dissolved and the dance came to an end, Richard twirled Maureen into a light dip, and she grinned at him from ear to ear.

"Maureen," he said as he brought her upright again, "you are remarkable."

"Thank you so much, Richard," she said, hand over her heart. "You have no idea what you've done for me, how you've taken me back to a time when..."

Her words trailed off, and he noticed a mist of emotion move up and over her as clearly as a morning fog.

"Where did you learn to dance like that?"

"I used to have a dance studio in Racine. My husband was a landscape designer, and there was...an accident. Before that, we used to dance together in the studio late at night—waltzes and the tango. I probably don't look the part, but I lay down a *mean* pasodoble!" An enormous smile cracked across her face and then melted down suddenly into a sorrowful, disappointed grimace. "But that was before his accident, before we packed up and moved down here to Holiday."

Her husband? "I had no idea."

"He's in a wheelchair now, and his dancing days are long behind him. But I've missed it so much."

"Maureen, you're married?"

"Thirty-six years. Marvin. The love of my life."

Richard was suddenly ashamed of his own arrogance. He'd been mistaking Maureen's longing for a dance partner for something else entirely. In the two years since he'd met her for the first time at a spaghetti supper at the church, he'd never even known that she was married. Or anything else about her life, he realized.

"Your husband doesn't come to church," he remarked.

"No. Marvin's a deeply religious man, but he's become very much of a hermit since the accident."

"Can I ask what happened?"

"It was a random mugging. He was on his way to the corner market, and a young boy held up a gun and demanded his wallet. The boy got nervous, the gun went off, and Marvin was paralyzed."

"I am so sorry," Richard said, and he took Maureen's hand into his. "Is there anything I can do for you?"

Maureen smiled through a haze of emotion. "You've just done it, Richard. Thank you for helping me recapture a piece of myself I'd thought was lost."

"How's your tango?"

Her brow arched immediately, and the corner of Maureen's mouth twitched. "A little rusty."

"The next dance is the tango. How about filling in for Laura?"

"Are you joking?" she exclaimed.

"Are you in?"

Grinning like a cat with a full stomach, she replied, "Oh, I'm all in."

"I'm serious, Tameka. It's almost impossible to reconcile the two different Richard Dillons: the one that drives me batty and the one that dances like Fred Astaire."

"I don't think I've ever seen Fred Astaire dance."

Cassie stared her down, mouth gaping. "How is that possible?" she finally asked.

"What?" Tameka exclaimed. "We didn't know anything about Fred Astaire where I grew up. We were more into Kool & the Gang."

"Hey," Cassie replied, wiggling her index finger at Tameka, "I liked Kool & the Gang. We used to dance to them on Friday nights at the YMCA."

"Oh, a wild girl, eh? Going to those Friday night dances at the Y."

"It didn't stop me from loving me some Fred Astaire, my friend."

Tameka chuckled, and Cassie began humming "Get Down on It" by Kool & the Gang, pulling out a few of her disco moves, pointing to the ceiling and then to the table.

Tameka added lyrics to Cassie's melody, and the two of them went into very different types of chair dances.

"Umm, can I...uh...get you anything else?"

Both of them turned instantly timid, squirming in their seats as the young waitress stood over them, and Tameka cleared her throat. "No. Thank you, dear."

Once the waitress put down the check and walked away, shaking her head, Cassie and Tameka broke into laughter.

"She can't even be eighteen yet, right?" Tameka cracked. "You know she's thinking, 'What a couple of morons.'"

"Yes, but I'm sure she has a much hipper term for it."

"Like what?"

"How do I know? I'm *your age*."

"Uh-huh, girl. I'll remember you said that. Mm-hm."

Cassie grinned and then realized that her cheeks ached from laughing so much over lunch.

"I'm so glad you met me here," she told her friend. "First of all, I've been planning to have this particular pizza since the day I left Boston, but there's been one obstacle after another until now."

"And second of all?"

"Second, I'm nuts about you."

"Back atcha." Tameka reached across the table and tapped Cassie's hand. "Promise me we'll do this again before you leave."

"Oh, we will. I heard a rumor that there's a soul-food dinner with my name on it at your place."

Tameka nodded. "You know there is, girl. Maybe we can invite Richard Dillon, too." She looked up at Cassie and tried not to laugh.

"Oh, now see there. You ruined it. We were having a perfectly good time, and you ruined it."

"I don't know. It looks to me like there's something more going on than just a bug and a windshield, Cassie."

Cassie raised her hand in the air. "Check, please?"

"We already have the check."

"Oh. Right."

Tameka grabbed the check, scraped back her chair, and rounded the table to give Cassie a hug. "I have to run," she told her. "I'll call you to set up that open house. I'd like to hold off until I can get some more information about this mysterious corporation. At the moment, I can't get any solid facts, just a lot of speculation."

"Just let me know."

"When I know something, you will, too."

They exchanged another wave once the check was paid and Tameka was on her way. Cassie paused to sip the last of her soda and then gathered up her belongings and made her way out the door.

Just outside the restaurant, she stopped to dig her sunglasses out of her purse and was nearly knocked down as the door flew open and smacked her hard in the arm.

"I hate you! And you can't make me work here another minute!" the girl on the other side of the tornado screamed, before ripping off her tomato-stained apron and pelting it to the ground. But instead of storming off as Cassie expected, the girl leaned back against the building and started to cry.

Cassie moved toward her with caution. This was the girl who had waited on them earlier. Her black eyeliner was running, and her black-and-pink-streaked hair was pulled into a long ponytail.

Her bottom lip was pierced with a round gold ball, and a tattoo of a rosebud peeked out of the scooped neck of her T-shirt.

"Are you all right?" Cassie asked her, and the girl jumped.

"No," she blurted.

"Is there anything I can do?"

"You can talk some sense into my father," she whimpered.

Her father? "Oh my. Are you Vanessa?"

"Yeah," she nodded. "Hi, Mrs. Constantine."

"Wow."

"I know. I've changed, huh?"

"You…yes. You certainly have."

"Sorry about Mr. Constantine."

"Thank you. Are you going to be all right?"

"I have a chance to graduate early, in January instead of waiting until June."

"That's great…isn't it?"

"You'd think so, wouldn't you!" she exclaimed. "I have a 3.8 GPA, and I was accepted to UF."

"Congratulations."

"I'm gonna study criminology and then go into forensics after that. You know, be a CSI like on TV."

"Oh."

"So if I graduate in January, I thought I'd go up there early, a'ight? You know, check the place out, rent a room in the area until I can get into the dorms, maybe get a job for half a year. But my father thinks I'm too young, and he won't let me go."

"Oh, I see."

"He is so bent."

Bent?

Just then, the glass door of the restaurant jingled open. "Nessa, come back in here," the young woman said.

"I don't need you all up in my grill. I'm talking here."

The other waitress looked at Cassie and angled her shoulders into a shrug before stepping back inside.

"You know, Vanessa, I understand your enthusiasm about getting out on your own as soon as you can, but didn't you say when we talked on the phone that you're just sixteen years old?"

"Seventeen next month."

"Still, that is very young to be out on your own. The world can be pretty terrible sometimes, and I can tell you from experience that there are very few people out there who will have your back, no matter what happens."

Vanessa glanced over at her, and then she lifted one shoulder.

"Your dad just wants to be there for you as long as he can. In another blink of an eye, you'll be in college and then working a job, maybe moving away. It happens so fast. And I can pretty much guarantee you that, after it does, you'll wish you'd stayed these last six months."

Vanessa gave a bitter chuckle. "I don't think so."

"You love your dad, right?"

"Most days."

"And he loves you."

"Till I choke."

"So you have a job here. You can make some money to sock

away and take with you when you move to the dorms. And in the meantime, you can take advantage of free room and board and a little extra time to spend with your family before you leave them behind and start your life."

The girl sighed. "Is that what your kid did?"

"Yes. It is."

"And she's glad now? I mean, she doesn't look back on it and think how whack it was that she had to live with you—and live by your rules?"

"I think she is glad now."

Vanessa made a fist and plunked it against the wall behind her.

"It's just something to think about," Cassie told her.

"Yeah. I guess."

"Feel any better?"

She surprised Cassie with a creeping smile that changed the whole look of her young face. "Kinda."

"Why don't you take a walk and do some deep breathing?" she suggested. "You'll feel so much better afterward."

"Thanks."

Cassie rubbed Vanessa's arm and then headed for her car.

"Mrs. C?"

She stopped and turned around.

"You're a'ight."

"You too, Vanessa."

It wasn't until she'd turned over the ignition and pulled out into traffic that Cassie remembered that morning's "Surprise Yourself" card.

Mentor a child who might benefit from your wisdom.

Vanessa was no longer the towheaded child with the bright orange bicycle that Cassie remembered. And she wasn't sure if their conversation warranted the label of mentoring…or even wisdom, for that matter.

But she had indeed surprised herself!

Chapter Ten

. . . .

13 DOWN: No one else like you (4 words)

"You must be Marvin!" Richard exclaimed, and he enthusiastically shook the man's hand.

"What was your first clue?" Marvin returned with a glance down at the wheelchair that held him, and then he let out a rolling and contagious laugh.

"Well, aside from that," Richard told him, "I saw my dance partner come in with you."

Maureen gave the spark of a smile from the sidelines, where she was buckling into her dancing shoes.

"You shoulda seen the way Mo's face lit up when she told of dancing again. You mighta thought she was suddenly raised out of her own wheelchair." He tilted his head thoughtfully and then added, "I guess that's sort of what it's like for her, too."

"Marvin Michael Heaton, you just stop that talk right now."

Marvin flashed Richard a crooked grin and then bit it off like a thread. "I just had to come and see it for myself. She's an angel on the dance floor."

"That she is," Richard agreed.

Without even looking back, he *felt* Cassie's entrance into the hall, and then there was the tickle her voice made at the nape of his neck. Richard shook his head at the soft but persistent alarm going off somewhere in his head. It was a throwback to his days in the navy! *Dit-da-dit-dit-dit-dit*—a sonar signal going off within him.

"Ohh, Marvin!" Millicent cried, and she toddled toward the man and leaned over to give him a warm and welcoming hug. "It's so good to see you out and about!"

"I had to come and watch my Mo dance."

Millicent looked confused, so Richard began rounding up the troops. "Okay, ladies and gentlemen. Laura couldn't make it today, but I was fortunate enough to stumble across someone with all the moves to make a great stand-in for our lesson today. Let's give a nice welcome to Maureen Heaton, my dance partner for today's tango."

They applauded, and Maureen squeezed Marvin's hand before she stepped up next to Richard.

"Some of you may know this, but I've only just learned it," he told them. "Maureen operated a dance studio in Wisconsin before she came to Holiday. I had the pleasure of dancing a waltz with her recently, and she was as strong a partner as any other one I've ever had."

"Oh, thank you." She actually blushed as she angled her face toward the floor. Richard thought it was rather sweet.

"The tango is an emotional dance, with lots of clipped movements like sharp head turning and immediate stops." He demonstrated. "The man's arm is higher than usual, and the couple is closer together. Like this."

Cassie's hazel eyes flared when they met his for only an instant, and Richard darted his gaze away as he led Maureen across the floor.

"There is no rise and fall in the steps of the tango," he told them. "You'll make very level, flat strides, with the knees slightly bent at all times."

Richard started the music, a piece from an Angelina Jolie/Brad Pitt movie, and Maureen hopped into his arms like a frantic rabbit. Normally he would have just shown them the most basic of steps, but Maureen was *invested*. He could feel it from her grip on the palm of his hand to the sharp, pointed plunk of her shoes on the wooden floor. And so he indulged her, and Marvin as well, as he watched them from the sidelines with an emotional mist in his eyes.

Clearly, one man's barn owl was another's perfect, carved cameo. Seeing his wife dance again was a simple gift to give, but Richard noted that it was a gift received like gold and silver would have been. When they finished the dance, the onlookers erupted into applause and Marvin looked as if he might spring right out of his wheelchair.

Richard started the music again. As everyone paired off and began their own versions of the tango, his roaming eyes made their way to Cassie and Millicent.

He watched Cassie as she tripped over Millicent's right foot and then her left. Two beats later, she dug her heel into her toes, and Millicent cried out in anguished pain.

"I'm so sorry," Cassie crooned.

The woman has all the natural rhythm of a monkey running away from a hummingbird.

Richard approached them. "How about we give Millicent a break?" he suggested, taking Cassie by the hand while her partner hobbled off to the side and sank into the first available chair with a whimper. "Kick off your shoes."

"Pardon?"

"Your shoes. Take them off."

Cassie pressed the back of her heel with the opposite foot and nudged off the tennis shoe. She repeated the motion with the other one and then rocked on both heels and waggled her sock-gloved toes.

"Now what?"

"Now," he said, leading her by the hand toward him, "gently… and please notice the emphasis on the word *gently*…step up on my feet so you're standing on top of them."

"Are you joking?"

"I never joke about golf or dancing."

Wrinkling up her face like a dried nectarine, she placed one foot on his shoe and gingerly followed suit with the other, grappling for a tighter grip on his hand so she wouldn't fall.

"Relax," he told her. "Don't try to move your feet at all. Let me do it for you."

There was that bumbling monkey again, all arms and rubber cement. As hard as she tried to stand there and enjoy the ride, Cassie just couldn't seem to manage it.

"Relax," he repeated. "Let me do the movements."

"I can't help it," she said from between clenched teeth.

"You *can* help it. Relax."

He felt the rise and fall of a very deep breath press against him, and then, for just a moment or two, they moved across the floor almost as one single dancer.

"Do you think you can try that?" he asked her. She nodded tentatively. "Okay, step down."

She did, allowing him to draw her along…and *she followed!* In perfect form, she actually followed his lead. Richard thought it might qualify as a minor miracle.

And just when he was about to allow the pride to move up from within him, to enjoy the rhythm of holding her in his arms and dancing in seamless synchronized harmony, the music dipped toward a close. And on the final beat of the song, Cassie Constantine turned back into a pumpkin, raised her foot, and planted it hard across all five of his toes.

"'During the 1920s,'" Cassie read from the large hardbound book in her arms, "'orchestras and bands played music meant for the fox-trot at a much faster rhythm than intended for the dance. Over time, a faster version of the fox-trot was developed, with elements of ragtime such as the Charleston incorporated into it. This resulted in the dance known as the quickstep.'"

Millicent set down two glasses of sweet tea on the coffee table in front of her as Cassie continued to read.

"'The quickstep is a fast and sporty dance with a great deal of tricky footwork involved. The tempo is slow-quick-quick-slow-quick-quick.'"

Millicent repeated it in a whisper as she moved her feet. "Slow, quick-quick, slow, quick-quick."

"'The majority of the slow steps are taken on the heel. And the quick ones are taken on the toe.'"

Millicent immediately adjusted the rhythm and stance. "Slow, quick-quick, slow, quick-quick. I think I've got it. Come here, hunny bunny. Let's try it together."

"Shouldn't we watch the video again?"

"No amount of watching is going to replace the doing. Now come over here and dance with me."

Millicent's vinyl copy of "You're the Cream in My Coffee" sounded grainy and scratched, but it was one of the songs listed in the book as ideal for dancing the quickstep. Cassie asked herself several times why she was working so hard at the next dance on Richard's list for the seniors, and she hadn't come up with an answer as of yet. She only knew that she'd found herself brimming with the desire to astound him. It may have had something to do with the "Surprise Yourself" card she'd drawn the day before: *Let each of you look out not only for his own interests, but also for the interests of others" Philippians 2:4. Think of a way to surprise someone else, rather than yourself.*

Or it may have just been the staggering attraction she'd felt while he tangoed her across the floor, with her standing atop his feet, as his dumbfounded prisoner. Either way, Cassie was determined to render Richard Dillon speechless when he saw her bombshell of a quickstep.

"Like this?"

"No, no," Millicent chided. "I don't think so."

"Oh. Well, let's try it again."

"Wait, I'll start the music over." And after a moment, "Cassie, you have to let go of me first."

"Oh. Right. Sorry."

Another few tries at mastering the dance and Millicent was breathing hard, with a little wheeze at the end of each pant.

"Why don't we take a break?" Cassie suggested.

Millicent only nodded since she wasn't able to speak, and then she pointed at the sofa and wheezed, "Divan. Sit."

Cassie hadn't heard a couch called a *divan* since her grandmother was alive.

"It's a dance of endurance, that's for sure," Millicent piped up after five minutes of puffing. "I betcha I'll drop a few pounds this week, don't you think so, hunny?"

Cassie nodded as she gulped at the cold tea in her glass. She leaned back against the sofa at the same time that Millicent did, and the two of them plunked their feet up on the coffee table in perfect unison. Cassie huffed out a sigh.

"So," Millicent groaned, "why don't you tell me about your hotsy-totsy?"

"My what?"

"Your big polka-dot crush on Twinkle Toes."

"What on earth are you talking about, Millicent?"

"You and Richard Dillon. What's going on there, huh?"

Cassie felt her heart kick into overdrive, thumping against her chest wall.

"It won't go any further, hunny. You can talk to me." Cassie just kept her eyes forward, as did Millicent, and when she didn't answer, Millicent pressed on. "Does he know yet?"

"Know what?"

"How you feel."

Cassie sighed again. "I don't know how he would when *I* don't even know how I feel."

"Has he told you how *he* feels?"

"Yes."

Millicent spun around sideways and faced her. "He has? When? What did he say?"

Cassie angled her head toward Millicent and then closed her eyes for several seconds. "Christmas. After dinner. We were out on the dock, and he said he was *very interested* in me."

"And what did you say in return?"

"I don't think I said anything. Stella came out and interrupted us."

"Oh, of course she did. That woman! And have you spoken since?"

"Not alone."

"So you haven't said anything back to him?"

Cassie looked up at her curious friend and asked, "What would I say to him? I don't know how to respond, or if I even want to."

"You have to figure that out first. I mean, even if we think we know somebody, we don't really know them, hunny bunny. But if he is who I once thought he was, men like Richard Dillon don't come around too often, take my word for that."

"I just don't know if I'm ready."

Millicent nodded, and then she asked, "Because of Zan?"

"Because of Zan, I guess. And because of that dumb crossword puzzle he left behind."

"*No com-pren-day*, hunny bunny."

"Every year, he would make these crossword puzzles for me on our anniversary, and they'd be chock-full of words describing me. Or his image of me."

"And this has to do with Richard…how again?"

"They're words like *orderly* and *astute*."

"Oh, I see. And those words pretty much describe Richard, don't they?"

"To a *T*. And they're the things I don't want to be anymore, Millicent," she said, sliding around and folding her leg underneath her. "I want to be *fascinating* and *surprising* and—and—*devastating*."

Millicent laughed. "Oh, I used to be *devastating* back in the dinosaur age. As I recall, it's not all it's cracked up to be, hunny."

Cassie chuckled and rubbed Millicent's hand. "Until I can at least be *interesting* and *breathtaking*, I just don't think I can give myself up to someone who is…"

"What? Who is what, Cassie?"

"The male version of Zan's straitlaced wife," she replied in a whisper.

"Well, I guess that's something you'll want to figure out first, then."

The two women sat in silence again, and then Millicent broke it with the tinkle of the ice in her glass as she swirled the refreshment and then took a drink.

"I hope you won't wait too long, though. Times are changing in Holiday."

"What do you mean by that?"

Millicent flexed her ankles on the table in front of them and then kicked off her shoes and let them thump to the floor.

"I got a visit from a Realtor here from Tampa this week," she told her. "He made me quite an offer on my house."

"Really? Was he representing that corporation I've been hearing about?"

"I think so."

"Millicent, what's that got to do with Richard?"

The older woman gulped down the last of her tea and rested the glass on her knee. "I think Richard Dillon *is* the corporation trying to buy up all of the property in Holiday."

Cassie folded both legs under her and sat sideways on the couch, her back against the armrest as she narrowed her eyes at Millicent.

"Richard? Why would you think that?"

"A few months back, he was asking a lot of questions over at the golf course. The place was…well, still *is*…in disrepair. It seemed like he was thinking of buying the course for himself, and the way he loves the golf game it seemed like a good move for him, now that he's retired. But then there was nothing. Not another word. Ask him about it, and he'll clam right up on you."

Fragments of thought dangled in the air like loose strings hanging from the ceiling. "I don't understand."

"I think Richard was asking questions and then when people started to catch wind of it, he had the Realtor from Tampa pick up from there. Rumor has it that the corporation is going to bulldoze all of the properties that back up to the golf course and over to the canal, and then make the whole place into some sort of golf resort."

"Bulldoze! Don't they have to get some sort of approval to do something like that?"

"Holiday is a small town, without a lot of resources. I'm afraid this would be just the sort of thing that would be approved because it would bring revenue and jobs into the area with no thought for much of anything else. But hunny, I've lived in Holiday since before my Bernie died. I don't want to go anywhere."

"So did you tell the Realtor that your property isn't for sale?"

"I did. But he didn't seem convinced, and Stella says they can get pretty rough when a homeowner stands in the way of their big corporate plans."

"And you think Richard is behind all of this?"

"I don't know. Maybe, though."

"Then why would you want me to take up with him, Millicent?"

"For one of two very good reasons." Tears stood in the woman's eyes as she replied, "To see if he has a part in all of this. And if he does, to talk him out of taking my home."

"I'll talk to him, Millicent."

"When?"

"I'll call him tomorrow."

"It's still early. Maybe you could call him now?"

"Let me work my way into that, Millicent." Cassie rubbed the woman's arm and smiled. "Maybe later."

"Will you call me after?"

"Yes."

"How?"

"What do you mean?" Cassie asked her. "On the phone."

"Do you have my number?"

Before she could answer, Millicent started speaking out the number, and Cassie plucked her cell phone from her pocket and programmed it into the memory.

In the span of the three minutes it took to walk across the street and up her driveway, Cassie decided that Millicent's fears were unwarranted. Stella was a bit of a drama queen, and she had no doubt conjured up some sort of theatrical production after Millicent reported on the visit from the Tampa Realtor.

Richard came to Holiday to retire, after all. Not to change the whole face of the city into which he'd moved and then to become some big resort owner. It just didn't fit together.

Cassie moved a chair from the patio down to the edge of the dock and settled there to watch the water and the stars for a while, and the scenarios continued to rumble around in her brain.

He sure does love to golf, though, she recalled. *If he was going to start up a new business, a golf resort would surely be the one he would start.*

Mr. Kendrick had mentioned a business venture that Richard was involved in—the one in which he feared Cassie was going to become involved, as well.

And hadn't Richard warned Cassie not to spend too much money fixing up her house to sell it? If he was going to bulldoze the place, that would be his thinking.

Cassie pulled the cell phone from the pocket of her capri pants and dialed 411.

"Directory assistance for what city?"

"Holiday, Florida," she replied. "Listing for Richard Dillon."

"Please hold while I connect you."

Chapter Eleven
....

15 ACROSS: Enticing; captivating; beguiling

Receiving an invitation from Cassie Constantine at seven o'clock at night to come over and have a latte seemed rather out of character, but Richard wasn't one to look a *gift-Gidget* in the mouth. By seven thirty, he was standing at her front door and waiting for her to answer the bell.

He glanced at the palm tree in the yard, its trunk illuminated like the stem of a red-and-green candy cane. At its feet were two freakishly ugly flamingos, both of them wearing collars of lights and so *neon* in their neon pink that they clashed with the Christmas lights, even in the Florida twilight.

"Richard, come on in," Cassie said as she pulled open the front door. "I'm glad you could come."

As he ruffled the fur behind Sophie's ears, he had the urge to look around with caution for signs of a trap door or a net that would scoop him up and hang him from the ceiling. He comforted himself with the reminder that she would certainly get to the point as soon as they were settled. Was she finally going to address the admission of interest that had spilled out of him on Christmas? He'd wished at least a hundred times since then that he could pull back those clumsy words, edit them a bit, and then reissue them as a better first draft.

"It's decaf," she told him, setting two mugs of foaming coffee on the dining room table. She sat across from him and began scratching something on the handle of her mug.

"Thanks," he said, and then he took a sip from the cup for lack of anything better to do. "Mmm. Pretty good."

"Yes?" she said with a smile that brought up those perfect round apples in her rosy cheeks. "Good. I'm…I'm glad."

They were as silent as a stockpiled bomb in the next seconds that ticked by, and it was just about all Richard could do not to call attention to it. But at last Cassie pulled open the casing and exposed the missile in the room.

"Richard, I hope you won't mind me bringing this up. I was wondering, though, if you could possibly tell me… I mean, I probably have no right to even ask…but I've heard some things and…"

"It's true," he said, breaking the ice with a steel pick.

"It is?"

"Yes," he said while nodding, "I tried out for *Dancing with the Stars.*" He took another drink of the latte.

"I beg your pardon?"

"I know I'm not a big star or anything, but I just can't live without that big glittering disco ball trophy. I have to take the chance."

She stared at him, a queer little question mark forming on her face.

"I'm kidding."

"Uh. Oh. Of course you are." She released a chunky little "Ha!" and then rubbed her temple. "That was…funny."

"Cassie, you obviously have something to say to me. Just relax and say it."

He took another drink from his coffee cup to give her preparation time, and then he set the mug on the table, leaned back in the chair, and folded his arms as she stared out the window for what seemed like an eternity.

"Are you going to build a golf resort?"

Just like that. A bubble in the air, popped with a pin, and bubble guts showering all over him.

"That's why you called me over here? To ask if I'm going to build a golf resort?"

"Yes," she stated, continuing to stare him down.

"Why would you ask me that?"

"Because I'd like to know."

"Why?"

She twirled the mug around in its spot once and then again before replying, "Because I think it will affect a lot of people in Holiday, and I'd like to know if you're the one behind it."

"Why do you care?" he asked her. "Aren't you leaving Holiday?"

"Well, yes. But there are a lot of folks who won't be leaving. Unless you have a hand in forcing them out, and—"

"Forcing them out? What are you accusing me of here, Cassie? Heading up the Tropical Mafia?"

"Well, no. Of—of course not," she stammered.

"Is this the only thing you called me over here to talk about tonight?"

"Yes."

"Never mind that you've left my declaration of interest in you lying on a plate like stale bread. You want to know if I'm going to be breaking people's kneecaps and forcing them out of their homes so I can build a golf resort."

Her hazel eyes fluttered slightly and then came to rest on the tabletop.

Richard stood up and looked down at her for several seconds.

"Thanks for the coffee, Cassie."

She was still in her chair when he reached the door and tugged it open, but she was pulling at his sleeve before he could take one step outside.

"Come on, Richard, we can talk about what you said on Christmas, too, if you want. But I really do want to know if you're behind this golf resort thing."

Richard twisted his arm until she released her grip.

"Mr. Kendrick told me you're starting up a new business venture," she reasoned as he walked away. "That was why he thought maybe I was going to take a job with you. Millicent said you'd been out at the golf course asking questions about the place. And then the Tampa Realtor came to her house. And—"

"And so you put all the clues together, and it must be Colonel Dillon. On the golf course. With the nine iron," he said as he made his way down the sidewalk, leaving her standing in the doorway with all of her questions.

"Richard, please come back."

"Thanks for the invitation, Cassie," he said, turning toward her and walking slowly backward down the driveway. "But I don't think so. Have a nice evening."

Cassie plopped down on the sofa with a groan. Sophie stood next to her expectantly, as if waiting for Cassie's next move. Immediately she noticed the crystal "Surprise Yourself" box sitting where she'd left it on the coffee table just that morning. The card had said something about taking care to be sensitive to someone else's feelings, and she felt a rush of heat move through her with the reminder that she had done just the opposite with Richard. She hadn't taken care with his feelings in the least.

She leaned forward and picked it up, pulling the card from the very back of the box, the same one she'd read just that morning.

"He who guards his mouth preserves his life, but he who opens wide his lips shall have destruction" Proverbs 13:3.

Try holding your tongue when you feel like saying something that might hurt someone.

Cassie felt the burn of Richard's disappointment inside her, all the way to her soul. He'd been waiting for her to respond to what he'd revealed about his feelings. Instead, she'd tried to dig up an admission about his personal business dealings.

But he did act very much like a man with a secret.

She looked down at Sophie, who was standing in front of her with a curious look in her eyes and her big floppy dog hanging out of her mouth by the ear.

"Sorry, Soph. Can we play later?"

Sophie dropped her toy, sighed, and sat down.

Cassie plodded into the master bathroom, started the water for a long, hot bath, and then pushed her hair up off her neck in three sections with long clips. She laughed into the mirror at the wacky results before her. Each section of hair pointed in a different direction like a three-armed scarecrow. Then she spread a thin layer of bright green mint julep mask over her face and flipped on the radio that sat high on the corner shelf.

Dan Brody was filling in for the night DJ on The Joy FM, and he introduced an old song by Brandon Heath as she shut off the faucet and stepped into the steaming water in the tub. Sophie placed her chin on the rim of the bathtub and whined as if she was singing along.

Cassie found herself humming with the tune that she hadn't heard in such a long time and then tapping her fingers on the sides of the tub. The music soothed her spirit and began to lift her up. In another moment it transported her, and she realized how much she wished for the very thing the song lyrics suggested. If only Zan could see her now. If only she could show him how she'd changed since coming to Holiday.

She leaned her head back against the edge of the tub, closed her eyes, and smiled. Struggling against all of the qualities he'd found worth appreciating in her had begun to carve out a new version of Cassie—a more fun-loving and adventurous Cassie and, oddly enough, a Cassie who would probably have delighted Zan to no end.

How ironic. Zan was gone and would never know the woman she was becoming. *And Richard!* Richard was just straitlaced and *just-so* enough to want the former Cassie over this current one.

She chuckled as she imagined the crossword puzzle Zan might create for her now.

Spontaneous. Disco dancer. Sensitive.

Well, she was trying to be sensitive. Even though she'd failed miserably with Richard.

She wanted to kick herself one more time.

Cassie sighed when the doorbell rang and Sophie tore out of the bathroom and down the hall while barking a piercing warning. Cassie had called Millicent to tell her that Richard was coming over, and she'd really meant to call her again after she spoke to him but then had completely forgotten. The woman had elicited a hand-raising vow that she would phone the minute he left. She'd probably seen him leave and then hurried over to see what she'd learned once she grew weary of waiting for the telephone to ring.

Cassie reluctantly climbed out of the tub and quickly ran a towel over her body as the doorbell rang again.

"Coming, Millicent," she called out as she slipped into the plush terry-cloth robe hanging on the back of the door. "Keep your dentures in," she mumbled as she padded down the hall and around the corner toward the front door.

She paused to tie a tight knot in the belt of her pale pink robe, and the doorbell rang yet again.

"Good grief," she said as she yanked the door open, and then she gasped when it wasn't Millicent standing on the other side at all. "Richard!"

His eyes opened wide and so did his mouth, as he stared at her, and Cassie felt relief flood over her like a sudden summer shower.

"I'm so glad you came back!" she exclaimed. "Come in, will you? Just have a seat while I go and throw on some sweats. I really was hoping to talk to you about before. I'm just so glad you came back."

Richard nodded, and he stepped inside and closed the door behind him.

"I'll be out in just a sec, okay?"

"Uh, o–kay."

He looked so odd to her, so uncharacteristically speechless. Maybe because she was wearing a bathrobe?

"I was just in the tub," she said, pointing over her shoulder. "So I'll just…go and change. Okay?"

"Uh-huh."

"Good," she replied, wondering if he was about to have a stroke or something. "Are you all right?"

"Yes."

"Because you seem a little strange."

"Do I?"

They stared into each other's eyes for several frozen seconds, and she noticed the corner of Richard's mouth twitch, as if trying to hold something back.

Cassie shrugged. "Okay. Well, make yourself at home, and I'll be right back."

She shook her head as she ambled back down the hall and into the bathroom. She pushed the lever on the front of the tub, and the drain gave a little *poot* as it released the still-warm water.

Turning back toward the mirror, Cassie froze with her hand in midair, and then she gasped and stopped cold.

A reflection of crazy scarecrow hair and neon moldy face surrounding huge, astonished eyes as round and shiny as quarters peered back at her.

"O-oh—" she panted, and then she repeated the strange noise, except this time a little louder. "O-ohhh— Nnn-noooo!"

Her neck snapped as she jerked back toward the door and thought of Richard. No wonder he'd been looking at her like he'd gotten a firm grip on a live wire!

"Aarrrrrrrgggh!" she screamed at the top of her lungs as she cupped water with both hands and threw it onto her bright green face in frantic splashes.

From the other room, Richard guffawed, and then he wheezed in little clucks before belting into laughter again. Sophie began barking excitedly. Whatever was inspiring Richard's hilarity, she seemed to want in on it.

"Oh, shut up!" Cassie shouted at him, which only seemed to make him laugh harder. She heard the squeak of the sofa springs as he fell down upon it, chortling and sniggering until it sounded as if he might choke.

"Come on, Mrs. Kabuki," he returned with a funny gurgle. "I—*hahaha*—I like your green face. And that hair!"

Cassie moaned as she tugged at the clips holding her hair in three opposing directions, and Richard exploded into another fit of laughter from the other room.

She could hear him through the closed bedroom door, trying to compose himself and seeming unable to manage it. She tied the waist of her sweatpants in quick jerks and pushed her feet into canvas mules before stomping down the hall.

"Can you quit that now?" she asked as she marched right on by and straight into the kitchen.

"I don't think so," he replied, still chuckling. And then he sprang to his feet and followed behind her. "Let me see your face. Is it still green?"

"No, it is not," she stated, turning back toward him for only a moment.

"You're right. It's pink again."

She produced a bottle of juice from the refrigerator, opened it, and took a swig.

"You're not going to offer me anything?" Richard asked her, a mock pained expression on his face.

"Oh, just grab what you want," she replied, and she walked away from him.

Cassie was already sitting on the sofa when Richard joined her a minute later with a bottle of lemonade in his hand.

"Why did you come back?" she asked him.

"I thought you were happy I came back."

"I was. *Until you spoke.*"

"That seems to be a theme with us."

"Well, if you would just stop irritating me all the time…"

"If you just weren't so easy to irritate…"

"Why did you come back?" she repeated.

"I'll tell you in a minute. First, you tell me why you were so happy that I did."

Cassie sighed. "I just wanted to say…" She sighed again, and then she clicked her tongue and groaned. "I wanted to say…that I'm sorry."

"For?"

She glared at him. He knew what for.

"Just to be sure," he said, the corner of his mouth twitching. "I want us to be clear."

"I'm sorry, Richard. You told me that you were interested in pursuing something more with me. At least I think that's what you were leading up to saying. And I didn't respond to you, and then I sort of…"

"Avoided me."

"Well, no."

"Yes. You avoided me."

"Okay, yes. I avoided you."

"Kind of rude, if you ask me," he added.

She glowered at him again. "I didn't ask you."

"Still."

"I know. And I'm sorry. Okay?"

"Are you really?" he asked her. "Because it doesn't seem all that sincere to me. In fact, you appear to be a little irritated just saying it."

Cassie growled and dropped back into the sofa cushions and closed her eyes.

"My turn?"

She opened one eye at him in silence. Then, "That depends."

"On?"

"On what you're going to say. I've reached my itchy irritation limit for this day."

Richard took a long draw from the bottle of lemonade, and then he placed one ankle atop the opposite knee. He just sat there like that for a long, frozen moment.

"I am not building a golf resort," he stated. He plunked his drink down onto the coffee table.

"Oh." Cassie inched forward and perched on the edge of the couch. "You're not."

"I am, however, thinking of buying the golf course, which makes all this corporate interest in the surrounding area a very special concern to me."

Cassie mulled that over and then scratched her head. "I don't understand."

"The golf course went into foreclosure earlier in the year, and it's going up on the auction block soon. I really want to buy it for as little as I can and then sink some dollars into refurbishing it. There isn't a course worth playing within forty miles, so I think it could be a pretty good investment."

"So why did that Realtor want to buy Millicent's house for you?"

"It wasn't for me," he declared. "A buddy who works for the county told me that some corporate entity is trying to buy up all the property around the golf course, and he thinks they'll try to snag the golf course, too."

"Ohhh. So that's where the rumor came in that someone, presumably you, was going to tear down all the houses and build a golf resort around the course."

"Exactly. But you can't talk to anyone about any of this, Cassie. I need to be able to trust you."

"Okay. But why? Why can't I tell anyone?"

"I'm trying to find out who I'm up against here and whether I even stand a chance. In the meantime, I don't want them getting wind that there's another party interested."

"Can I just tell Millicent?"

"No."

"Why not?"

"Because Millicent has the Southern-bred ability to spread gossip faster than a speeding crawfish."

"Even if I ask her not to say anything to—?"

Cassie cut herself off. She hadn't even finished the thought before realizing that there was no fighting it. Giving Millicent something juicy to tell and then asking her not to tell it would be like putting a screen door on a submarine. She wouldn't be able to help herself.

"You're right," she breathed. "I can't tell Millicent."

"Thank you."

"But you know, everyone in town thinks it's you."

"I know."

"And it's only going to spread from here. Doesn't that bother you?"

"The only part that really bothered me," he said, leaning forward and staring at the floor, "was letting *you* think it was me."

"Really?"

"Really."

"Why?" When he didn't respond right away, Cassie grinned. "Because you're *sweet on me*?" She elbowed him and giggled. "Huh? Is that why?"

Richard raised his head and narrowed his eyes, burning a hole straight through her.

"Do you still want to know what I think about that?" she asked him.

He looked as if he was going to simply shrug, but then he turned it around with an abrupt nod. "I do."

"Well," she began, and then she heaved a hefty sigh. "The truth is…I don't know how I feel about it, and that's why I didn't respond to you sooner than this. Even after all these months, I can't really wrap my brain around the fact that Zan is gone, but he is. And he's not coming back. And I have to move on but, frankly, I just don't know how to do that."

Richard nodded. "I get that."

"So I can't give you any definitive answer. Even though you didn't really ask any questions. I mean, I can't deny there's something going on here—an attraction or chemistry or something. But the thing is, Richard, you know…I…uh—" Cassie broke off and blew a puff of air up under her bangs. "I'm babbling, huh?"

"Yes."

"I'll stop now."

"Good idea."

"So we're good?" she asked him timidly. "For the moment?"

"For the moment."

"Good."

"And you're keeping my secret?"

"For the moment," she replied with a smile.

"Good."

And with that, Richard leaned back into the sofa cushions behind him and sighed. "So about that green stuff you had on your face. What in the world *was* that?"

Chapter Twelve

....

17 ACROSS: Causing one to gasp; thrillingly beautiful

Cassie had to read it a second time. She didn't know what the twelve-letter answer was for 17 Across, but the clue made her heart beat a little faster to know that Zan was able to think of a word that meant "causing one to gasp" and "thrillingly beautiful" and still manage to associate it with her.

She looked hard at her reflection in the sliding glass door as she wondered if he'd ever included such lovely clues in his crosswords before. The answers she could remember from years past were words like *dependable*, *loving*, and *sensible*.

But *thrillingly beautiful*?

Cassie squinted at her image again, trying to find something thrilling or beautiful there, and then she grinned from one ear to the other.

Causing one to gasp!

She especially liked that clue, but it poked her with an instant reminder of Richard's reaction when she'd unwittingly opened the door to him while donning a full Kabuki-style facial mask. The recollection caused her to chuckle out loud while she smeared another blob of peanut butter onto a saltine.

The sun would be coming up soon. As soon as she finished

eating, she'd grab a quick shower and get dressed in the hope that she might have time to share some coffee with the sunrise before Tameka arrived at eight thirty. Florida certainly held the top spot in the country for amazing sunrises, and she'd been kind of dreaming about experiencing one of them close-up from outside at the end of her dock. This morning might just find her in the right place at the right time to do that.

Cassie downed the last of the cold skim milk in her glass and then reached forward to move the crystal "Surprise Yourself" box closer. She plucked out the first card and read the scripture verse on the front.

"He who has begun a good work in you will complete it"
Philippians 1:6.

She popped another cracker into her mouth as she turned over the card.

Think about the bigger picture today.

Funny, that was just what she intended to do.
And then the second sentence gave her a bit of a scrape.

Who are you destined to become?

Cassie sighed, fixing her focus on the chair rail on the wall across from her for no good reason except that it was there.

"I wish I knew," she told the card, and then she tucked it into the back of the box and closed the lid.

The question hummed inside her as she put away the jar of peanut butter and placed the knife in the dishwasher. It continued to sing softly throughout her shower and while she applied some makeup and put on her clothes. Pumping up the volume, it throbbed to the beat of her heart as she dragged a chair out to the edge of the dock and sat down, resting a cup of coffee on the knee of her denim jeans. She reached over the arm of the chair to scratch Sophie's neck. The collie sat beside her, erect and looking out at the water, a stuffed reindeer hanging out of her mouth.

Who am I destined to become? Cassie asked herself in harmony with the echo of the message on that card.

She thought back to the morning that she and Zan had brought Debra home from the hospital. Sitting there in the bright white rocking chair, surrounded by pale green walls and a border around the room illustrated with happy dancing bears wearing soft yellow hats and light blue ribbon sashes, her destiny became so clear. Her future was all about that tiny baby in her arms, as pink as the cashmere blanket that held her. Cassie knew then that her destiny was to become the best mother she could possibly be.

Debra was all grown up now, and she'd probably had those very same thoughts on the mornings when she'd brought Zach and Jake home from the hospital. When Zachary had been christened at the little stone church near Debra's home in suburban Baltimore, Zan had wrapped his arm around Cassie's shoulder and squeezed her toward him.

"Well, Mac," he'd said, "this is one of those defining moments. Our girl has officially broken free of us, and it's just you and me now."

The horizon beamed with pink and orange as the memory tickled Cassie's heart. Zan was gone, and she was alone. She'd never imagined she would grow old without him.

Think about the bigger picture today. Who are you destined to become?

It was a very good question, and she was just on the brink of that place where she needed to answer it soon. While she pondered the subject, the bright pinks and oranges on the horizon gave way to purples, and then the blue Florida sky emerged. The occasional cotton ball of white fluff appeared, but for the most part she saw an endless indigo canopy stretched out over the river canal, beyond the roofs of the houses on the other side of the wooden docks, and clearing the tops of the tallest palm trees in the distance.

By the time Tameka arrived at 8:35, Cassie had spent more than enough time with her own questions and thoughts. She was ready for a second cup of coffee and some digging for information.

"I spent the morning watching the sun come up," she told her friend, as she set down two mugs of hot coffee between them at the dining room table. "You really have to give the place credit for those sunrises, don't you?"

"I try to see as few of them as possible," Tameka replied playfully. "I much prefer to sleep through them and concentrate on the sunsets instead."

"Well, those are good, too."

Tameka's smile was so engaging and warm. Her teeth were as white as pearls against her light tea-colored lips and dark brown skin, and her cocoa eyes sparkled like glass in sunlight.

"I think I have some pretty good news for you." She gleamed, and Cassie straightened in anticipation.

"You do?"

"I haven't been able to find out who's behind the offer, but those mystery guests I told you about are willing to pay you eleven grand more than the asking price for your house."

"You're joking."

"I'm not. Their representative paid me a visit yesterday."

"Do you have a guess about who he's representing?"

"Well, the Holiday rumor mill has been circulating a theory about Richard Dillon being behind this. He used to be an attorney for a big developer, so it's not so far out of the realm of possibility."

"Is that what you think?"

"No, I don't think it's Richard. The questions this guy was asking just don't seem to be questions Richard would need to ask. He's been living in this community long enough to know."

Cassie nodded, trying to keep her expression as close to blank as possible without going over the edge to unconvincing.

"So who does that leave?"

"I hope I'm wrong, but I think this guy is a front for the Mandalay Corporation."

"Who's that?"

"They're developers out of California. There's a history there of buying up property that backs up to a central location of interest, like a lake or some developed tourist attraction like a national park."

"Or a golf course?" Cassie asked, trying to maintain a display of casual curiosity.

"Right. This would be small potatoes for them, but I can't get a line on anyone else. They usually come in and strip the place down to the bare bones and start again. It's great for bringing jobs into a community, but it's not so great for the residents when their taxes go sky-high and their quiet surroundings turn into an amusement park of tourists and traffic. I'd hate to see that happen to Holiday."

"I don't really see it happening, Tameka. I mean, Millicent, for one, isn't going to sell. They can't just build around her."

"Oh, Cassie, if it's Mandalay, they can and they will. And when it becomes unbearable for her to remain, they'll give her a pittance for her house and she'll take it just to escape. The golf course is the main attraction here, I think. As I said, that's very small potatoes for Mandalay, but it goes to auction next week. Once they have that, there will be no stopping the progress."

"What if someone else buys the golf course?"

"Someone who can afford to outbid Mandalay? Not likely."

Cassie's spirits dropped. She wanted to ask Tameka if she could help Richard get the golf course before it went to auction, if she had any information or connections that could aid him, if only for the good of the community of Holiday. But she couldn't break his trust, and she'd promised her silence.

"So you have a decision to make," Tameka told her. "Do you want to take their offer?"

"Oh, Tameka, I don't know. It seems like such a betrayal of Holiday."

"I understand. But your goal is to leave here, so I have to present the offer to you and let you decide based on your own priorities."

"Why do you have to be so fair-minded?" Cassie said, chuckling. "Can I have some time to think about it?"

"I'll call you in a day or two."

Cassie stood in the doorway and waved at Tameka after she pulled out of the driveway. The minute her Dodge Caravan shifted into DRIVE and headed down the street, Cassie closed and locked the front door, raced through the living room, grabbed her purse and keys, and flew into the garage.

She'd only been to Richard's house that one time, the first night they met, when she gave him a ride home after the Hootzes' boat sank. She wasn't sure she remembered how to navigate the twists and turns of his neighborhood, but she defied her own doubts and drove straight to the one-story ranch with the brick planter out front.

She knocked on the door and then tapped her foot while she waited for him to answer.

"Cassie!" Richard exclaimed when he opened the door.

"I should have called," she said. "Are you busy?"

"No. Come on in."

She brushed by him into the foyer, and while he closed the door behind her, she peered into the living room and immediately met the gaze of a large albino fish with red eyes and a thick mustache. Its glass tank was built into an enormous wooden cabinet that acted as a separation wall between the living room and dining room.

"What's up?" Richard asked as he led her inside.

She couldn't take her eyes off the odd fish, and she approached the aquarium and gave the glass a soft tap. "Hi there."

"That's Chi Chi."

"Chi Chi?" she repeated with a laugh. "Well. Good morning, Chi Chi." Several other varieties of fish swam out from behind the plants at the back of the tank.

"Chi Chi Rodriguez. He's an Albino Aeneus Cory Cat. There are a couple more like him in there."

"What are these others, here?" she asked, pointing at the smaller, rounder occupants that looked as if they'd been dipped in gold.

"Gold Veil Angels," he told her. "Jack and Arnold."

Cassie looked at Richard, and he gave her a sheepish grin.

Pointing at the darker, striped guy keeping to the far side of the tank, she said, "Let me guess. This one's Tiger?"

"How did you know?"

"My husband loved golf, remember? Jack Nicklaus, Arnold Palmer... What is it with the game of golf?" Cassie asked him, shaking her head. "Men become absolutely giddy and obsessed!"

Richard stared at her in disbelief. "Uh, it's *golf*," he stated. "The greatest sport in history."

"Oh, please. Can I sit down?"

"Be my guest. Can I get you something? Coffee?"

"No, thank you. I wanted to tell you about a conversation I had with Tameka this morning. She got an offer on my house, without them ever setting foot inside."

"Ahh," Richard groaned, and the two of them sat down at opposite ends of the micro-suede camel sectional. "Any idea who's behind the offer?"

"Have you ever heard of the Mandalay Corporation?"

Recognition sparked in Richard's crystal blue eyes, and he nodded. "Of course."

"Tameka hasn't been able to confirm it yet, but she thinks that's who it is."

"I thought they stayed out West," he remarked. "California, Arizona, New Mexico; those are Mandalay's usual stomping grounds, if I remember correctly. And Holiday seems like small-time for a company like Mandalay. Why did Tameka zone in on them?"

"She didn't say. She just said that's who she suspected."

Richard leaned forward, his elbows pressed into both knees, and Cassie watched as the wheels of thought churned in his expression.

"Thank you, Cassie," he said.

"I knew you wanted to know who you were up against."

"I don't know how much good it will do to know, but I appreciate it," he told her.

"You know, I've really been thinking about this," she said. "And I can't figure it out."

"Figure what out?"

"Well, why are they offering so much more than the appraised value? I mean, if they're buying up all the property in the area, shouldn't they be trying to get it for as little as possible?"

"I can't begin to tell you what the logic is behind any of it," Richard admitted with a shake of his head. "Are you going to accept their offer?"

"That's why I wanted to speak to you. How much damage will I do if I take the money and run?"

Richard turned his head and watched the fish swim for several moments before answering. "I'm debating on giving you the selfish answer or the one that's good for you."

Cassie smiled. "Why don't you give me both?"

"I don't want you to go," he admitted as he looked into her eyes with such intensity that it rocked something inside her. "So, no, I don't think you should take their offer. I think you should hold out for a legitimate buyer, someone who is going to appreciate the work you've put into making that house a home for them."

"And?"

"Oh. Well, the flip side is that, yes, you should take their offer. You can be back in Boston by the new year and put sinking pontoon boats and ballroom foot-stomping lessons and everything else about Holiday far behind you, once and for all."

Not so fast, she thought. *What if I don't want to put everything about Holiday behind me?*

The sudden consideration astonished her, even as it jiggled around in her mind.

"Speaking of the new year…," she began. She pressed her pant legs with both hands. "The seniors are having a costume disco party at the church on New Year's Eve. The flyer says it will say good-bye to the seventies—never mind that most of them have already said good-bye to their seventies."

Richard grinned. "I heard. Also never mind that they'll all be home and in bed by 9:30."

"Could be," she replied on a laugh. "Do you have a date?"

"Did you just call me a senior?" he asked.

"Certainly not!" she exclaimed, punctuating it with a giggle. "But I know they all adore you. So I wondered if you'd like to go with me."

Richard gazed at her without speaking, something akin to curiosity in his expression.

"We can wear spandex and polyester and big hair," she teased. "It will be a happening!" She paused. "Will you be my date, Richard?"

"Millicent won't mind?"

"Well, she'll be with us, of course."

"In that case, I'd love to," he said, and then he pointed at the ceiling in an overly casual Travolta move.

"That's great! I'll stock up on hair spray and dig up some spandex."

He'd almost decided not to invite Cassie along, but as Richard turned and glanced at her now, he was really glad that he had. The window on the passenger side was rolled three-quarters of the way down, and there was a chilly breeze pushing back her hair. She closed her eyes and tilted her face into the sunlight, and he thought what a beautiful, porcelain face it was.

"I can't get over 76 degrees in December," she said without opening her green eyes. "How long was it before you did?"

"I'm still not there," he replied. "Any climate that allows me to golf in short sleeves in December has me at 'Hello.'"

Richard pushed the gear into Park and flipped the switch to roll up Cassie's window.

"It's hard to believe you got me to come golfing with you," she said with a chuckle. "I hope your friends won't mind me riding along."

"They're expecting you."

He rounded the back of the car to open her door, but she'd already opened it for herself by the time he reached it. So he took her hand instead and helped her out.

"Why do you drive so far away just to golf?" she asked him as they walked through the parking lot.

"Just?"

"Oh, I mean, to golf," she corrected with a chuckle. "An hour in the car ju— um…to *play golf* seems a little excessive to me. I don't even like to drive from my house into the city for a linen sale downtown."

"The Pine Barrens course at World Woods is ranked one of the best public courses in the state," he answered.

"I'll just pretend I know what that means and nod like I'm impressed."

"You really need to get out more."

"*Yyyeahh*," she said with a slow drawl. "You're so right. Chasing a small white ball around acres of grass, sand, and water…that's really something that's been missing from my life."

"Now you're talkin'."

"That was sarcasm."

"It was reality."

They walked toward the clubhouse, and Richard touched her arm and stopped her before they reached the door. "Listen," he said, "no one knows that I have any designs on the course out in Holiday. Let's make sure we don't tip my hand?"

"Sure," she said with a nod. "But find some way to show me the things you like about it, the things you'd like to recreate if you do buy the course out there."

"What," he laughed, "like a secret code? I'll touch my index finger to the side of my nose and give you a nod."

"Yeah," she replied. "Like that." He wasn't entirely sure that she'd been joking until she walked through the door and looked back at him with that big, goofy grin of hers.

Ray Velasquez had bailed on them, but his other two buddies were there already, waiting on him. Richard led Cassie toward the table where they'd parked.

"Gary Todd and Steven Hearns, meet my friend Cassie Constantine."

Each of them stood up and greeted her with enthusiasm.

What a couple of pushovers. A beautiful woman enters the picture and they mask every trace of the Neanderthals they really are.

"I hope you don't mind me coming along," she told them. "I won't back you up by playing. I really just wanted to ride along in the cart and enjoy the sunshine."

"We're pleased to have you with us," Steven said. "You'll help us pretty up the place."

"It already looks pretty to me," she replied, nodding out the window. "Richard was telling me that this is a pretty spectacular course."

"Par 71, 134 slope rating," Gary told her as he led her, with his hand on the small of her back, away from the rest and out the door.

"One of the best courses in Florida, right here in our own backyard."

"I don't have a clue what you just said except that it's a really good golf course," she answered him, casting a glance back at Richard over the curve of her shoulder.

"By the time you leave here today, Cassie, you'll be fluent in Linkspeak," Richard heard Gary tell her, as if he was the foremost authority.

Pretty funny, coming from a guy who finished twelve shots back from me the last time we played.

Gary helped Cassie into the golf cart and then climbed in beside her.

"Uh-uh, Todd. No," Richard warned, pointing his finger at his friend. "You ladies are in *that* one."

Gary turned to Cassie and grinned. "I'll see you later."

Richard shook his head as he slipped in next to Cassie instead. "Sorry."

"Oh, he's harmless."

"Don't you believe it for a minute," Richard said, turning the wheel and steering them up toward the first tee.

"It really is beautiful," she said, looking around.

"And a pretty complicated course," he replied. "I don't have any illusions about trying to create something like this out of the Holiday property, but there are things I'd like to emulate."

"Par 4, Dillon," Gary called out as he and Steven came to a stop next to their cart. "Even you should be able to handle it. Let's start out strong and impress your lady friend, huh?"

Richard rolled his eyes slightly at Cassie. She laughed and

it sounded like a song, making it more difficult than usual to concentrate.

He stepped out from behind the wheel and deliberated as he weighed the distance to the green.

Driver off the tee box. Maybe then a four or five iron with the windup. Eight iron onto the green.

"Let's go, Dillon. We don't have all day."

Richard looked back at Cassie. "Excuse me for a minute while I go teach this guy a lesson."

Chapter Thirteen

....

10 DOWN: Genuine; real; dependably trustworthy

The afternoon sky was gray and dismal, and the breeze had a brisk nip to it. Cassie hurried back into the house and grabbed a hooded sweater from her closet. She slipped into it as she strode down the length of her newly repaired dock, sat down at the edge, and dangled her legs over the side.

The water in the canal had a choppy current to it, and the tops of the small waves were foamy with white-gray caps. She chuckled as she zipped the sweater. Since when did 60 degrees constitute a chill?

"What's so funny?"

She whirled around and saw Richard crossing the grass toward the dock.

"I had to get a jacket," she told him. "It's 60 degrees, and I needed a jacket! That's spring weather in Boston."

He squeezed her shoulder when he reached her and then folded down beside her and swung his legs over the edge of the dock, too. "Looks good," he said, running his hand along the wood.

"They did a nice job. And much faster than I'd expected."

Sophie rushed out through the open sliders, excited to say hello to Richard, and she dropped her ball on the dock beside him.

"How much more do you have to do to the house?" Richard asked, and then he tossed the squishy fleece ball across the lawn.

"I decided against the French doors, and that was the last thing on my list," she replied, and then she turned to face him with half a smile. "The place is all ready to sell."

"What did you decide?"

"About the offer?"

He nodded.

"I really don't know. I thought I'd put it off until after New Year's."

Sophie trotted back with the squeaky toy, which looked very much like a large speckled cotton ball protruding from the side of her mouth. Instead of dropping it, she just chewed the thing and it squeak-squeak-squeaked. Richard pried it out of her mouth and tossed it again.

"That's just a couple of days."

"I know."

Richard surprised her by reaching over and taking her hand and then lifting it to his lips. He planted a soft and sincere kiss on her knuckle before guiding her hand to his face and nuzzling it gently.

"I don't want you to go."

She had absolutely nothing to say in reply. Not one single thing crossed her mind except to ask herself what she could say to ease his mind.

Nothing. There's no promise I can make, no hope to lay out there for either of us.

"I'm sorry," she managed.

"I'm sorry, too," he replied on a whisper, releasing her hand.

Cassie looked into Richard's eyes and felt stranded there, disoriented. She couldn't pull away from his gaze.

He's so handsome, she thought as she watched him.

The wind kicked up a blustery stream around them, and his chestnut hair feathered back from his face in sections. His blue eyes darkened like a night sky, and the parenthetical dimples that she loved so much were nowhere in sight. He would have had to smile for her to get a glimpse of them, and Richard wasn't smiling.

He lifted his hand and pressed it softly against her cheek. Then he guided her toward him with two fingers beneath her jaw. Cassie knew she had the choice to pull away, but she just couldn't manage it. She couldn't even entertain the idea.

When his soft lips touched hers, it was a tender kiss, as smooth as the flight of two soaring birds or a petal falling from a flower. They lingered in that kiss, both of them lost in the poetry of the circumstance.

The heavens rumbled faintly and then rain began to plummet, but Cassie and Richard were spellbound, absorbed in one another and the perfect moment they'd been given. When they finally parted, Cassie felt as if she'd just been awakened from a deep and abiding sleep. Her eyelids were heavy, and her lips ached for more. It wasn't until Richard was on his feet and extending his hand toward her that she realized it had begun to rain.

"Come on," he called, and she scrambled to her feet.

By the time they made it to the sliding doors and rushed into the dark house, they were both drenched. Richard peeled the hooded jacket from her and stretched it out over the back of a chair, and then he brushed his hands through his hair and shook the moisture from it in splashes. Sophie quaked as well, adding to the mist of flying water.

"That downpour came out of nowhere," he said, but Cassie couldn't reply. She just stood there in the open doorway, trembling slightly.

"Are you all right?" he asked her.

She nodded without looking up. She didn't think she could speak to him even if she gave it her best effort. Words had drained out of her, along with much of her strength and most of her reason.

"Cassie?"

She glanced at him and then felt trapped by his eyes again.

"What's wrong?" he asked her.

She struggled to look away, and then she sighed. She felt it—*but what was* it?—moving up, up, and over the top of her head, and she could hardly move beneath the weight of it. A warm, heavy glaze of emotion and dread and fear and—

"Cass?"

With that one syllable of familiarity, the fire was stoked. She was freed. She moved toward Richard, clenched the front of his soaked shirt with both hands, and dragged him into another kiss.

"Well, I've probably been more embarrassed before, but I certainly can't recall when."

Rachel's laughter taunted Cassie through the telephone. "What did he say?"

"He said he had to leave."

"Just like that?"

"Just like that."

"He left?"

"He flew out of here like the wind. I probably scared the poor guy half to death, Rach."

"You didn't. He probably left like that because he's a good guy and he didn't want the two of you to do anything you couldn't take back." Rachel gasped. "Would you have? Would you have done something you couldn't take back?"

"Of course not," she scolded. "I didn't accost him, Rachel. I kissed him."

"Depending on the kiss, maybe he felt like he was being accosted," she said. She started to giggle again.

"Thank you very much. I call you for some comfort, looking for you to tell me that I haven't acted like a foolish teenager, and this is what I get."

"I'm sorry. Really. I'm sorry, Cassie. So...*how was it?*"

"How was what?"

"The kiss."

"Rachel."

"You can tell a lot about a man by the way he kisses. Was it soft and sweet?"

"Very."

"Not vulgar."

"Of course not. I'm hanging up on you now."

"No, wait."

"Vulgar!" she exclaimed. "You're vulgar."

"I am not. I'm just—"

"Hanging up."

"Cas–sie."

"Love you, but you're about to hear a click." And in the next second, Cassie made that click happen.

She sat at the table, twirling the disconnected phone in her hand as she stared at the "Surprise Yourself" box in front of her. She entertained herself with imaginings about the next card in the box: *Chuck your whole life back home and dive right in to a new life with someone who looks a little like Dennis Quaid.*

Or perhaps *Viva la romance! Talk about surprising yourself! We thought you'd never be kissed again. Way to go!*

Cassie dropped her face into her hands and cackled with a half groan, half laugh. The truth was that she'd sometimes given great, flapping wings to that fear. She'd worried that Zan was the last man who would ever kiss her, that she'd spend the rest of her time on earth eating whatever she wanted until she grew into a rotund old woman who drank coffee by the window and dreamed about that last kiss so very long ago while her ancient dog snored and many, many felines rubbed against her leg, meowing for her to share her cat food with them.

Zan had always kissed her with the same enthusiasm and sheer joy he'd displayed in everything he did. They were often slightly sloppy kisses, filled with eager and appreciative emotion. She loved those kisses of his.

But Richard…

She dug her fingers into her hair and combed it away from her face and then sighed. Richard's kisses were monumental in their unexpected passion, burgeoning with frightening ingredients, like promise and hope. Two kisses from Richard and Cassie felt changed, as if her soul had suddenly crawled out from its hiding place. But now what was she going to do with it? In fact, she decided, her soul needed to just slink back inside and hush up and stop all that singing.

Oh boy, she thought. *I might be in real trouble here.*

"Yoo-hoooo!"

Sophie popped up from the floor and tore through the kitchen, barks escaping her faster than she could run.

"No no no, Sophie, it's just me. I'm a good guy, not a bad guy."

"Sophie, come here!" Cassie called. Sophie whipped past her and peered at Millicent as she walked through the door from the garage.

"I'm sorry. The garage door was open."

"It's fine."

"Some of us are heading over to the thrift store to find some disco getups for tomorrow night. You wanna come along, hunny?"

"What a great idea," Cassie said, hoping that she still had a New Year's Eve date. "Let me take Sophie out, and I'll meet you out front. Do you want me to drive?"

"Would you, Cassie? Then we can take two cars and I don't have to be all jammed in the backseat with Stella. She's in the middle of a dissertation on the history of disco. I can hardly take it anymore."

Cassie laughed. "I'll pull out the car. Just give me a couple of minutes."

Sophie tended to her business in the backyard, and Cassie had barely closed the slider after bringing the dog inside when she heard her car door slam shut in the garage.

"I sent them on and told them we'd catch up in a few minutes," Millicent told her from the passenger seat of her car once Cassie reached her. "That Stella just twists my earlobes."

Cassie snickered as she started the car and pulled out of the garage.

"I don't have one of these," Millicent told her, clutching the remote for the garage door and pushing on the button.

"You have a carport," Cassie reminded her.

"I know, but I like the button." She pushed it again and the door stopped mid-close and went back up again. "Oh dear."

"Here," Cassie said, taking the remote from her. "You just push once."

They watched the door lower, and Cassie clipped the remote back to the visor above Millicent's head before pulling out of the driveway.

"Where are we headed?" she asked.

"What do you mean?"

"I mean, where is this store we're going to?"

"Oh. I don't know."

Cassie paused at the stop sign and shifted into PARK. Turning toward Millicent, she asked, "How can we meet them there if you don't know where we're going?"

Millicent tilted up one shoulder in a tentative shrug and admitted, "I didn't think of that."

"Okay, well, let's call Stella on my cell phone and find out where they are. What's her number?"

"Stella doesn't have a cell phone, hunny."

Cassie popped with laughter at that and then sighed. "Do you feel like some lunch?"

"That sounds lovely."

They grabbed a salad at Angelo's, and while they were there, Cassie referenced the phone book to find the address of the secondhand store in Holiday. When they finally arrived, sure enough, Stella, Georgette, and Maureen were still there, going through the racks of clothes.

"What took you so long?" Stella snapped.

"We stopped at Angelo's," Millicent sort of sang, and Cassie realized that she was bragging a little. "Cassie wanted to take me out for lunch."

It hadn't occurred to her before then that Millicent was the only one in the group of women from the church who didn't have a husband or children with whom she could spend time. Presenting herself as the one Cassie chose to spend time with was a bit of a win for her.

"I want to spend as much time with Millicent as I can while I'm here," Cassie told them, and Millicent beamed. "Have you ladies found anything yet?"

Georgette held up a fringed flapper-type dress and a hat with netting and a feather. "It's no disco outfit, but I sure do love it."

They all laughed, and Cassie took Millicent by the arm and headed past the row of dresses and toward some bell-bottom pants and tie-dye T-shirts.

"Let's look through here and see if we can find something shiny," she suggested.

The first hanger Millicent produced wore a red satin halter dress with cleavage cut out down to the belly button.

Cassie covered her mouth and shook her head. "Nnn–o. Let's keep looking."

"Cassie, look what we found," Georgette called to her. She held up a pair of silver glitter platform shoes. "I think we'd break our neck in these for sure, but you might be able to wear them! Can you wear a size 7?"

"That's my size," she said with a nod, and Georgette passed them to her across a clearance table.

"What about this?" Millicent asked. She fluffed a pair of hot pink satin bell-bottoms out over the table. When she finally found the tag, she grimaced. "Size 6. About eight sizes too small for me. What about you?"

"I might be able to wear them," Cassie said, and she took them from Millicent and held them up in front of her in the mirror.

On another clearance table, Cassie spotted a dark knit top with a sequined ripple pattern across the front in red, gold, green, magenta, and blue. Over the next hour, they found outfits for every one of them, plus a polyester leisure suit for George with a bright scarf to tie around his neck.

"You'd better practice walking in those shoes tonight," Millicent told her as they stood in line at the cash register. "You fall off those things and it's a long, long way down."

After Cassie finished paying for her purchases, she excused herself and went to the car to wait for Millicent. The minute she tossed her bag into the backseat and closed the door, she plucked her cell phone from her purse and dialed.

"Hi, Richard. It's Cassie. I'm sorry I missed you, but I just wanted to say that…well, I hope we're still on for tomorrow night. I, um, wondered if you wanted to…you know…talk about anything first. If you do, you can call me. I'll be home tonight, taking my new platform shoes for a few laps so I can figure them out before I try to disco dance in them. Okay…well…give me a call when you get this?"

A flock of butterflies took flight in her stomach as she pressed the button to end the call. She wondered what Richard was thinking today. He'd left in such an immediate rush after she'd grabbed him and kissed him the way she had.

Maybe he thinks I kiss like a platypus. I am out of practice, after all.

Perhaps after all those years of kissing only Zan, she'd lost touch with the correct way to pucker…or the proper angle of the head. Or maybe she'd given him whiplash, the way she'd grabbed his shirt with both hands and yanked him toward her.

Cassie gasped and covered her mouth with her hand as she suddenly wondered, *What did I have for lunch that day? I can't remember. But…maybe my breath smelled like a shrimp-and-garlic sandwich!*

While she knew she hadn't had either shrimp *or* garlic, she worried about the state of her breath just the same. Richard's breath was minty-fresh, she recalled. Sweet and clean and inviting. No wonder he left in such a hurry. Her breath couldn't possibly have been right.

"Oh…man!"

"Are you talking to someone, hunny?"

She hadn't even realized Millicent had opened the car door, much less climbed in beside her.

"Oh, no. I was just thinking about something. Millicent, do you mind if we stop at the pharmacy? I need to stock up on a few things."

"Sure. Like what?"

"Oh, toothpaste and floss. And some mouthwash. And a few packs of mints."

"Getting ready for the big kiss at midnight, are we?"

Millicent hiccuped and chuckled, so pleased with herself for making the joke. But the truth was, Cassie hadn't thought of kissing Richard at midnight until her friend mentioned it.

Maybe I should get something for a queasy stomach, too.

Chapter Fourteen

....

16 ACROSS: Compelled by intense emotions; fervent

Donning black biking shorts and an oversized white T-shirt that she knotted at the waist, Cassie piled her hair on top of her head, laced up her shoes, fired up her MP3 player, put the dog on the leash, and hit the pavement. As one of her old favorites by Bryan Duncan cued up, Cassie felt inspired. She'd planned for a brisk walk, but now she found herself at a full run, much to Sophie's sheer glee.

By the time they rounded the corner and headed home, however, the poor dog looked like she was going to keel over. Cassie, on the other hand, might have been able to take another lap around the subdivision. Instead, she apologized to Sophie with a scratch behind the ears and a full water bowl before tossing protein powder, skim milk, and a handful of frozen raspberries into the blender.

She flipped on the stereo and listened to The Morning Cruise on The Joy FM while she sipped her smoothie and pressed her crossword puzzle flat on the table with both hands. She filled in a couple of the words and was working on the next one when Sophie exploded with a noisy announcement just an instant before the doorbell rang.

"Hush," she told her, and then she pulled open the door. Cassie's heart raced, and a flush of heat radiated through her. "Richard. Good morning."

"Is it too early?"

Early? I was expecting to hear from you yesterday, so I think you're late.

"No. Come on in. Do you want a smoothie?"

"No, thanks."

She led him through the living room and then sat down at the dining room table once more, folding her leg beneath her. Richard followed and took the chair across from her.

"I'm interrupting your breakfast."

"Not at all," she replied. "What's a ten-letter word that means *compelled by intense emotions; fervent*?" He was thinking it over when she added, "Fifth letter *I*, last letter *E*."

When he didn't respond, she looked up at him. "Richard?" She set her pencil on the table and folded her hands beside it. "What is it?"

"I wanted to talk to you about…what happened the other day."

The memory of that kiss pulsed in her ears like a rumba, but for some reason she casually asked him, "What happened?"

Richard sort of snorted and then stared her down.

"Oh, you mean the kiss."

"Yes."

"Which one?"

"Pardon?"

"The one you gave me, or the one I gave you afterward?"

"Collective, I guess," he replied.

"So you want to talk about *all* the kissing."

"Yes."

Here it comes. The part where he tells me he has nothing against the platypus in general, but—

"Cassie, don't get me wrong. I'm really attracted to you."

Nothing good can come from a beginning like this one.

"And if you were staying here in Holiday, I'd probably love to pursue a relationship with you and see where it led."

But your breath is just out of control.

"But I assume you're making plans to go back to Boston any day now, and I'm staying right here. Do you see where I'm going with this?"

"I think so."

"I just wanted to apologize to you if I gave you any reason to feel conflicted or—"

"Richard," she interrupted, keeping a cool mask in place to disguise the turmoil and disappointment brewing just beneath the surface. "It was just a couple of kisses. Nothing more. And we are not teenagers. I'm not expecting you to give me your ID bracelet and ask me to go steady."

He sighed, and Cassie felt like slapping him for it. *You're so relieved that you had to sigh?*

"You're a very nice man, and I've enjoyed getting to know you. But I have a life elsewhere, and you have one here."

"I'm happy to know we're on the same page."

"Same paragraph. Don't worry about a thing. Now, are we still on for disco dancing tonight?"

"We're on," he said, and he gave her a quick flash of those parenthetical dimples before snatching it back again. "I'll be dressed to kill."

"You and me both."

"Pick you up at eight?"

She nodded, forcing that false, pasted smile back to the surface. "I'll be ready."

Richard got up and rounded the table. He leaned over her and planted a peck on her cheek. "Thanks, Cassie."

She waved him off with her hand and chuckled. "Are you kidding? Everything's fine."

"Passionate."

She winced. "Come again?"

"Ten letters meaning *compelled by intense emotions*," he clarified. Then he touched her cheek where he'd kissed it.

"Oh, that can't be it." *Not exactly a word Zan would have used to describe me.*

He shrugged. "Okay, then. See you tonight."

"I'll have my dancin' shoes on!"

The moment the front door closed behind him, Cassie's face fell, and she leaned forward against the table with a sigh.

Buyer's remorse.

She'd met a few guys before Zan who had commitment problems and grass-is-always-greener mentalities. They moved in for the kill until they had the girl right where they wanted her and then, without warning, they set down their guns and went home. Perhaps they'd save the actual kill for another day. A bigger trophy. A better "get."

Buyer's remorse.

Cassie determined that she would not let Richard—or anyone else—know that she'd been had. She glanced down at the crossword puzzle and counted out the boxes with the tip of her pencil.

P-A-S-S-I-O-N-A-T-E.

It fit, into the spaces anyway, but certainly not into Zan's usual crosswords about her. If Richard had been making the puzzle, it might have been a different story, after the other day. *Passionate* might very well have been one of his descriptors.

Along with patsy and gullible.

But that was going to change right here, right now. Richard Dillon would never know the thoughts she'd been having about him or the ridiculous (albeit momentary) fantasies about entirely changing her life in order to be closer to him. He was never going to see her sweat!

Except on the dance floor.

Richard started the car but was still parked in Cassie's driveway fifteen minutes after he'd left the house. His visit hadn't gone the way he'd planned, and he was toying with the idea of going back again to set things straight.

He jerked when a knock on the window next to him startled him out of his wits.

"Good morning, Richard."

Millicent grinned at him from the other side of the glass like a toothy cartoon character he'd once seen.

He pressed the switch to roll down the window and said, "Hello, Millicent. How are you?"

"Is everything all right?" she asked him. "You've been sitting here for a long time."

"I—just—I was just leaving," he said.

"Oh, I see." Millicent gave the backseat of his car a once-over before she smiled again and returned her focus to him. "Are you still coming to the party tonight?"

"Yes, I am. Would you like to ride along with us?"

"Thank you, hunny. I'd like that."

"I'm picking up Cassie at eight."

"I'll see you then."

Millicent lingered for several moments, looking for all the world as if she was going to burst if she didn't say something to him. But then she sighed, tapped the car door, and muttered, "Right. I'll see you then."

Richard imagined it had something to do with the big secret buzzing around Holiday. She'd probably wanted to ask him if he was the front man for the big, evil corporation coming to town. And Richard wished he could tell her he wasn't, that he was as curious as she was about the whole thing. He wished he could give her some peace of mind.

Instead, he smiled and waved good-bye as he backed out of the driveway.

He arrived earlier than expected at the Heaton house, and while he was debating whether to wait in the car for a few minutes before ringing the bell, Maureen opened the front door and waved at him.

"Come on in," she hollered.

He nodded and turned off the engine.

Maureen had set out quite a spread in anticipation of Richard's visit. The aroma of coffee greeted him at the door, and the kitchen table offered an array of china cups and plates, a tray of pastries, and a crystal bowl filled with chunks of fresh fruit.

"It looks like the buffet brunch at the Ritz," he complimented her. "This is beautiful, but you didn't need to go to so much trouble."

"No trouble at all," she told him. "Sit down and I'll pour you some coffee. Marvin got a bit of a late start this morning, but he should be out in a few minutes."

"I hope he's feeling all right."

"He has his good days and bad. Last night was a little rough, so we stayed up watching reruns of *Murder, She Wrote*. We both love a good mystery."

"I'm sorry to hear that." She cocked her head slightly, and Richard laughed. "Sorry about him not feeling well. Not about enjoying Angela Lansbury."

By the time Richard finished his first cup of coffee, Marvin wheeled into the kitchen and navigated his chair up to the table. He was clean-shaven, and his thinning hair was damp and combed back from his round face.

"Good to see you again," he said, extending his hand toward Richard.

"Same here. I want to thank you both for seeing me."

"Are you joking? The man who got my wife dancing again is welcome at this table any day, any time."

Maureen blushed, pouring Marvin a cup of coffee and refilling Richard's before pouring one for herself as well.

"I have something rather sensitive to talk to you about," Richard began. "I hope I can trust you both to keep this between us?"

"Absolutely."

"Of course."

"Well, Marvin, your wife tells me that your former career was as a landscape designer."

The man arched a curious brow. "Yes."

"I'm hoping you might want to freelance a little and help me out."

"Freelance?" Maureen repeated. "Like a job?"

"Yes. I've looked into a few of the bigger jobs you did up in Wisconsin, and I think you might be just what I need."

Marvin glanced at his wife and then rubbed his chin. "Listen, Richard, I'm grateful that you helped Mo find her dancing feet again. But if you're about to ask me to be involved in this whole golf resort thing, I'm afraid I'll have to turn you down flat. I don't want any part of—"

"No, no," Richard interrupted, and he held up his hand. "I know what people are saying, but I'm not the front man for the corporation that's been sniffing around. I give you my word."

"You're not?" Maureen exclaimed. "Because everyone in town feels certain that you are. Not that it makes one lick of difference in how we feel about you, Richard. But you can just tell us straight out if it's true."

"It's not."

She exchanged a look with Marvin that told Richard they might actually believe him, and he sighed.

"The only interest I have is in the golf course," he explained. "I know it's going to auction next week, and I've been hoping to buy it and refurbish the place."

"Just the golf course," Marvin clarified.

"Yes. I'm hoping that enough of the residents in Holiday will stand up against the machine trying to buy them out, and that this corporation—or whoever they are—will give up on the resort idea. If they can't buy up the surrounding properties, then there would be no reason to buy the course."

"I think there are a lot of mixed emotions about it," Marvin speculated. "Some of them have received offers they can hardly afford to turn down."

"And others think it might be a really good thing for Holiday," Maureen added. "It would bring jobs to the community, and some are just waiting and hoping they'll get an offer, too."

"What community?" Richard remarked. "If half the families sell off their properties, this will only be a place where tourists and resort-dwellers go for two weeks out of the year."

"Didn't I make that very point to you just last night?" Marvin asked his wife. "Part of Holiday's charm is that we're a sort of bedroom community where everyone knows one another and neighbors are *neighborly*. It won't be that way if Corporate America moves in and takes over."

"There are other things at issue, as well," Richard pointed out. "Like higher taxes. But my interest, as I said, is specifically in the golf course itself. That's where you come in."

"I don't understand."

"We couldn't really afford to invest in a golf course, Richard," Maureen admitted.

"Oh no, I don't want an investor. I want a landscape architect to help me design the restoration." He turned to Marvin and added, "Like what you did to the Rolling Rock course in Racine."

Marvin scratched his chin again and smiled at Richard. "Came out great, didn't it?"

"It was art," Maureen remarked.

"Marvin, I need someone with your skills, yes, but also someone I can trust to keep the endeavor private until we see how this is going to play out. I'll pay you for your time either way it goes, but I've been thinking and planning and praying about this. I just have this feeling about getting things started."

Maureen dropped her head, and Richard noticed that she was sniffling.

"I'm sorry. I, uh—"

"Marvin's been needing something like this," she said without looking up. When she did, her eyes were red and filled with tears. "He's still so vital and talented, but that wheelchair has him convinced otherwise."

"That's enough, Mo." Marvin tilted his head and looked at Richard. "My wife is my biggest fan."

"I can see that." Richard shared a smile with him, and then he looked to Maureen. "Does that mean I can count on you both?"

Maureen looked to Marvin and grinned, and then Marvin nodded.

"We won't tell a soul."

Richard's adrenaline started to pump, the way it always did when he wrapped his thoughts around the potential of the project.

"I have some preliminary notes, but I thought we might take a drive over to the course and have a look around, maybe see if you get inspired."

"We can take the van!" Maureen exclaimed, and she hopped out of her chair. With a sudden jerk, she changed directions and sat back down again. "You have something to eat, Richard."

They all shared a laugh, and Richard plucked a bear claw from the platter. "I think I will. Thanks!"

"I'll go powder my nose and then we'll get started."

Marvin dropped a ladleful of fruit, first onto his own plate and then onto Richard's. He snatched an éclair from the platter and took a big bite out of it. He was still chewing it when he said, "Mo worries. I hate it when she worries."

"It's part of the deal, isn't it?" Richard asked him. "Your wife loves you, and she's going to worry. It's like the egg roll that comes with the entrée at China Jade; it sort of comes with the dinner."

"I don't appreciate the Chinese food so much. Gives me gas."

Richard let out a laugh, both because he thought Marvin's remark was funny and also because he was so relieved to have someone else in on his plans. It had been a long and lonely few months while putting it all together and worrying about the sudden appearance of Mandalay—or whatever corporation was behind the buyouts.

"Are you boys still eating?" Maureen exclaimed as she hustled back into the kitchen. "Let's light a fire under you. Time's a-wastin.'"

Maureen grabbed the handles of Marvin's wheelchair and started pulling him away from table. He tossed the last of his pastry to the plate as she pushed him toward the door. "Hold your horses, woman!"

"I'll get Marvin into the van and we'll meet you out front," she told Richard over her shoulder. "Could you press the lock on the knob when you go out the door?"

"Sure," he said, grinning.

Richard imagined that Maureen wanted to get the show on the road before Marvin changed his mind. The thought of her husband having something creative to do, something that would exercise his brain a little more than those mystery reruns she'd mentioned and that would pay him a little something to boot, well, it probably looked like a whole set of golden opportunities to Maureen.

He popped the last bit of bear claw into his mouth, wiped the icing off his lip with a napkin, and then hurried out the front door before Maureen came in and dragged him out, too. By the time he locked up and stepped foot outside, Maureen and Marvin were in the van and waiting for him in the driveway.

Richard climbed into the passenger seat, and Maureen was at the corner stop sign before he'd even clicked his seat belt into place.

"Slow down, Mo. Richard might wanna get there in one full piece."

"Sorry. Okay. So are you coming to the disco bash at the church tonight?"

"I am," he replied. "Against my better judgment, I'm even going in costume."

"Oh, c'mon, Richard. Loosen up," Maureen teased. "You'll have a ball!"

"I'm not exactly the 'loosen up' type of guy, or hadn't you noticed?"

Maureen grinned. "We've noticed."

"I thought I'd turn over a new leaf; just a test drive to see how it fares."

She chuckled and then asked, "Are you bringing a date?"

"I'm bringing Cassie and Millicent."

"A man with a harem," Marvin teased from the back.

"I'd have thought Cassie would be coming with Stella's nephew," Maureen remarked. "I thought they were the new couple in town."

Richard swallowed around the sudden lump in his throat. "Cassie and Hunter?"

"Yes, that's his name. Hunter."

"Is he still in town? I had assumed he went back to New York."

"Mm-mm. Not until after the new year. In fact, he and Stella's son-in-law are in charge of the music tonight."

He didn't particularly like Hunter when they'd met on Christmas, but he certainly wasn't aware that Hunter had been seeing Cassie since then. No wonder she'd been so clear about a kiss being just a kiss. She wasn't just on the same page with him, she'd said; she was parked in the same paragraph, with no designs whatsoever on a future with him.

"Stella says he has quite a torch for Cassie."

"Really."

"You didn't know?"

"Nope. She never mentioned it."

"I hope I'm not causing a problem. If you're her date tonight, then—"

"No, Cassie and I are just friends. I'm escorting both her and Millicent."

Just friends.

It stuck in Richard's throat, leaving it scratchy and dry. There wasn't anything *just friends* about his feelings for her. There never *had* been, from the very first day he'd seen her at the other end of the dock from George Hootz's sinking pontoon. That was why he hadn't been able to stop himself from kissing her and why everything male inside of him had responded to the female in her when she'd hoisted that return kiss upon him.

Passionate.

That was the answer in her crossword puzzle, although she denied it because she couldn't manage to see herself that way, nor believe that her own husband had been able to. But that kiss she'd laid on him told a different story, one of passion and fire.

Whether she could see it or not, Cassie Constantine was 2 parts intellect, 1 part adorable, and 1 very full part passionate. Richard couldn't even entertain the idea that Zan had missed that in her. In fact, the only one that seemed to be missing it was…Cassie.

Maureen veered into the parking lot and then circled into a space. "Do we want to get out?"

"No, let's drive around the outside of the course and have a look," Richard replied.

"Isn't that Smitty?"

Kenny Smits, the owner of the golf course, was standing at the far end of the parking lot with two other men. Smitty leaned on the trunk of one of the two cars parked there.

"Who's that with him?" Maureen asked in a whisper, as if they could be overheard from 200 yards away. "Maybe the corporate raiders?"

Richard diffused a laugh. Maureen was no doubt a frustrated mystery solver. To her, this was just a live episode of *Murder, She Wrote*, sans the murder.

The men shook hands, and Smitty turned and headed toward the office. When the two other gentlemen stalked toward their car, Richard's breath caught in his throat once again. He squinted to make sure.

"Well, we know one of them," he told them. "The one in the blue shirt is Hunter."

"Stella's nephew?"

"The very same."

"We were just talking about him!" Maureen exclaimed.

"Well, what on earth is he doing meeting with Smitty at his closed-up-tight golf course a week before it goes on the auction block?" Marvin observed.

"That's a very good question," Richard replied.

Chapter Fifteen

....

6 ACROSS: Smart dresser; neat in appearance

Cassie grazed over her reflection in the bathroom mirror and felt like she might need to shield her eyes if she looked too long at the hot pink satin bell-bottoms, sequined top, glitter platform shoes, and something called "stardust" sprinkled over her *very big* hair. One of the clues in Zan's crossword puzzle left an echo of laughter as she thought about it.

Smart dresser; neat in appearance.

"Yeah, there's nothing smarter or neater than sequins and glitter," she told Sophie, who was seated at her feet with her ears forward and head cocked, watching Cassie as if she might sprout wings at any moment.

Cassie applied another few spritzes of hair spray to make sure her big hair stayed big, and then she danced out of the bathroom to the disco music and glitter ball in her head.

"Dog fed and walked. Check!" she said, and Sophie wagged her fringed tail in response. "Dancing shoes buckled and ready. Check! Stardust and sequins in place and ready to catch the light. Check, check!"

She couldn't help but think how much pleasure Zan might have taken in a night like this one. She could almost see him in a turquoise leisure suit and platform shoes, probably working to inspire his stick-in-the-mud wife to give it a chance and have some fun. One look at the shimmery disco-diva persona she'd become and poor old Zan might have had to check his heart.

Sophie announced Richard's arrival before the bell did, and Cassie flung open the door and exploded into an immediate fit of laughter. Richard stood there frozen in his best Travolta pose, wearing a very shiny polyester shirt in watercolors of peach and pink, with a huge butterfly collar and starched French cuffs. His peach-toned pants were accessorized with a white riveted belt and a rhinestone buckle that read, "Disco!"

"You look…ready to shake your groove thing." Cassie chuckled.

"Are you ready to party down?" he returned.

Cassie grabbed her sequin purse and patted Sophie on the head before she closed the door. Richard led her down the sidewalk and to the driveway, and they reached his car just as Millicent tottered across the street with her arms waving.

"You two are so shiny," she called out.

Richard and Cassie both erupted into laughter when they saw her in her paisley caftan and huge Afro wig with the matching scarf tied in a knot just behind her left ear.

"How do I look?" she asked, fluttering her glittering blue eyelids at them.

"Oh, Millicent, you're a slice of heaven!" Richard wailed, and he wrapped his arms around her and rubbed the top of her wild hair with his knuckles. "Two hotter dates a dude never could have."

"Well, then," Cassie said, miming a couple of gum chews. "Let's split, then."

"Solid."

Once they were all in the car, Richard flipped on the radio.

"I searched the Internet for the best oldies station in town, and what do you know," he exclaimed. "They're playing disco hits until midnight!"

He cranked up the volume just as Gloria Gaynor began to sing. In the next moment, Cassie sang along with her.

When Millicent chimed in, Richard shot them both a bewildered expression.

Suddenly the two women began to sing at the top of their lungs, gyrating in their seats and pointing their fingers at Richard, crooning about how he should just go right ahead and walk out the door!

The mood was so merry and fun that Cassie couldn't help recognizing the contrast. How long had it been since she'd laughed so much or taken a lighthearted attitude about anything in life? She was reminded of the infrequent times in college when she and her friends would take a break from studying and get so silly that the laughter made their cheeks ache. She remembered when Zan would force her into activities she thought ludicrous for people over thirty, like ice-skating, a trip to a comedy club, or a pizza-making class. *Serious* went right out the window when she wasn't looking on those occasions, and she remembered finding herself, just like tonight, feeling uncharacteristically exuberant. It was so unlike her, really, but Zan just managed to bring that out in her sometimes.

Cassie wondered if Richard felt that way now, but the look on his face told her that he was only partially there; the rest of him, merely puzzled. That was okay, though. She'd spent a long time feeling utterly baffled in her first years with Zan, but he'd brought her around every once in a while. Maybe, she speculated, she could have that same effect on Richard.

Well, if I was going to be around long enough to keep at it, she thought.

But for now, she really was on a *holiday* in Holiday, Florida, and she speculated about all of the really entertaining Christmases and New Year's Eves that she and Zan had missed while she stuck to her traditional guns about fencing the holidays in to Boston Proper.

It was a little like Halloween inside the recreation hall. Leisure suits and polyester abounded, and the whole crowd looked just a little bit taller, thanks to the fad of platform shoes. A silver glitter ball hung from the middle of the hall, and colored spotlights from all four corners intersected at the center of the dance floor. Tables overflowed with punch bowls and ice buckets of soda cans. Platters offered varieties of chicken wings, pigs in blankets, cheese pinwheels, and shish kebabs.

Richard snapped a few photos of Cassie and Millicent just as someone shouted, "Oooh, Cassie's here!"

It seemed as if the whole roomful of seniors erupted with applause.

"Lead us in the hustle, Cassie!"

It was a bit like filtering the disco '70s through a circus sideshow tent from the '60s hippie era as she looked around at them: George Hootz in his pale blue suit and psychedelic shirt unbuttoned to the middle of his chest; Stella Nesbitt in fuschia hot pants over bright blue spandex leggings; and someone else in a gold glitter dress so shiny that Cassie couldn't make out her face past the reflection.

"Night Fever" by the Bee Gees invited her to the dance floor, and Cassie grabbed Richard's hand on her right and Millicent's on her left and dragged them along with her.

"I'm not doing this alone," she told them as they moved toward the center of the floor.

※ ※ ※

Cassie was waiting for him on the stone wall outside the recreation hall, and Richard offered her one of two paper cups of punch.

"I think this might be fruit punch mixed with ginger ale," he warned her. "Sugar rush to follow."

Cassie giggled. She sipped it and then wrinkled her nose in response. "Mmm-hmm. I think you're right."

"They have bottled water, too. Would you prefer that?"

"This is fine," she told him. "Sit down."

Richard parked on the wall beside her.

"I'm glad we got a few minutes alone," she said. "I wondered if you'd learned anything else about the auction next week."

He smiled. Cassie had a sort of intuitive nature, and he wasn't at all surprised that she'd sensed something else had happened.

Richard took a final swig of punch and crumpled the paper cup between his palms. "I'm pretty sure I know who at least one of the representatives is. I saw Hunter Nesbitt over at the golf course with Smitty and some *suit* this morning."

"Hunter! Are you sure?"

"Oh, I'm sure."

"Maybe it wasn't about the auction?"

"Maybe. But the place was vacant, and they had their heads together with Smitty. What can you tell me about Hunter?"

"Not much," she replied. "Just that he's from New York and has a job where he crunches numbers."

Richard nodded, and then he sighed and shook his head.

"I don't like him," she added. "He's very pushy."

"What do you mean?"

"Oh, I don't know. I had a little episode with him when he was saying good night after dinner on Christmas."

Richard bristled. "Do tell."

"It was nothing really. But he moved in without any warning. Or interest on my part, let me add. It was really uncomfortable."

"What do you mean, he *moved in*?"

With the casual wave of her hand, Cassie replied, "He…kissed me."

Richard popped to his feet before his feet even knew what the rest of him was doing. "He kissed you!"

Cassie looked a little stunned, and he took a step backward.

"It was no big thing," she assured him. "Just unexpected."

"Idiot," he muttered.

Cassie grinned, taking his hand. "All things being relative," she said with a gentle lilt, "it wasn't much of a kiss."

It was pretty pathetic how his heart soared at her reassurance, and he pressed his fingers into her palm. "Well, not when you have so much to compare him to."

"That's what I'm saying."

Richard smiled and returned to the wall. He shook his head and muttered "Idiot" once again.

"Oh, Richard! Do you think Stella knows?"

He looked up at her, the sudden revelation somewhat of a shocker. He didn't know why he hadn't wondered that himself.

"No!" Cassie blurted, answering her own question. "Stella loves this place and these people. She couldn't possibly."

"Are you sure?"

"Richard, she wouldn't."

"So you think he's just down here on the guise of visiting his aunt...," he surmised.

"But he's really here doing his dirty corporate duty," she completed the thought. "Hey, I wonder what revealing the truth to Aunt Stella would do to his whole plan."

"Or—"

She interrupted him. "Or what it would do to Stella."

The two of them sat there, side by side and in silence, as they mulled over the possibilities.

"I guess we'd better get back," Richard said. He stood up and offered her his hand.

She took it and then gave it a gentle pull. "I'm not going to take that offer on my house, Richard."

"Even though it's much more than you might get from an individual buyer?"

"Even though," she said with a nod. "It's just not right. I can wait for the right buyer to come along when all this is sorted out. Tameka can take care of the details and let me know when it's done—and *done right*. I'm not going to help some corporation turn Holiday into a tourist trap."

"You're sure?"

"I'm sure," she said. Then she got up and wrapped her arms around his neck and gave him a gentle squeeze. "I want you to get your dream," she added on a whisper. "And I want the people in Holiday to keep theirs."

Richard wanted to kiss her so badly. Instead, he pecked her cheek and pulled away from her embrace. "You're doing a good thing," he said. She slipped her arm into his and they meandered back toward the hall.

"Oh, wait!" he said. He produced a small digital camera from the front pocket of his shirt. "Let's take a photo."

Placing one arm around her shoulder and pulling her in close, Richard held up the camera and snapped. The image in the viewfinder was one of strangers. Two groovy dudes from the '70s, all decked out and ready to dance.

As they headed toward the door, Richard stopped and said, "You know, Maureen Heaton told me that Nesbitt would be here tonight. Have you seen him?"

"No," she replied. "Until you said you'd seen him this morning, I'd assumed he'd gone back to New York."

"He and his cousin are supposedly in charge of the music."

As he pulled the door open, they were smacked right in the face with KC & the Sunshine Band and the call to shake-shake-shake their booties.

"Well, I can say one thing for him," Cassie yelled over the audio. "He sure does that right!"

A smile masked the silent prayer Richard was sending upward as he looked into her sparkling hazel eyes.

Lord, this is the most adorable creature I've ever spent thirty seconds with. I don't know how You're going to work this out or if You're even inclined to work it out. But I'm in love with this woman, and I'm asking You not to make me spend another day without her.

She turned around and tugged at his sleeve, clueless about his thoughts.

"Are you hungry?" she asked him. "They have chicken wings! I love chicken wings."

Richard watched her hurry to the buffet table and grab a large plastic plate.

"C'mon," she said, nodding him toward the food. "Chicken wings."

She snatched a pair of tongs from the platter and started to load her plate.

"Happy New Year, Cassie."

Hunter Nesbitt.

"Same to you," she commented, focusing on her plate and then glancing at Richard tentatively. "I didn't know you were still in town. You remember Richard Dillon?"

"Yeah. How are you, Dillon?"

"Nesbitt."

A dozen scenarios flew through Richard's mind, not the least disturbing of which was the memory that this guy had laid his lips on Cassie's. Since that seemed like the lamest one to bring up at just that moment, Richard took a different tack.

"Saw you over at Smitty's golf course this morning," he stated without inflection. "Who was the suit with you?"

"Oh, uh, that was a guy I know from New York. We thought we might play a round of golf but then found out the place is closed down. Apparently in foreclosure."

"It seems like Stella might have told you that," Cassie piped up. "Before you went over there, I mean."

Nesbitt just stood there, his beady little eyes darting back and forth between Richard and Cassie. "Yeah," he said at last. "Well, Happy New Year."

"Same to you," Richard said as Hunter turned away.

"Have a good night," Cassie called.

Cassie stepped up next to Richard, holding her full plate with both hands. "Oh yeah," she said, both of them watching Hunter meld into the crowd. "He's up to no good at all. Did you see his reaction?"

"It's good to know for sure," Richard answered. "Let's eat."

He'd just filled his plate when Maureen appeared on the other side of the table, a crooked pirate smile on her face.

"Hey, Maureen," Cassie said. "Have you tried these wings? They're amazing."

"Yes, I have," she replied. Richard thought her tone was quite odd. "They set up some tables outside, and some people are eating out there. Marvin's already settled, and we were hoping you could join us for a minute, Richard."

"Let's do, Richard," Cassie exclaimed.

"Actually, we just wanted to speak to Richard, if you don't mind."

"Uh…oh. Okay."

He realized that Maureen and Marvin had something to tell him about Nesbitt. "Cassie knows," he said quietly.

"Oh, good."

"I know what?"

"Let's go outside," Richard said. He placed his hand on the small of Cassie's back and led her through the doors behind Maureen.

Marvin's wheelchair was parked at the farthest table, with no one at the other tables nearby. The three of them made their way over to him, and Richard smacked Marvin's shoulder in greeting.

"Happy New Year."

"Same to you."

"Do you know Cassie?"

"Not officially," he replied. "How are you?"

"Great. It's so nice to meet you."

Once they were all seated, Maureen could hardly contain herself any longer. "They're after Stella's house," she whispered, leaning forward.

"What do you mean?" Richard asked her.

"Stella told Marvin just a few minutes ago. Some guy approached her this afternoon and offered her ten grand more than her home is appraised at."

"So she *is* in the dark!" Cassie exclaimed.

"I thought as much, when we saw her nephew at the golf course this morning," Marvin said to Richard. "That guy is a slug."

"You all were at the golf course together?" Cassie asked.

"Marvin is a landscape designer," Richard explained. "I drove over there with them hoping he might get some inspiration for a redesign once I purchased the course."

"That's when we saw Stella's nephew," Maureen added, "all cozied up to Smitty. And he was with someone else. We think it's the guy who's been going around making offers on all the properties."

"It makes sense," he said to Cassie.

She shook her head. "And he's using Stella as a front for it. That's despicable."

"They've offered to buy out his own aunt, and she probably still doesn't even know," Marvin told them. "Stella told me the news tonight, and she's really shaken up over it. She's completely against this whole idea of a big corporate takeover of Holiday, but she also doesn't want to stick around if everyone else caves in and moves away."

"Well, at least one person isn't caving in to the offer," Richard said with pride, and he smiled at Cassie. "Cassie has decided to reject it."

"Oh, that's wonderful," Maureen told her. "I hope the others will follow your lead."

"Any thoughts on how best to proceed from here?" Marvin asked him. "Maybe we should tell Stella it's her nephew behind all this drama."

"That will break her heart," Cassie said. "But if someone was using me like that, I'd want to be told."

"Me, too," Maureen commented.

"Me, three," said Marvin.

His own interests aside, Richard had a clear picture of what had to be done. "But we need to figure out how to handle this delicately.

And no one says anything about this to anyone until I've had time to dig a little. Agreed?"

"But, Richard, why?" Cassie asked him. "We should confront him and tell Stella. We need to make sure she isn't strung along any further."

"I'll see that Stella's not hurt in this," he promised. "But I need everyone's word here. We don't tell anyone what we think we know. Not yet. Agreed?"

"Yes!"

"Proceed with caution."

"Agreed."

Maureen had that look again. She stared into Richard's eyes so hard that he could feel the burn on his eyelids. Then, without a word, she offered him her hand and smiled.

"Right," he said.

And then the four of them joined hands and bowed their heads. Cassie squirmed a little.

"Father, we need Your guidance in this situation," Maureen began. "Please lead us on how best to proceed for Stella's benefit and for the benefit of everyone affected."

"Shine Your light in the dark places," Marvin added. "Don't let anyone get away with deception or underhandedness."

"Let the truth come out in that gentle way You have, Lord Jesus," Cassie stated, and Richard opened his eyes and glanced at her just as she opened her eyes, too. The smile she gave him was like a gift, all packaged up with ribbon. "And send Your ministering angels to do Your will, so that the crooked places will be made straight and Richard's dream will come to fruition, anointed with Your grace."

"And let that happen, Lord," Richard said, his voice hoarse from the emotion of the prayers of these good people on his behalf, "with Your protective hand guiding the outcome."

"In Jesus' name, we pray," said Maureen, and they all added their amens.

"Does anyone mind if I eat these chicken wings?" Cassie asked them afterward, and they all laughed in unison.

"The woman is obsessed," Richard teased.

"I'm just starving," she corrected before biting into one of them. "And they're so good!"

Chapter Sixteen

....

9 ACROSS: Without a flaw; porcelain-skinned; beautiful

"Richard Dillon, I have a bone to pick with you!"

Cassie turned around and watched as Stella Nesbitt stomped
her way up to Richard at the drink table, planted her hands on her
bony hips, and stared him down. Cassie hurried to his side, but Stella
glared at her.

"This doesn't concern you, Cassie," she said. "I'm about to give
Richard Dillon a piece of my mind."

Cassie looked at Richard, wondering if she should walk away, but
Stella slid into her tirade without waiting for her departure.

"You cannot just appear in this community one day, stick around
for a couple of years, and then act like you own the place," she told him,
pointing one skeletal index finger at his nose. "Those of us who live
in Holiday are here because we love the place. Oh, it might not be all
upper-crust and ritzy, Mr. High and Mighty, but we like it just fine."

The confrontation was beginning to draw a crowd. Cassie watched
as Hunter noticed, then scurried through the nest of gathering people
and placed his hands on Stella's shoulders.

"Aunt Stella," he croaked, "this isn't the time or place. It's a party."

"How are we supposed to celebrate?" she asked him. The question
seemed all the louder because the music had faded to silence with

Hunter's absence from the DJ table. Then Stella turned to the others. "Are we supposed to let this individual flit into our town and act like he's one of us and then shake us out of our homes like ants on a tablecloth?"

"Stella," Cassie interrupted, but Stella waved her off with a violent thrash of her arm. "You're really out of line here, Stella. Honestly, you're going to be so embarrassed."

"I'll be embarrassed?" she sort of screeched. "Me? I think Richard Dillon is the one to be embarrassed."

"First of all, Stella," Richard began, "I rarely *flit*."

"Don't you dare be flippant with me, young man!"

"And secondly, if you would like to have this discussion privately, I would be more than happy to do that."

"So you can get me away from any witnesses?" she accused him. "Why? Then what?"

"Aunt Stella, please calm down," Hunter said through clenched teeth.

"This man is creeping around trying to buy up property until he has enough land to put together a big, gaudy development. He won't stop until all of us are out of our homes and replaced by hotel villas, s–spa treatments and—and—a golf course!"

"Richard," Millicent asked him from the sidelines, "is this true?"

"No, Millicent, it is not," he said. "Thank you, though, for bothering to ask me."

Cassie touched Richard's arm. When he looked into her eyes, she recognized the pain of betrayal shining back at her.

"I think I've had about all of the happy '70s that I can stand," she told him. "Will you take me home?"

"Glad to."

"Millicent? Do you want a ride home now?" Cassie asked.

"We'll get her home," Maureen assured her. "You kids go on."

"That's right," Stella snapped. "Put your tail between your legs and go running home."

Anger swelled inside Cassie, and she turned toward Stella, poised and ready to fire back, but Richard shook his head in one short jerk. She swallowed her fury somehow—she wasn't quite sure how—and she and Richard walked out the door.

"I don't understand!" she yelped the minute the car doors were closed. "Why didn't you tell them? You could have exposed Hunter right there and then and gotten everyone on your side. Why didn't you?"

"It's not time."

"What does that mean?" she pressed. "How could it not be time? Stella Nesbitt, that old shrew, stood right there and talked to you like that, disrespecting you in front of everyone. Why, Richard? How could that not be the right time to tell that self-righteous old—"

"Cassie," he said softly. He rubbed her arm before turning over the engine. "Sometimes we have to keep things close to the vest. Timing is everything."

"Yes, but—"

"I know you don't understand at the moment," he told her. "You'll just have to trust me. Can you do that?"

Her heart was pounding, her mind was racing, and Cassie's mouth was gaping open in a perfect round *O*. And then she growled and tossed herself back against the passenger seat and closed her eyes. "Whatever."

He let a few minutes of silence act as a balm, and then Richard asked her, "Did you really just say 'Whatever' to me again?"

"You are very frustrating," she admitted.

"And you are very sweet. But my skin is thick enough to bide my time with this."

"But why?" she asked him again.

He only smiled at her and then shifted into REVERSE and pulled out of the parking space.

Every time she thought about it, she wanted to scream. She spent the whole drive home trying to suppress the proliferating throb of bitterness and resentment toward Stella, toward Hunter, toward all of them who just stood there as Richard was accused. Just about the time she would start to breathe normally, Stella's pointy features would hop across her mind's eye once more and she'd feel herself infuriated all over again.

Richard pulled into her driveway, cut the engine, and flipped off the headlights. Then they sat there in the dark, both of them staring straight ahead.

"Is there anything I can do?" Cassie asked in a raspy whisper.

"There is."

"Oh, good!" she said, turning sideways in her seat. "What is it?"

"You could invite me in for coffee."

"Coffee? You want coffee?"

"I do. Very much."

"Should I spike it with something really strong?" she asked, letting out a nervous laugh.

"No need," he replied. He turned and smiled at her. "Just your company and a latte at midnight will be just fine."

She gasped and her gaze darted to the clock: 11:36.

"It's nearly midnight! Come on."

Twenty minutes later they stood out on the dock in their shiny disco clothes, each with a steaming mug of coffee in their hands. Sophie sat at attention beside Cassie.

"Why did you want to come out here?" Cassie asked him.

"We're waiting for midnight."

"How will we know? Are you wearing a watch?"

"I am. But that's not how we'll know."

"How then?"

Richard leaned toward her and bumped her with his arm. "You really have to work on the whole patience thing, Cassie. Are you cold?"

"No, but what time is it?"

Across the canal from them, people stepped out onto their docks, and the one next door was dotted with silhouettes, as well.

"Happy New Year!" Cassie called to them, and they waved at her.

"Same to you!"

"Richard, what are they all doing out here?"

"Waiting."

"For what? Will you please tell me what's going to happen?"

"Just watch and see."

"Well, what time is it? I just want to know when it turns to midnight."

"You'll know, Cassie."

"But how?"

Richard set his coffee on the wooden dock beneath them and then took Cassie's cup from her and did the same. Slipping one arm around her shoulder, he glanced at his watch.

"Are you ready?"

"What's happening?"

"Just wait. Wait for it."

And just as Cassie opened her mouth to ask him what on earth she was waiting for and why so many people were gathered around the canal, it happened—something that sounded like the pop of a cannon. A long, sputtering wheeze preceded the explosion of color.

Oh, of course, she thought. "Fireworks."

One after another after another, fireworks crackled in the distance, filling the dark night sky with explosions of color.

Ooohs and ahhs stemmed from all around them, and Cassie added to their harmony on instinct. An enormous, shimmering blue star popped above them, and then a wiggling green kite with a spiral tail. Reds, golds, and silvers darted upward, popped open, and then shimmied downward.

Cassie dropped her head to Richard's shoulder. He nuzzled the top of her head with his chin and drew her deeper into his embrace.

"It's beautiful," she said. "They do fireworks in Boston, too. We went into the city one year to watch, but traffic was a zoo. And our house is just too far out to see them very well from there. This is spectacular."

"See what you've been missing by staying away at this time of year?"

Cassie didn't reply. There were a lot of things in Holiday that she'd been missing. Earlier in the car, Richard had told her, "Timing is everything." She felt those words resonate somewhere deep inside of her.

"Happy New Year, Cassie."

She tilted her face up toward him and grinned. "Happy New Year, Richard."

As his warm lips touched hers with a tender kiss, a tight fist clenched inside Cassie, pressing against that hollow just above her ribs. Her knees went weak, and her head started to spin ever so slightly.

As they parted, she found that her eyelids were so heavy, she could hardly lift them. She felt like a rag doll in Richard's arms, and she looked into his blue eyes and sighed. She tried to peel her gaze away from his to no avail. She was stuck there. Trapped. And Cassie realized at that moment, as she swam around in the blue waters there with no real hope of breaking free, much to her surprise...she didn't actually mind the imprisonment.

"Oh, Richard," she breathed. "I...love..."

Cassie broke into a full sweat.

No. No! Are you kidding me? What are you saying?

"I...l–love...new beginnings," she said. "Midnight at the new year al–always promises something new and...um...fresh. Do you know what I mean?"

Richard narrowed his eyes and nodded.

"Y–you're covered in glitter," she told him on a rolling, nervous laugh.

The glitter she'd sprayed on her hair and skin was smeared down one side of Richard's face. He lifted his hands, and they were shimmering, too.

"Nice," he chuckled. "It must be my sparkling personality."

"Too bad I don't have a pool. We could both jump in and wash it off."

"And clog up the filter," he pointed out. "There's always the canal."

"You first," she teased.

"I think I'll go home and have a shower instead."

Two little words, and they cut like a sharp knife.

Go home.

"Do you have to?" His astonished expression told her that she needed to expound. "I mean, are you hungry? Because I am."

"I'm beginning to think you're always hungry," he said with a grin.

"I wish so much that I could deny that."

"I really should be going," he told her. "Besides, I can't eat this late and keep my girlish figure."

Cassie giggled at that. "I wouldn't want to tempt you out of your golfing weight."

She walked him inside and then stood by the front door feeling awkward. Fortunately Richard broke the silence.

"Aside from the whole gang mentality there at the end," he said seriously, "I had a really good time tonight. Thanks for being my date."

"Thanks for putting up with all the glitter."

"It was nothing."

"Tell me that in the spring when you're still vacuuming it out of your car," she remarked.

"Hey, yours is a rental," he remembered. "I should have let you drive."

"I guess you're playing golf tomorrow?" she asked.

"No plans. What about you?"

"No, I'm not golfing either."

Richard laughed right out loud at that.

"Unless it's miniature," she continued. "There's nothing like the feeling when that ball goes straight into the clown's mouth."

"I'm not so much into the whole miniature thing. But if you'd be interested in going to the driving range instead, I could pick you up around noon."

"Really? Me and a golf club. I didn't peg you for being quite that courageous."

"Not so courageous," he replied, "as just…fast."

"If you're serious—"

"I'm serious."

"—then I think it might be fun."

"Lunch first?" he asked.

"I'll make something here and we can head out afterward?"

"Don't go to much trouble. Just a light soufflé would be fine. Some truffles. Maybe something flaming for dessert."

"Golf clubs *and* a flaming dessert. You're not brave; you're stupid."

One chuckle popped out of Richard, and he put his hand on the back of Cassie's head and drew her toward him. He planted a lingering kiss on her forehead and then immediately blew through puckered lips as he brushed the glitter off them.

"My sparkling personality," she quipped. "It's everywhere."

"See you tomorrow," he said, still making raspberries and dusting off his mouth as he headed out the door toward his car.

Cassie stood under the hot shower for ten minutes, rinsing off the glitter and washing it out of her hair. Then, with her locks still dripping wet, she ran a warm bath in the garden tub, grabbed an apple from the crisper, dimmed the lights over the tub, and climbed in to soak for a while. While Cassie munched on her Gala apple, Sophie stretched and yawned before curling into a large strawberry blond ball of fur on the bathroom rug.

It was nearly 2 a.m. by the time she dried her hair and pulled on her favorite pajamas: pale pink boxers and a T-shirt with dancing ducks across the front.

Not exactly the jammies of a fifty-something, she thought, *but no one has to know.*

Her feet had no sooner left the floor than Cassie's cell phone began to ring. She'd left it out in the dining room, but no one called her at two in the morning without a pretty good reason, so she took off at a full run down the hall. She stubbed her toe on the table leg and was groaning as she flipped up the phone and hobbled toward the light switch.

"Ow—hello?"

"Cassie?"

"Millicent?"

"Hunny bunny, I have a…*situation*." Her words were clipped, and she didn't sound like herself. "Would you mind coming over right away?"

"Are you all right?"

"Please just come over right away. Oh, and come around to the back door."

"Um, okay. I'll be right over."

"Hurry, please?"

"Will do."

"And don't come to the front. Come to the back?"

"I'm on my way."

Cassie tucked her cell phone into the pocket of her boxer pajamas, stepped into the rubber flip-flops by the sofa, and yanked open the door.

"Sophie, stay," she said when the dog bolted toward her. "I'll be right back."

She closed the gap between her house and Millicent's and then started up the front walk. Suddenly remembering Millicent's instructions, she cut across the grass and went around to the back of the house. The yard was dark and her feet were drenched, but she made it to the back door and pulled it open.

"Millicent?" She saw the woman standing in the middle of the L-shaped living and dining area, her back to Cassie and still clutching the telephone. The woman was *completely stark naked*.

"Oh my gosh! Millicent?"

"Don't come any further," Millicent warned her. "Stay right where you are!"

Cassie covered her eyes on instinct and exclaimed, "What are you doing?"

"Don't panic, okay?"

"Why would I panic?" Cassie asked her, an octave higher in pitch than normal.

"There's something over by the front door." Millicent was slow and deliberate in the delivery of the statement.

"What? What is it?" Cassie's heart was pounding so hard that she could barely hear Millicent above the thump of her pulse resounding in her ears.

"I'll tell you, but not until you promise not to react."

"Is it human? Can you just tell me that?"

The muscles in Millicent's back tensed. Her arms outstretched from her sides, she flexed her fists as she replied. "No."

"Is it a bug?"

"Hunny, it's not a bug. But every time I move a muscle, it rears up. So I need you to very slowly and carefully open that door behind me, to your left, and get out one of the big towels. If we throw a towel over it, I'll have time to run out the back door with you."

"Okay, Millicent. But will you please tell me what it is?" she asked as she tiptoed toward the linen closet and cringed as she eased open the door.

"It's a very…big…*snake*," Millicent answered—and Cassie could almost hear the screech across the record of the moment.

"What *is* it about Florida and reptiles?" she said loudly, with feeling, as she squinted at the dark side of the house to try to see the thing.

"Please. Don't. Shout." Millicent's voice trembled.

"Okay, okay. I'm sorry," she said in a hushed voice. "Here I come, towel in hand."

"Um, hunny? Could you grab a second one for me? I don't want to run out of the house without a stitch."

"Oh. Right." Cassie took a second one from the shelf and crept back toward Millicent.

"Now, very carefully, hand me one of the towels. And then unfold the other one and hold it open."

"Why?" There went her panicking heartbeat again. "Because if you're thinking I'm going to catch it or something, Millicent—"

"The open one is for me to run into before I leave this house."

Cassie considered it for a moment and then got the visual. "Makes sense."

"Slowly, hunny bunny."

"Where is it?"

"About five feet in front of me."

"What's it doing?" she asked, craning her neck to peek past Millicent.

"It's considering where to strike before it eats me alive. Give me the towel, please?"

Millicent's hands reached backward toward Cassie, and she placed one of the towels into the hand nearest her.

"I don't think this will be big enough."

"What do you mean?"

"It's really big, Cassie. Maybe get a blanket instead?"

"Millicent, maybe you should just back out of there without trying to cover it up. Just take a few steps backward."

"I can't. Every time I've moved for the last hour, it has come closer to me."

"You've been standing there naked and facing off with a snake for an hour?"

"Hunny, could we maybe have this discussion a little later?"

"Sorry."

The moment Cassie made a move toward the linen closet and yanked out a blanket, Millicent let out a blood-curdling scream and ran into her so hard that the two of them flew backward into the wall. Millicent, still screaming, thudded past her and then grabbed Cassie by the arm and yanked.

"Oh, my Lord, help us!" the woman screamed. Cassie looked down to see a fat black snake with yellow stripes *at least six feet long* now less than two feet away from her.

She and Millicent screeched all the way down the hall and into the bathroom where Millicent slammed shut the door and continued to shriek.

"That is the biggest snake I've ever seen, in person or not!" Cassie cried. She stepped over the side of the bathtub and stood there pitching from one foot to the other, clutching the towel and the blanket as if her very life depended on them. "Seriously, I don't think I ever even knew there was such a thing as a snake that big. How did it get into your house?"

"I wish I knew," Millicent said, panting.

"Oh," Cassie breathed, "here." And she handed Millicent the towel, which the woman wrapped around herself.

"Thank you."

"Now what are we going to do?" Cassie asked.

Millicent turned toward her, her face pinched like a dried prune, and she held up the telephone that she was still clutching. "But who do I call?" she asked.

"I'm thinking 911 would be appropriate."

Chapter Seventeen

....

20 ACROSS: Displays originality and wit

Cassie was stretched out in the dry bathtub with her feet propped on the faucet and her arm draped over the side, looking very much like she was trying out the sled for a downhill luge race in the Winter Olympics. Across from her, Millicent had lowered the toilet seat and was perched on the edge of it, wrapped in two large towels.

"What's taking them so long?" she grumbled.

Cassie shrugged. "I dunno."

"Did Richard say he was coming over?"

"Yes, but I told him to stay outside until the fire department arrived so he doesn't get eaten."

"That thing sure did look big enough to have any one of us for a midnight snack," Millicent remarked.

"At least he's too fat to get through the opening under the door."

Millicent's eyes darted to the doorjamb, and she lifted her feet to their tiptoes.

"It's okay," Cassie reassured her, rubbing her knee. "I told you, he's way too big to get through."

The woman sighed and reluctantly relaxed her feet and planted them on the floor again.

"Cassie?"

Cassie bolted upright and scowled at Millicent. "Richard? Don't come in! Wait for the men with axes."

A rumble of activity on the other side of the door told her that the cavalry had arrived. A sudden turn of the doorknob jolted Millicent, and she screamed as she pulled the top towel in closer around her.

"Don't open the door!" Cassie cried.

"Why not? You can follow me right out the back door now," Richard said through a minuscule opening.

"The thing is, Richard…Millicent is sort of…*naked.*"

Total silence. And then came the snickers of several men, including Richard.

"Maybe instead of laughing, you people could get her a robe!"

"She's right," Richard told them. Then he called to Cassie, "I'll go and get it."

"It's hanging on the back of the bedroom door," Millicent sang as she looked at the ceiling. "Down the hall, first door on the right."

Cassie opened her cell phone and checked the time: 4:11 a.m.

"It's after four," she told Millicent.

The door eased open, and Millicent hopped to her feet and shielded herself behind it, her back to Cassie. As the robe entered, Cassie shielded her eyes and told Millicent, "Put that on, will you?"

"Happy to," the woman snapped.

Just as Cassie pushed herself to her feet, a ruckus from the other side of the door caused Millicent to slam the door and catapult over the side of the tub, standing inside it right beside Cassie.

"Whoa!" one of the men yelled. "That thing is *huge!*"

"I told you!" Cassie shrieked, and Millicent yanked the shower curtain shut in front of them.

"What in the—!" someone shouted.

"What is it?" someone else asked, and then a chorus of men suddenly roared in unison.

"What? What? What happened?" Cassie cried.

Thumps and bumps and shouts and groans from the other side of the bathroom door drew Cassie and Millicent together in a desperate embrace. When there was finally silence for a few seconds, the women looked at one another in sheer terror. Fear stuck in Cassie's throat like a large cotton hook.

"Uh, Richard?" she managed in a shaky rasp. "Are you out there?"

No one answered.

Cassie felt the dread swirling around them in a torrent like dirt on the floor of a drafty old warehouse. Clutching Millicent, she cleared her throat.

"H–hello?"

Nothing.

"Sweet Jesus, protect them," Millicent prayed.

"Sweet Jesus, protect *us,* too!" Cassie added.

Footsteps…the turn of the doorknob…

As the bathroom door flew open, Cassie and Millicent shrieked.

"It's me!" Richard exclaimed, but when he yanked open the shower curtain, they screamed again. "Calm down, it's me."

Both women threw themselves into his arms.

"Thank God you're all right!" Cassie cried.

"Did they find it?" Millicent asked concurrently. "Is it gone?"

"It's gone," he told them, and he took Millicent's hand and helped her over the edge of the tub. "You can go on out. It's gone."

"What was it?" Cassie asked him when he offered his hand to her, but Richard paused to look her over.

"Nice outfit," he remarked. She tugged at the boxers and T-shirt to make sure it was all in place. "It was a Florida king snake."

"Are you kidding me?" she said as she stepped over the tub and followed him out of the bathroom. "What's that?"

"It was a King," one of the firemen stated. "You could tell by the yellow crossbands."

"Ewwww." Cassie cringed. "Why did he come inside the house? Why would he do that?"

"Happens more than you'd think. They're most active at night, and the weather has still been warm, so—"

"Where is it *now*?" Millicent asked him.

"Animal Control just arrived. They're loading it into their truck."

"Cody!" One of the other firemen entered at just that moment and declared, "Man, the thing is five feet eleven inches!"

"Ohhh." Cassie cringed again and turned away. "And I thought those little anole lizards were disgusting, running amuck wherever they please the way they do!"

"Probably lives out in the canal," the fireman told them. "I'm surprised a gator didn't get it."

"What? There are *alligators* in the canal?" Cassie shouted.

"Nice," Richard said to Cody with a smack to his arm. "Thanks for that."

"How on earth did it get into my house?" Millicent exclaimed.

"I'd advise you to get a pest control inspector out here as soon as you can," Cody, the twenty-something fireman in the tight gray T-shirt, advised her. "They'll be able to answer that question for you."

"Meanwhile, you'll stay at my house," Cassie added. "Go pack a few things."

Millicent gave a ferocious nod and scurried toward the bedroom.

"Alligators, lizards, snakes," Cassie muttered. Richard moved to touch her arm and she jumped a foot out of his grasp.

"Sorry," he said and grinned.

"I hate Florida."

"No, you don't."

"I do. I always have."

"No, you haven't."

"Richard, I think I would know if—"

Millicent appeared, wearing a cotton housedress and clutching a bulging overnight bag. Putting one arm around her shoulder and the other around Cassie, Richard began walking them toward the back door.

"You don't like the wildlife," he told Cassie, "but you don't hate Florida."

"Well, I think it's icky anyway," she said as they headed outside. "The humidity in the summer and bugs the size of Volkswagens... It's just not natural."

"It's very natural," he replied in a soothing voice. "It's just not what you're used to."

"I don't think I want to get used to it."

"Me neither," Millicent chimed in.

"Okay, well, we'll get you both across the street and settled," he comforted them as they rounded the house and headed down the driveway. "The only scary creature over there is Sophie."

Cassie giggled, and then so did Millicent.

Richard had a very calming influence, Cassie realized. And she took a moment to shoot a prayer upward to thank God for it.

Millicent was tucked safely into Cassie's guest room, and Cassie was in her bedroom changing out of her pajamas into something less pajama-like. Although Richard didn't think there was anything indecent about what she'd been wearing before in her light pink boxer-type shorts and T-shirt with the row of very respectable ducks swimming along in top hat and tails. The last one in the row, however, was tossing off his hat, holding up his cane, and grinning from ear to ear, and that image screamed "Cassie" to him.

She does tend to stand out in a crowd.

He dunked a couple of tea bags into a small ceramic pot of hot water and then pulled two large cups from the cabinet. By the time Cassie reappeared, the tea was steeped and poured, and he carried the cups out to the living room and set them down on the coffee table.

"Thank you," she said. She curled her legs underneath her and held the warm steam close to her face. "It must be almost morning, huh?"

"Not long now."

"I'm afraid noon will roll around awfully fast today," she said.

"We'll hit the driving range another time," Richard replied—and then he found himself wondering if she would still be around for him to keep that promise.

"I'm hoping to sleep the whole day away."

"You've had a lot of excitement today."

"So have you," she said. When he glanced at her, she was smiling sweetly at him. "You doing all right?" Cassie asked.

"Fine."

"Honest?"

"Honest."

"I know!" she said, straightening. "Why don't you come over for dinner later today?"

"I appreciate the thought," he answered, "but I can't."

"Better offer?"

"I'm not sure there is one," he said with a grin. "But I made dinner plans in Tampa with an old buddy of mine."

"Oh."

"Steven Hearns. You met him at the golf course."

"Oh, right."

"In fact," he said, the moment it occurred to him, "maybe you'd like to come along."

"I don't want to intrude on your male bonding ritual." She grinned.

"No male bonding taking place over dinner," he corrected. "Steven has his own company. He checks the backgrounds of potential employees for companies all over Central Florida. I've asked him to use a little of his magic to find out more about Hunter Nesbitt and Hunter's mysterious friend."

"Did he find anything?"

"I don't know. He just left me a voice mail asking me to meet him for dinner over in Tampa because he's leaving in two days for a weeklong business trip. Why don't you get some sleep, and I'll pick you up around six for dinner." Her expression was a little blank, so he added, "If you want to go."

"I'm worried about leaving Millicent alone," she told him. "Do you think she'll be all right here by herself?"

Richard smiled. "I don't think any other creatures are coming up from the lagoon."

"Promise?"

He laughed. "Almost."

"Where are we going?" she asked. "So I know what to wear."

"A place out in New Tampa called Stonewood Grill."

"Casual?"

"Steak and seafood. But it's Florida. You can pretty much wear anything, anywhere."

"Okay."

He considered suggesting the pink boxers with the dancing duck shirt and then thought better of such a joke. "Anything you wear will be fine."

Despite the fact that she was exhausted, Cassie had a hard time falling asleep. She'd crawled into bed just a few minutes after Richard had left her house and the sun wasn't even peeking its head over the horizon yet. Too many things were rumbling around in her brain, and the buzz was just about driving her mad.

When she finally did doze off, it was almost seven o'clock. Morning sleep almost always brought with it strange dreams, and New Year's morning was no different. Cassie dreamed of a house-sized snake with Hunter Nesbitt's face, a group of naked neighbors wrestling alligators in the canal, and an embarrassing ride with Richard into Tampa where all she had to wear was a large towel made of glitter.

She tossed and turned in her sleep, and when Sophie finally insisted that she wake up late in the afternoon, Cassie didn't feel much more rested than she had that morning. She opened the back door and stepped outside with the dog. While Sophie sniffed around the backyard, Cassie leaned on the wooden railing of the deck and concentrated on the water beyond the dock.

I wonder if there really are alligators out there, she thought.

Fortunately, Sophie derailed that train of thought by trotting past her and back into the house.

"I had the strangest dream last night," Millicent told her, as she brought two cups of coffee and a plate of toast into the dining room and set them on the table in front of her neighbor.

"Me, too," Cassie said, shaking her head.

"I dreamed that a large snake got into my house and I didn't have a stitch of clothing on!"

Cassie gazed at her for a moment and then the two of them broke into laughter.

"It does feel a bit like a nightmare, doesn't it?"

"Hunny bunny, I can't thank you enough for coming to my rescue."

"All I did was hide in the bathtub with you," Cassie said, chuckling and then taking a bite of wheat toast with jam. "It was Richard and those cute firemen that did all the rescuing."

"Still."

"Well, you're welcome."

"Is it all right if I stay another night?" Millicent asked her timidly.

"Of course."

"I can't get anyone out here until tomorrow."

"No problem," Cassie replied. Then she tried a sip of the strongest, blackest coffee she had ever encountered. "Oh, hey, do you mind being here on your own for a while tonight? I've got some plans with Richard at six."

"Certainly not. The two of you are seeing a lot of each other, aren't you?"

"Millicent, I want you to know something," Cassie said. She put down her cup and looked her friend right in the eyes. "Richard is not behind any of that mess Stella was talking about."

"All right." She didn't seem convinced.

"You have my word on it. I've been helping Richard try to get to the bottom of it, and I can assure you that he's not the one trying to buy your house—or Stella's."

Millicent's eyes grew as big and shiny as oil. "You're helping him?"

"Richard adores you. And he wouldn't do anything underhanded. I promise you."

"Does he know anything about what's going on then?"

"A little," Cassie replied, but she knew she couldn't say any more about it without betraying Richard's confidence. "I know he'll fill you in when he has something solid. But in the meantime, I don't want you to worry about anything. Promise me."

"I promise."

There was a vague mist of emotion in Millicent's eyes, and Cassie wished she could better reassure her. She wondered if Steven Hearns would offer up any information to help settle the whole matter once and for all.

"Sophie and I will keep each other company until you get home." A beat or two passed, and then Millicent asked, "What are these?"

Millicent had the crystal box in front of her, with the hinged lid gaping open.

"Oh, it's called a 'Surprise Yourself' box. Each day you pull a card from the front of the box, and read the scripture there. And then you turn the card over and find an idea of how to live that verse. Go ahead and pull one out."

Millicent produced the card at the front of the box and read it out loud. "'Do not be afraid of sudden terror, nor of trouble from the wicked when it comes; for the LORD will be your confidence, and will keep your foot from being caught.' That's Proverbs chapter 3, verses 25 and 26."

"Now turn it over."

She did as requested but read it in silence and then lifted her eyes to Cassie as if she'd somehow been shamed.

"What does it say?"

Millicent looked down at the card, swallowed hard, and then read it. "'Say a prayer right now about what concerns you most, and then believe God for the solution to your most unsolvable problem.'"

Cassie grinned. "Those cards are so timely, aren't they?"

"Well, this one is."

Cassie leaned over and kissed Millicent's cheek and then headed down the hall toward her bedroom. As she pushed her door closed, she could hear Millicent whispering.

She's praying, she thought. And the realization warmed her soul. Cassie found herself wishing she had the time to do a little praying herself.

She opened the closet door and then plopped on the edge of the bed and stared into it. She hadn't really brought any clothes with her that would be suitable for a dinner out, and she hoped she would still fit into the ones that had been hanging in the closet already.

A blue dress caught her eye, so she pulled it out and hung it on the closet door by the hanger. The tags were still on the dress, and she wasn't sure she even remembered buying it.

Size 4. Well, that might be a problem.

She slipped the steel blue sheath off the hanger and over her head. The straight skirt barely made it over her hips. It was too tight. Then she tried the little black dress Zan had seen in a store window in a New Port Richey shopping plaza years back. She'd only worn it once, she remembered, as she pulled it out of the closet.

Richard had said to dress casually. This was more of a cocktail dress.

Too dressy.

A splash of blue inside the closet caught her attention, and she removed the hanger and admired the light blue cardigan with silver-and-white beading across the front. She'd brought it down with her two or three springs back and then left it hanging in the closet because the humidity made it unappealing. It would be just right for a Florida winter, though.

A so-called winter, anyway.

She decided to pair the cardigan with black pants, a string of pearls, and an updo. When she walked out into the living room and saw Millicent's expression, she knew she'd made a good choice.

"Oh, hunny bunny, you look lovely."

"Thank you. The pearls aren't too much?"

"They're just right. You're a dazzler."

Cassie caught Sophie's attention mid-stride, and she jumped back and held both hands down toward the dog.

"No, no, Soph!" she exclaimed, and Sophie sat down right where she was. Cassie grimaced and told Millicent, "Black pants and Sophie are not a good mix."

"Well, Sophie, you come over here and sit with your aunt Millie then," she said, patting the sofa. The dog hopped up before Millicent was finished.

Cassie opened the drawer in the table next to the chair by the front window and produced a small lint brush. She began running it over her pants while Sophie looked on, dejected.

"So where are you all going?"

"New Tampa," Cassie replied tentatively. "A place called Stonewood Grill. Do you know it?"

"I do. It's quite nice."

"I'm dressed right then?"

"Just right. The pearls will play nicely." Millicent's grin put Cassie at ease.

"Can I get you anything before I go?"

"You can show me how to use this complicated thingy for the television set."

"Oh," Cassie said on a sigh. "Sorry. It's not too difficult. Press the green button to turn it on and off. Here's the volume, and here are the channels. And if you want to watch something on the DVR—"

"No, no," Millicent interjected. "Volume and channels are about all I can handle."

Cassie chuckled as the bell rang. Sophie sprang from the sofa, all barks and snarls until Cassie opened the door and they saw that Richard was there.

"Hey, Sophie."

The dog turned tail and headed back to Millicent and the sofa.

"You look beautiful," he told Cassie. She exhaled for what felt like the first time in an hour.

"Thank you. I wasn't sure what to wear."

"It's just right."

He looked so handsome that her breath caught, but Cassie didn't tell him so. Richard was wearing black trousers and a light blue shirt that really brought out the blue in his eyes, and Cassie realized they looked like they'd coordinated their clothing.

"Ready," she said, grabbing her purse and heading for the door. "Millicent, you have my cell number in case you need me?"

"This isn't my first time home alone," the woman commented, and then she shot them both a smile. "You kids have a good time."

"We'll bring you home some dessert," Richard said in a mock whisper, his hand cupped around his mouth in a conspiratorial way.

"I wouldn't turn that down," Millicent returned, and Richard and Cassie headed out the door.

Chapter Eighteen
....

19 ACROSS: Rare excellence; appealing perfection

Stonewood Grill was leather and wood and casual elegance. Cassie decided she probably could have left the pearls behind after all, but they wouldn't hurt anything now.

Steven Hearns had already arrived, and he was seated at a large booth.

"You remember Cassie Constantine?" Richard said. She could see from Steven's expression that he was rather stunned by her presence.

"I do. Good to see you again."

Once they'd slipped into the booth across from him, Richard reassured Steven. "Cassie knows pretty much everything. It's fine to talk in front of her."

"I was wondering," he replied. "Good—because I have a lot to tell. Shall we order some appetizers?"

Richard nodded. "What do you suggest?"

The waiter arrived as if on cue, and Steven asked him for smoked salmon and baked Brie. Richard added three mineral waters, and Cassie could sense his anticipation.

"What have you got for me?"

"Richard never was one for suspense," Steven told Cassie. "He doesn't enjoy the buildup."

"I'm not a big fan of it either," she admitted.

"All right, all right," he said, producing a file folder from the seat beside him and opening it on the table.

Steven reached into the pocket of his sport coat, pulled out wire-framed glasses, and placed them on his substantial nose. He scanned the paperwork for a moment and then looked up at Richard over the top of the lenses.

"I think you were correct in your assumption that something's up with Nesbitt," he said. Richard squirmed slightly and then leaned forward to the edge of the table. "He did work for Mandalay once upon a time—you were right about that—but he's not involved with them now. For the last three years, he's been employed by a corporate entity out of New York called Pressman Ventures. They're basically a much smaller version of Mandalay. Land development, resort properties, and the like, but not on the scale of Mandalay."

Richard cast Cassie a quick glance, and she could sense that his anxiety level was cranking upward.

"Last year Nesbitt was a key player in a questionable development in Pennsylvania. It was a sweet deal for him, really. Somehow he knew that Mandalay was going to develop a resort community, despite the fact that he didn't work there anymore. He swooped in, bought up three or four properties in the area, and then had them in his pocket as bargaining chips."

"I don't understand," Cassie interjected. "He bought the properties and then held on to them?"

"Until Mandalay had acquired every other property necessary to make their deal happen. And then he emerged as the last man standing and demanded quite a hefty profit on those properties. He made something like half a million dollars on that one deal."

"Half a million!" she exclaimed. *He should spend some of it on charm school.*

"So it is Mandalay that wants to move in on Holiday, then?" Richard asked him.

"That's the interesting part," Steven explained. He paused while the waiter delivered the appetizers and drinks.

"Can I take your orders now?" he asked.

"We're going to wait a bit," Steven replied. "We'll give you a shout when we're ready."

"My name is Tim, if you need anything."

"Thanks, Tim." Steven waited for a moment and then picked up where he left off. "Anyway, it's not Mandalay that's invested in developing anything in Holiday. It appears to be Pressman Ventures, his own company."

"That doesn't make sense," Cassie said to Richard. "He didn't work for Mandalay anymore when he bought the properties in Pennsylvania, so it didn't matter. But now he works at Pressman, and they're the ones who want to develop Holiday? Would he take a chance on outsmarting his own company and possibly losing his job? Surely Pressman Ventures wouldn't take kindly to him moving in on their deal. With Mandalay, he had nothing to lose because, as you said, he didn't work for them anymore." She looked at Steven as she finished.

"Maybe he has a partner," Richard offered. "Maybe someone from his old days at Mandalay, someone who gave him the information about Pennsylvania. Then Hunter went in and did the actual buying."

"My guess would be," Steven said, pausing to finish his mineral water, "that's the suit you saw with him at the golf course."

"So Hunter has a friend who still works at Mandalay who advises his own company to buy in that particular area," Richard surmised. "Then he feeds the information to Hunter, who steps in and acts as the front man for the deal. Afterward, he siphons in the information to Pressman about the place, and his friend from Mandalay plows the road on that one."

"Oooh," Cassie said, shaking her head, "Stella will flip her wig when she realizes the game he's playing."

"The good news for you, my friend," Steven told Richard, "will be if this guy's aunt has any influence over him at all. If she can put a stop to him starting the ball rolling in her own little neighborhood—"

"And no one will sell to Pressman once they hear about this, Richard."

"I don't think we can assume that," he replied. He looked at Steven. "Do you have solid proof about Nesbitt's involvement in the Mandalay deal?"

"Would his signature on the paperwork be enough proof for you?"

A smile slid across Richard's face, and Cassie's heart thumped at the reappearance of those parenthetical dimples of his.

"He didn't buy the property, but he did arrange for the inspection beforehand. Now there's no guarantee that it will all work out the way you want it to," Steve told him. "But it's some core information."

"That's what I wanted."

"And that's what you have," Steven said with a smile. "Now you gotta try this salmon. It'll knock you out."

Once they were in the car on the way back to Holiday, Cassie was pretty sure she had eaten that much in one sitting before, but she certainly couldn't remember when. The satisfied fullness gave a half-court press against her ribs, and she leaned back into the seat in an effort to give her digestion some room to operate.

When they pulled into her driveway back in Holiday and Richard shut off the car, Cassie jerked and realized she'd been dozing.

"I wasn't very good company on the ride home," she said on a grin. "I'm sorry. I'm like a fat and happy dog. Feed me and then I go to sleep."

"You bear no resemblance whatsoever to a fat and happy dog," Richard assured her.

Cassie squeezed his wrist. "Nice to know."

"Looks like Millicent received some company."

A dark blue Taurus was bellied up to the curb in front of the mailbox, but Cassie didn't recognize it.

"I wonder who it is."

"Let's go find out," Richard said, and he pushed open his door.

He grabbed the take-out bag from Stonewood Grill and then quickly rounded the car and opened Cassie's door, taking her hand to help her out.

"It's official," she said. "I'm a salmon-stuffed sausage."

"It would be worth the drive out to New Tampa just to have that on a regular basis," Richard concurred. "But I'm developing some fins myself. I'm thinking that second platter we ordered might have been a little much."

Cassie chuckled. "Ya think?"

Richard placed his hand on Cassie's shoulder as they meandered up the sidewalk, and she pushed open the front door and stepped inside.

The television was tuned to Animal Planet, and Sophie was sacked out on the sofa, watching it intently. Millicent was seated at the dining room table with the overhead chandelier turned to full-on bright. A game of Scrabble was in progress, and Cassie blinked when she saw who was seated across the board from Millicent.

It can't be. But that looks like—

"Debra?"

"Hi, Mom."

Her daughter's smile brightened the rest of the house and the neighborhood, too.

"What are you doing here?"

Debra pushed up from the chair, and Cassie noticed her little baby bump right away. She hurried toward her and wrapped her arms around Debra, rocking her from side to side as tears sprang to her eyes and cascaded down her face.

"It's so good to see you."

"You, too," Debra sniffed, and Cassie realized that her daughter was crying, too.

She pulled back and dabbed the tears from Debra's face with her index finger. "Stop that now."

"I've missed you so much," she told Cassie.

Cassie grinned at Millicent and then turned back toward Richard where he stood in the arched doorway to the living room. "I'm sorry, Richard. Please come and meet my daughter, Debra. This is my friend, Richard Dillon."

They exchanged greetings, and Richard grasped Debra's hand between both of his. "I've heard so much about you that I feel like we've already met," he told her. "Congratulations on the baby."

"Thank you," Debra told him. "I haven't had the same pleasure. Mom's told me nothing about you at all."

Cassie recognized the arch of her daughter's brow—most likely subtle and barely noticeable to anyone else, but not to her.

"Millicent roped me into taking a ballroom dancing class with her at the seniors' ministry over at church, and Richard is the instructor."

"But we really met before that," Richard reminded her. "When the Hootzes' boat demolished your dock."

"Oh, that's right!" she replied, and the two of them laughed. "Do you remember George and Georgette Hootz, Deb?"

"I think so."

"I made tea," Millicent said. "Can I get some for you two?"

"Oh, dear, no," Cassie answered. "I ate so much at dinner that I might just spring a leak if I add anything before it settles."

"Millicent, we brought you dessert," Richard said. "Do you want it now, or shall I put it in the refrigerator for later?"

"Fridge, dear. Thank you."

"Where did you go for dinner?" Debra asked as Richard popped the bag into the refrigerator and stepped back into the dining room.

"A place called the Stonewood Grill," Cassie said as she sank into one of the chairs. Debra and Richard followed suit. "It was fantastic."

"Stonewood Grill?" she asked. "Mitch and I ate at one of those in North Carolina, I think. It was awesome."

"Oooh, it's a chain? Do they have them in Boston, I wonder?"

"I don't know," Debra replied. She reached over and rubbed her mother's hand. "I love the improvements you've made on the house, by the way. It's so inviting."

"Isn't it wonderful? Did you see the glass hanging in the window of the master bath?"

"I did. Millicent gave me the full tour. It's really spectacular. She says you might have a bite for a sale, though. From a big corporation or something?"

Cassie and Richard exchanged glances.

"I'm not going to be taking that offer," Cassie said. Millicent darted her attention toward her.

"You're not?"

"No. Richard and I found out some things tonight, Millicent. Very important things about who that corporation is and what's really going on."

Millicent hopped to her feet but didn't leave the spot. She just stood there looking somewhat terrified and glanced first at Cassie, then at Richard, and then back again.

"We'll tell you everything, Millicent, I promise," Richard told her. "But I'd like to wait until tomorrow, if that's all right with you."

"And we'd like to tell you with Stella here," Cassie added.

"Stella."

"She's going to want to hear what Richard has to say."

"Is it…bad news?" Millicent asked, her hand clutching her dress just over her heart.

Richard got up from his chair and walked around the table and then put his arm around Millicent and kissed her on the top of her head.

"It is not bad news, my darling. Not for you. You're not going to be moving out of your house, and neither is Stella."

Millicent looked to Cassie. When she nodded at the woman, Millicent gave a shaky sigh so heavy that Cassie thought it must have been building up inside her lungs for a very long time.

"How about we start a new Scrabble game?" Debra suggested. "Mom and Richard can play, too."

Millicent nodded, and Richard helped her back to her chair.

"She was wiping the floor with me, anyway," Debra told them as she emptied the tiles on the board back into the box. "I'm happy to have an excuse for a do-over."

"Do-overs are good," Cassie commented as she turned over the tiles so that all of the letters faced downward.

"So, Mom."

"So, Debra," Cassie retorted as she swept eggs from the pan to the plate the next morning.

Debra leaned against the counter, jutting out her already-protruding belly. "What's going on with you and Richard Dillon, huh?"

"There's blackberry jam in the fridge. Why don't you grab it and come to the table?" Cassie responded as she passed her with two full plates in her hands.

Debra scurried to the refrigerator, found the jar of preserves, and followed her mother to the dining room table. She sat down across from her and placed a napkin on her lap as she remarked, "The two of you seem to be connected. How long have you been seeing him?"

Cassie thought about telling her daughter that she wasn't *seeing* Richard, that it was only a casual friendship and nothing more. But she couldn't seem to manage it. "The truth is," she began, before pausing for a bite of scrambled eggs, "if I was staying in Holiday, I'd be excited about pursuing something with him to see where it led. But I'm going home soon."

"When is that?"

"I'm not sure. A few days, or maybe next week."

"So the two of you aren't…?"

"Aren't what?"

"Pursuing anything."

"No," she replied. "It's just kind of rolling along."

"What does that mean, exactly? I mean, where are you rolling?"

"Debra Constantine Rudolph, you watch your tone."

"I'm just worried about you, Mom. Daddy hasn't been gone very long, and I'm afraid you might slip into something because you're lonely. I mean, Daddy was a big presence."

"Yes, I know."

"Learning to live without that presence can't be easy."

"No, it's not."

"And I think that would leave the door open for someone to walk right through and lead you somewhere that you weren't... I don't know...meant to go."

"Debra, there are no doors open here, no leading or going. It's just two people, both of whom have lost their mates, finding some common ground in one another."

"That's it?"

"Are you asking me if I'm attracted to Richard?"

"I wasn't going to ask. But are you?"

"Yes, I am."

"Mom!" Debra gasped, and she set her fork down across the center of her plate.

"What? Your father died, Debra. I did not. It's going to happen every third or fourth blue moon that I am going to meet someone that I connect with in some way. It doesn't mean I didn't love your father or that I've moved on from losing him...because, frankly, I'm not convinced that could ever happen. All it means is that I'm a human being searching out some joy and passion in what's left of my life."

"Joy and passion," Debra repeated. "And Richard Dillon makes you feel joyful? Passionate?"

"Actually, he does...surprisingly enough."

"Have you... Have you kissed him?"

Cassie set down her own fork, folded her hands on the edge of the table, and stared Debra down for a long moment.

"Let me be crystal clear about something," she replied. "This is none of your business. And just because you and I have a close relationship, which I'm very glad about, that does not mean by any stretch of the imagination that you are entitled to every detail of my life. Do you understand that?"

"Yes," Debra said on a sigh as she looked away. "I'm sorry. You're right. I've just got to get used to the idea that my mother—"

"But, yes, I've kissed him."

Debra's eyes darted back to her, but she didn't say a word.

"I like him very much, Debra," she said, stopping herself short of the whole truth. "He's a dear, sweet man, and he's been very kind to me. I like almost everything about him, and we're very compatible. But that's as far as it goes. All right?"

"Yes."

"But if that wasn't as far as it went—"

"I know."

"It wouldn't be—"

"—any of my business."

"Up until the time I decide to marry him or move to Holiday to be closer to him, this would be none of your business. Correct."

Debra picked up her fork and began pushing her eggs around on the plate.

"I'm sorry."

"You're forgiven." Cassie twisted open the lid on the preserves and spread some on her toast. "Now tell me about your plans. Why did you come, and how long can you stay?"

"I was reminiscing with Mitch the other night about all the fun times we had down here, and it occurred to me that I wanted to do this with you."

"Do what?"

"I wanted to be here with you one last time, and I wanted to help you get the place ready to sell."

"It's pretty much ready, honey. I don't think there's much else to do except the packing, and we're not having you do any of that in your condition."

"I just didn't want you to have to do it alone."

"Thank you, sweetheart," Cassie replied.

"I couldn't believe it when I pulled up and saw those flamingos out on the lawn." Debra cackled with the remembrance. "I remember Daddy telling me about them when he bought them…and about the fights the two of you were having over where they would stay."

"Or if they would stay at all," Cassie said on a chuckle.

"I would have thought that you'd have thrown them away without a single hesitation. And then there they were, in the yard, underneath the palm tree that was strung up with lights. What brought that about?"

Cassie pointed at the crystal box sitting on the table.

"A 'Surprise Yourself' box. I got one of those for Lacy for Christmas. She's the girl I work with in the nursery at church."

"I pulled a card that said something like, 'Do something you said you never would do,'" Cassie confessed.

Debra laughed, and then Cassie started giggling right along with her.

"Well, keeping them was certainly something you said you'd never do. Planting them out there in the yard for the world to see, well, that was downright beyond."

"Those flamingos are *beyond*," Cassie teased.

"Can I have them?"

Cassie looked up at Debra, inspecting her face to see if she was serious.

"You hate them, and if you're going to throw them away—"

"I'm kind of attached to them now," Cassie admitted. "But I promise if I ever get the urge to toss them into the trash, I'll save them for you instead. Deal?"

"Deal," Debra said with a smile. "By the way, I was looking at one of the crosswords Daddy made for you last night. The one that Millicent was working."

"What?" Cassie's heart tried to stop, and then it thumped over the obstacle in the road. "What do you mean?"

"When I arrived, she was sitting here at the table working one of Dad's crosswords. See? Right there."

Cassie snatched the folded piece of paper tucked under the flowers at the center of the table. When she opened it and laid it flat before her, tears sprang to her eyes. The entire puzzle was filled in.

"Mom, what's wrong?"

"I've been taking my time with it, working it a little bit at a time," Cassie told her. "Kind of savoring the last things your father thought about me."

"Ohhh. So you didn't tell Millicent it was all right to finish it."

"I wouldn't have told *her* that or anyone else."

"Oh, Mom. I'm sorry."

Cassie ironed the page with a flattened hand and then stroked it gently.

"I thought they were really nice words to describe you, though," Debra said in a tone that overemphasized the hope that she could find some way to make her mother feel a little better. "I mean, *exquisite* and *flawless*? Those are pretty romantic notions for a man to have about his wife of twenty-five years."

Cassie scanned the page, searching for those particular words. She stared at them, her brow furrowed and her eyes narrowed to a squint.

Those really are *romantic and wonderful.*

The adjectives that stood out in her memory from years past pinched her with regret rather than encouraged her. She'd spent years upon years wondering often whether Zan was describing his wife or a dependable used car.

Her thoughts fluttered back to Richard. He'd suggested that the clue for the ten-letter word Zan had used to describe her pointed to *passionate*, and she'd assured him that he was wrong, quite certain that Zan wouldn't have referenced her in that way. He saw her more like eager and enthusiastic, like the cocker spaniel down the street. But passionate?

16 Across: Compelled by intense emotions; fervent.

And Millicent had penciled in the answer in confident block letters: *Passionate.*

"I'm going to grab a shower, okay?"

"Hmm? Sure, honey. Go ahead."

Cassie inspected the completed puzzle more closely, and she scratched her head.

Perhaps Zan had begun seeing the things in Cassie that she was *going to be.* After he was gone and it was too late to enjoy those qualities in her. That was the only explanation. She was always an average woman with average strengths. There was nothing really out of the ordinary about her that she could think of.

I've never been what one would consider passionate.

She swallowed hard and then checked the clue again.

Have I?

Chapter Nineteen

....

12 ACROSS: Delightful; wonderful; completely enchanting

Stella Nesbitt was a tough nut to crack. Millicent opened the door and welcomed her in, but Stella waltzed into Cassie's house with her nose in the air and a scowl on her face.

"I'm here because my good friend Millie asked me to come, as a favor to her. There is nothing else that could have gotten me here."

"I understand," Cassie replied. "Can I get you some coffee?"

"I don't want any of your coffee. Where's Richard Dillon? Let's get this started and take it on the road."

"He should be here any minute. Millicent, can I get you some coffee?"

"I'll get it, hunny bùnny."

Cassie would much rather have been the one to leave the room.

"Stella, I'd like you to meet my daughter Debra."

"Pleased to meet—"

"When's the rug rat due?" she interrupted, giving Debra a gentle poke in the belly.

"Early summer."

"Don't let it be said that you should be punished for the sins of your mother," Stella snapped. "Congratulations to you."

Cassie looked up and saw Richard standing in the doorway. He'd let himself in.

"I feel that way, too," he said, and Stella jumped. "So we won't hold you responsible for the sins of your nephew."

"How dare you!"

"Stella," Richard began, and he walked over to her and sat in the chair across from her. "I have something to tell you, and I'd appreciate it if you would hear me out to the end."

"If you're here to talk about my house—"

"No," he interjected, "I'm not. At least not directly." He turned to Cassie and asked, "Where's Millicent?"

"I'll get her."

They all settled in the living room, Stella and Millicent on the sofa, Richard in the chair across from them, and Cassie perched at the edge of the rocker by the window. Cassie noticed that Debra had moved to the dining room, and she was trying not to appear obvious about her interest in what was going to come next but failing just the same.

"Let me start by saying this," Richard said, looking directly into Stella's glare without flinching. "I am not the person who is trying to buy up properties here in Holiday."

Stella sniffed and looked away, but Cassie noticed that Millicent was enrapt, wide-eyed, and silent.

"You have my word on it, both of you."

Millicent nodded. "That's good enough for me." Stella shot her a glare.

"I've been looking into it, though," he continued, "and I've discovered who *is* making offers on some of the houses here."

"Who?" Millicent asked him.

"Hunter."

Stella skimmed the room and then turned her sharp nose right back into the air. "Not possible."

"Actually, Stella," Cassie chimed in, "it's true."

"No," she snapped.

Richard produced the manila file folder that Steven Hearns had provided, and he opened it in his lap.

"A couple of years ago," he explained, "Hunter was working for a company called the Mandalay Corporation."

"I know that," she barked. "Anyone could know that with a little checking."

"He was one of the team that recommended locations for Mandalay to develop resort communities." Richard directed his attention to Millicent. "And he proposed a town in Pennsylvania. He then teamed up with a buddy who was completely unrelated to Mandalay, and with this friend in the driver's seat, they bought three properties in the area for themselves and held those plots back until they were the only ones the company couldn't get. Consequently, Mandalay had to pay a pretty penny for them, and since they'd bought them from Hunter's friend, they had no way of tracking it to him. Hunter and his friend walked away with a hefty profit."

"How do you know this?" Stella asked him. Before Richard could answer, she turned to Millicent. "This is not possible."

"I have the inspection paperwork right here," Richard said, and Stella leaned forward to take a closer look. "Hunter Nesbitt, right here. That's his signature."

Millicent tried to stroke Stella's hand, but she jerked it away.

"Hunter left Mandalay soon afterward," Richard continued, "and went to work for a similar development company called Pressman Ventures, where he's now pulling the same thing. He's recommended *Holiday* to them as a location for a resort, centering in this area around the golf course." Richard tilted a map toward them with a large circle around the course and the neighboring properties.

"No!" Stella exclaimed, and she leaped up to her feet and stood over Richard with a menacing glower. "He would never do something like that."

"Stella," Cassie said, rising from the rocker to stand at the woman's side, "just hear him out."

"Hunter wouldn't," Stella insisted, but Cassie could sense the change in her tone. She was no longer insisting out of anger. Instead, she seemed to be pleading for this not to be true. "He couldn't."

Cassie helped her sit down on the sofa again, and she perched next to Stella on the armrest.

"His partner is the one who approached Millicent, and we think he's also the same guy who went to Tameka Plummer and made the offer on Cassie's place."

"You're saying that's why Hunter came to Holiday over Christmas?" Millicent asked.

"That's what I'm saying," Richard replied.

"Let me see that," Stella nipped. She yanked the folder from Richard's hands.

As she looked over the documents, Stella's expression remained rigid and unyielding as she flipped through page after page. But then something on the paperwork caused her face to drop, the sternness melting away to disappointment and then devastation.

"What is it, Stella?" Millicent asked.

"Never you mind," she said, her embers weak.

"Stella."

"Bristol Banks," she said.

"The name on the sale of the Pennsylvania properties," Richard clarified.

"He's the person who came to my home and tried to coerce it right out from under me," Stella told them.

Cassie and Richard exchanged glances. Stella's disappointment was palpable, as real and sour as lemon rinds.

"You're certain my Hunter made the suggestion of Holiday?"

"As certain as I can be. That's how it worked the last time around, anyway."

Tears beaded up in the corners of Stella's dark eyes, and she focused on something well beyond the windows through which she stared.

"He told me he came to Holiday for Christmas so I wouldn't be alone, because he missed me. He said what a charming little town I lived in, how he understood why I'd stayed for so many years and loved it so much. But then he even suggested maybe it was time I thought about leaving, coming up to New York and taking one of those doggone retirement apartments so I could be close by."

"We're so sorry, Stella," Cassie told her. "After he found this information, Richard agonized over how to tell you. We didn't want to hurt you, but we thought you needed to know."

Cassie offered her the tissue box, and Stella pulled one out and dabbed her moist eyes. When she was through, she angled her head toward Richard and said, "Why have you been meeting with Smitty over at the golf course and driving around the perimeter all the time if you're not the one buying up the properties? Elaine Gilbert saw you parked over there, at the edge of the golf course, a half dozen times."

Richard glanced at Cassie, and she nodded. It was time to tell his secret.

"Ever since I heard that Smitty went into foreclosure," he admitted, "I've been dreaming about buying the golf course and refurbishing it."

Stella grimaced. "Just the golf course?"

"Just the course."

"Never the houses around it?"

"Never that."

Millicent tapped her heart and let out a nervous little laugh. "Oh, my goodness."

"Why didn't you tell anyone?" Stella inquired.

"I wanted to find out who I was up against," he confided. "I'm not a wealthy man. My hope was to get the golf course before it went to auction, but when all this corporate interest developed, that just wasn't possible any longer."

"Oh, Richard." Stella let out a rolling groan before smiling at him through a well of tears. "I haven't been very nice to you. When Bristol Banks threatened me and I thought you were behind it—"

"Wait a minute. He did what? He threatened you?"

"When he told me why he was knocking on my door in the middle of supper, I gave him what-for. I told him that my home was not for sale. I tried to close the door, but he dug in his heels and put his foot in the jamb. He looked at me just as mean as you please and said I'd be good and sorry if I didn't entertain the idea of leaving Holiday."

"He was very menacing when he came to my house, too," Millicent told them. "He didn't put his foot in the door like that, but he was as slimy as that king snake."

Cassie met Richard's scowling eyes, and she raised an eyebrow.

"I think we need to call the police and report this, Stella," Cassie suggested.

"No need," Stella told her. "Now that I know Hunter is behind this, that he's responsible for trying to put my hometown on the auction block and even going so far as having his friend threaten *me* and try to take *my* home…well, that boy is going to be running back to New York City so fast he'll have windburn."

"So no one is selling their house and moving," Richard told them.

Millicent blinked at him and tried to smile. "Except for Cassie."

All eyes centered on her, and Cassie felt a conspicuous heat rise over her.

"Don't remind me," Richard commented. "But no one else."

"Well," Millicent said after a moment, "I don't know about that. I may be."

"Millie, don't be stupid," Stella scolded. "You're not going anywhere."

"I haven't had a chance to tell you, Stella," Millicent said, folding her arms over her padded stomach. "I had a little uninvited houseguest on New Year's Eve."

"Little?" Cassie said on a chuckle.

"Not so little," Millicent said. "Six feet tall, and he scared the spit right out of my mouth."

"Six feet? What are you talking about?"

"A Florida king snake," Cassie told Stella with a grin, and she raised her hands to show her how huge the thing actually was.

"No!"

"She's been staying here with me ever since."

"The pest people are coming tomorrow, but if they don't find out how he got in, I'm going to be abandoning that house for good. In fact, maybe I'll have to buy your house from you, hunny bunny, so I'll have somewhere to live."

Richard laughed and reassured her. "We'll make sure your place is sealed up tight. Don't you worry."

Cassie's pulse was tickling the insides of both ears. She wasn't quite sure why she was so nervous, but when she nearly applied cover stick to her lips, she realized that Richard's invitation for her and Debra to come over for dinner wasn't quite as simple as she tried to make it.

She'd tried on three different outfits, each of them too dressy for a casual meal at the home of a friend, so she settled on jeans, a tailored white blouse with dark blue pinstripes, and white tennis shoes. She scrutinized herself in the full-length mirror and decided to add a watch, a simple gold necklace, and gold filigree hooped earrings. The end result didn't shout "Trying too hard!" which was just what she was going for.

Debra looked adorable in her mint green baby doll dress, with the tiny bulge in her stomach pushing softly against it. She'd curled her brunette hair and then pushed the curls upward into a high ponytail, slipping into flat white sandals to complete the look.

"I haven't seen anyone who wore pregnancy so well in all my years," Cassie told her as she pulled at one of Debra's curls and then let it spring back into place. "You're adorable, honey."

"This is okay, then?" she asked. "I don't know why, but I just couldn't decide what to wear."

"It's perfect," she reassured her daughter.

"You look nice, too. Are you ready to go?"

They chatted about the boys on the short drive to Richard's house, and Debra told Cassie about Jake's attack of nerves when he went to the door to pick up blond-haired, blue-eyed Jessica Winthrop for the seventh-grade dance.

"His face was all blotchy, and his hands were shaking," Debra said, chuckling. "You'd have thought he was walking down the aisle to say 'I do' or something."

As they climbed out of the car and headed to Richard's front door, Cassie thought that she could sort of feel Jacob's pain—although it may have been more about Debra's pending impression of Richard than anything else. She didn't know why it mattered so much, but—

"Mom!"

"What?"

It wasn't until she saw that Debra was scowling at her tapping foot that Cassie even realized she was making the motion.

"Are you nervous or something? Stop thumping your foot like that."

Cassie forced an enormous, radiating smile to her face as the door opened and Richard greeted them.

"Right on time," he said, and he gave each of them a kiss on the cheek as they passed. "I'm really glad you could come."

Richard led them through the living room and beyond the huge, gurgling aquarium. Cassie stopped for a moment to tap on the glass and say hello to Chi Chi and Jack. At least she *thought* that was them glup-glup-glupping at her through the glass.

A large wooden table was set up next to the pool, and the chairs around it were padded with four solid inches of foam that invited them to sit down before Richard could even say the words.

"Make yourself comfortable," he told them. "Would you like iced tea?"

"I can't believe this weather!" Debra exclaimed as Richard poured. "Just after the first of the year, and I'm sitting here with bare legs and no coat!"

"Your mother had quite a time adjusting to that, too," he told her. "She kept saying things like, 'It's Christmas, and it's 73 degrees!' and 'I can't believe I don't need my jacket!'"

They all laughed at that, and a rush of warm embarrassment coursed through Cassie.

"Richard, how long have you lived in Florida?"

"A couple of years." He sank into the chair beside Debra. "Right after retirement."

"Retirement!" she exclaimed. "You're too young to be retired."

"What he hasn't told you yet," Cassie interjected, "is that Richard is a planner. He and his late wife planned out his early retirement since they were toddlers."

Richard guffawed. "It's true," he admitted. "Hello. My name is Richard Dillon, and I'm a planaholic."

"You and my mother should get along great."

"Hey, I've really loosened up since coming to Holiday," Cassie pointed out. "I'm not nearly the regimented person you've known all your life."

"Well, I do admit that I see a change in you," Debra said. "But what was it Granny MacLean used to say? A leopard never changes its spots and a—"

"A method never finds its madness," Cassie finished for her. Shooting a grin at Richard, she explained, "My father was very structured and sensible. My mom used to say he wouldn't know spontaneity if it surprised him in the shower."

"Granny was so funny," Debra observed. "I'd forgotten how really funny she was."

"So, see? It was in my genes. I just had to let it out of the cage."

"And all it took was a little disco music," Richard said, and he and Cassie doubled over with laughter.

"What?" Debra asked them with a curious grin. "What about disco music?"

"Picture this," Richard said. "Your mother leading a whole group of geriatrics on how to do the hustle!"

"What? No way."

"Way," Richard countered. "I think that was the moment I realized she wasn't going to be predictable in the least."

"And Richard appreciates predictability," Cassie tossed in.

"There's a lot to be said for knowing what to expect," he finished.

Debra shook her head emphatically. "My mother? The crazy one in town? I don't know how to wrap my brain around that." She narrowed her eyes and stared Cassie down for a moment and then asked, "Who are you? And what have you done with Cassandra Constantine?"

"I'm sorry. Who?"

"Oh, that reminds me…," Richard began. He produced an envelope from the top of the bar behind him. "These are for you."

Cassie opened it and pulled out several glossy 4 x 6 photographs from the night of New Year's Eve.

"Oh no!" she cried when she examined the first one, her and Millicent standing at the front door of the recreation hall. They were barely recognizable beneath the big hair, makeup, and disco garb.

She passed the photos to Debra, one by one, pausing at the last one. The one he'd taken by extending the camera and snapping it himself.

Cassie and Richard. His arm was tight around her, and her head was nestled casually into the shoulder of his shiny polyester shirt.

"Mom, I can't believe this is you!" Debra cried. And then, "Wait. Are you joking? Is this Millicent next to you?"

Richard cackled, leaning over toward Debra and looking at the top picture in the stack. "She couldn't decide whether she was a hippie or a disco queen."

"You have got to make me copies of these," Debra said on a rolling laugh. "Mitch and the kids will never believe this is my mother!"

"Oh, no you don't. There will be no duplication of these photographs," Cassie declared.

But Richard leaned in toward Debra and nodded. "I'll make you some 8 x 10s."

Chapter Twenty

....

5 DOWN: Bright with joy; as if emitting rays of light

The dinner menu had been a simple one: shrimp orzo and steamed asparagus, with fresh raspberries and blackberries in vanilla cream for dessert. Cassie and Debra had seemed to enjoy it and as he poured coffees for the three of them, Richard felt satisfied. It had been a very pleasant evening, and Debra appeared relaxed and comfortable. That was all he'd hoped for.

"Do you play?" she asked him, nodding toward the piano as Richard walked into the living room and offered her a cup of coffee from the tray.

"I do."

"Would you play something for us?"

He hesitated for a moment and then lifted one shoulder in a slight shrug. "Sure. What would you like to hear?"

"Surprise me."

Richard gave Cassie her coffee, and the two of them shared a grin. He wasn't sure why, but it had been an unspoken certainty that they were both invested in the evening going well.

After placing his own cup on the coffee table, he made his way to the piano and slid across the bench in front of it. He thought for a moment and then suppressed the grin that tried to rise over his face.

A few slow, serious notes sounded very much like they were leading into something classical…but then his fingers flew across the keys into a rendition of "Night Fever." Cassie and Debra exploded with laughter, and Debra added some off-key vocals to the disco favorite as Cassie stood back, shaking her head at him and giggling.

Afterward, Cassie and Debra sat down and enjoyed their coffee while Richard played some Christmas carols, starting off with "O Holy Night."

"That's Mom's favorite carol," Debra told him.

"Mine, too," he admitted.

He couldn't help but think about how many things he and Cassie had in common, and it went far beyond Christmas carols. Even more significant were the things they didn't share—*like a love for disco dancing, for crying out loud.* She'd somehow managed to finesse him into appreciating it, despite his doubts that she could. Everything seemed more interesting, more entertaining, just…*more!* with Cassie at his side.

As he played the chorus of "The First Noel," Richard gazed at Cassie and smiled. She brushed her long bangs away from her face and nodded as Debra spoke to her softly; then she tucked her bouncy hair behind her ear and tipped her head to one side. She grinned, and it was a faint, slow smile that clung to the edges of her lips like a ray of light.

Richard played out the song and then joined them in the living room, sinking into the sectional next to Cassie.

"I've always wanted to play the piano," she said to him.

"I could teach you."

Cassie seemed to consider that for a moment, and then she asked him, "You know how suited I am to ballroom dancing?"

He grinned and then wiped the smile off his face and nodded.

"If only I were that musical," Cassie stated.

Richard snorted.

"You—" Debra closed her eyes and shook her head. "Ballroom dancing?"

"Richard's the ballroom dancer," Cassie explained. "I'm the quicksand that slows him down."

"You are the very lovely boulder determined to break my toes."

Cassie hooted. "I'm so sorry, too."

"A small price to pay for the pleasure of dancing with your mother," he told Debra. She arched a curious brow and glanced at her mother.

"Well, this has been lovely," Cassie said, "but I'm afraid we're going to have to be on our way. Tameka has an open house planned for tomorrow, and I have a lot of details to attend to before then."

Richard's heart dropped an inch or two. "Really. Is there anyone interested?"

"I guess we'll know tomorrow."

"Best of luck."

"Thank you, Richard," she said as she rose from the sofa. "And thank you for dinner."

"It was wonderful," Debra told him. Then she crossed the room and gave him an eager hug. "And it was so nice to get a chance to know you. Thank you so much."

"I hope I'll see you again before you leave."

"I hope so, too."

He walked them to the door and touched Cassie on the arm.

"Tell Millicent to put me on speed dial," he said, and then he grinned at Debra. "It's her first night back in her house after the snake incident."

"That's what we're calling it," Cassie added on a chuckle. *"The Great New Year's Eve Snake Incident."*

"I haven't had as much adventure in my whole life as I've had since your mother has come to town," Richard told Debra.

"My mother? Adventurous?"

"She's just the breath of fresh air this town needed."

"I'm sorry," Debra said, shaking her head again. "You're referring to my mother? This woman, right here."

"Hey," Cassie laughed. "I have a fun side. You just never could see it from the glaring spotlight of *your father's* fun side."

"Richard, if you think my mom is a free spirit, my dad would have given you a stroke."

"Oh, I'll bet I would have liked him. He was a golfer, wasn't he?"

"Addicted to the game, and it drove Mom batty."

"Uh-oh. Note to self," he teased.

"Everything he did made her nuts, in fact. From the Hawaiian shirts he wore to the sucking noise he made when he ate soup. Oh, and he refused to call her by her first name. He'd always just call her *Mac*."

"Mac! Now *that* I just can't see."

"You know," Cassie said with a grin, "now that I think of it… *Richard* is an awfully formal name."

"Richard Alan Dillon," he stated with a regal tone. "What's formal about it?"

"You don't mind if I call you *Dilly* for short, do you?"

"That depends," he replied. "Do you expect me to answer?"

Debra cackled at his reply. "I can't believe this. The two of you are soul mates."

Cassie leaned in and planted a soft kiss on Richard's cheek, and he squeezed her shoulder as she did.

"Thank you again."

"Good night, ladies."

He closed the door and stood there for a long moment just staring at the grain of the wood. Then, with a flinch, he turned and crossed the house, walked outside to the patio, and sat down in the chair he'd occupied over dinner. He blew out the pillar candle that was still flickering at the center of the table then leaned back into the jade green cushion and sighed.

The underwater blue lights made the pool glisten, and a slight breeze helped pick up the rhythm of the shimmer as the wind moved in waves across the water's surface.

Richard ran both hands through his hair then propped his elbows on the edge of the table and leaned on his clasped hands.

"Now what?" he said aloud. He closed his eyes and drew his lips thin and straight. *You're not really going to let her sell her house and leave Holiday, are You?*

It was at that moment that Richard Dillon realized he had no interest in any segment of the life that he'd been planning for so many years…life in Holiday, refurbishing the golf course, taking up sailing…. None of it held any draw whatsoever for him if Cassie Constantine wasn't a part of it.

He blew out a sigh and rubbed his temple then repeated the sentiment again.

"Now what?"

✳ ✳ ✳

"Did you know Richard before you came down this time?"

Cassie came to a stop at the traffic light as she shook her head. "No. We just met."

"Funny."

As she eased her way through the intersection, she tossed a quick glance Debra's way. "Why is that funny?"

"You two seem like you've known each other forever. In fact—" She stopped herself mid-sentence and just shook her head.

"What?"

"Well…"

"Debra."

"Well, I don't think I remember you being that comfortable with Daddy."

Cassie sighed. "Don't be silly. Your father and I just had a different dynamic, that's all. There's no comparison in my relationship with Richard and my twenty-five-year marriage with your father."

"I guess, but…"

"But?" Cassie pressed. "Debra, does it bother you that I've struck up a friendship with a man?"

"Not anymore," she replied. "Now that I know Richard somewhat, I'm not bothered at all. What does bother me is that you could find someone who obviously suits you so well and you'd be willing to walk away from him. It seems a little cavalier to me, and I never saw you as cavalier."

"What a thing to say." Cassie's heartbeat thumped as she pulled into the driveway and fumbled to press the button on the garage door opener.

"Yeah, I'm sorry. The truth can kind of rock your world sometimes, can't it, Mom?"

You have no idea.

Once they were inside the house, Debra announced that she was going to make some tea. "Would you like a cup?"

"Please. I'm just going to tidy up my bedroom so I won't have to worry about it in the morning."

But Cassie plopped down on the edge of her bed when she got there, and she chewed on Debra's words. She'd been almost accusatory in her tone. She'd called her *cavalier*!

Oh, Lord, what am I supposed to do here? Abandon my whole life in Boston for a man I've just met? Is it cavalier to want to be cautious? I've already had a quarter of a century with a wonderful man. What are the odds I'll live out another quarter of a century with someone just as wonderful?

She entertained herself for a moment with thoughts of Richard Dillon the serial killer and Richard Dillon the bank robber but then brushed away the fantasies along with the bangs in her eyes. She popped up from the bed and straightened the items on the dresser, pushed shut the drawer that was open just a smidge, and scurried into the bathroom to run a Clorox wipe over the counter and sink.

Cavalier. I am not cavalier about love or anything else, she reassured herself. *And I'm not going to give it another moment's thought. I have a house to sell tomorrow.*

Cassie shed her clothes and dropped them in the hamper, replacing them with cotton flannel pajama pants with clouds on them and a sky blue T-shirt that was two sizes too large. When she joined Debra at the dining room table moments later, the spicy scent of chamomile tea tickled her nose.

"I used honey instead of sweetener," Debra told her, filling her cup from the ceramic teapot. "Just like you used to make for me."

"It's been a lot of years since we were alone together for a cup of tea," Cassie replied. "I'm so glad you came down on your own."

"It seemed like the perfect time to spend some time with my mom," Debra said with a smile. "I've missed you so much. Especially since I got the news about this baby, for some reason."

"It took you by surprise. A woman always wants some comfort from her mom when she's taken by surprise. But you know, honey, you are such a spectacular mother to the boys. That's not going to change with this little one."

"Mitch and I were just so settled in our family. Two kids, a mortgage, and a minivan. And then…*pow*!"

"Change can be a good thing sometimes," Cassie assured her. "Your father used to tell me that all the time."

"Any chance you could listen to him now?"

Cassie raised her eyes and met her daughter's concerned gaze.

It caught her off guard, and she lowered her teacup to rest on the tabletop.

"What's that supposed to mean?"

"Consider a change," she suggested. "Haven't you had enough of walking around in the past? Clunking around in that big old house you shared with Daddy?"

"Oh, Debra—"

"Mom, all I'm saying is…maybe it's time to consider a change."

Cassie grimaced and turned her attention toward the sliding glass doors and the dark water beyond them.

"Change can be a good thing sometimes," Debra quipped, and Cassie looked back at her daughter and lifted one corner of her mouth in a quiet smile.

"Don't you need your rest?" she teased. "You're sleeping for two now, young lady. Get out of my hair and go to bed."

"Yes, ma'am," her daughter replied, and she took her cup of tea with her as she left the table.

Debra backtracked to plant a quick kiss on her mother's cheek. "I love you," she said in a whisper.

"Yeah, yeah," Cassie called after her as Debra headed down the hall, and she heard her daughter giggle as she closed the guest room door.

It started off as another restless night for Cassie, and two hours after she'd crawled into bed, she crawled out again and ran a hot bath in her garden tub. As she soaked in Warm Vanilla Brown Sugar–scented suds, she propped her feet up on either side of the faucet then piled her hair on top of her head and fastened it there with a large-toothed clip.

With a heavy sigh, she tilted her head back against the edge of the tub and appreciated her bathroom makeover. It would be difficult for her to say good-bye to such an ideal and inviting getaway, and she wondered if she would ever be able to recreate it in her house in Boston. She'd established a sort of relationship with this room, and she loved it from the top of the clear glasswork hanging in the high window to the bottom of the blue, wine, and gray mosaic tiles.

Cassie dipped her favorite scrub mitt into the hot suds and then gently rubbed her arm and shoulder. She was almost envious of the person who would buy the place, hopefully at the open house in the morning, because they would have the pleasure of unwinding in this spa-like haven she'd created for them.

In fact, this might be my last chance to soak in this tub, she realized. At that thought, she wished she'd lit some candles or something.

Sleep was tucked into bed and waiting for her when she returned to the bedroom. The next thing she knew, the alarm was going off and it was time to get up and greet the day.

Tameka brought cookies and muffins from a bakery near her office, and Cassie helped her by arranging them on a platter while she waited for Debra to get dressed and join them. She made one last lap around the house, making sure that everything was in order, and then the two of them dropped off Sophie at Millicent's before they all headed out for breakfast…while strangers wandered around inside, gawking and evaluating and considering.

"I almost hope no one is interested," Millicent admitted to Cassie over scrambled eggs and jellied toast. "I just hate the idea of you packing up and leaving Holiday for good. I'll miss you so much, hunny bunny."

"I'll miss you, too," she admitted. "And I never thought I'd see the day when I would utter these words, but I'm going to miss that house and this town so much more than I ever thought I would."

"Yes," Millicent nodded seriously. "No snakes or gators or giant water bugs."

Cassie chuckled. "And no more little lizards with the"—she formed a sack under her chin with both hands, making a strange noise as she made it pulse—"the big weird things under their necks."

"No more Hootzes taking down your dock or disco dancing with a bunch of old geezers."

"Ohhh," Cassie moaned, pulling a sad face and pushing out her bottom lip. "No more rumbas with you."

"No more stomping on my toes," Millicent added happily. "I have to admit, I won't miss that."

"Richard said you stomped on his toes, too, Mom," Debra pointed out. "I see a pattern here."

Millicent gasped, her big eyes round and her doughy features pulled taut. "Hunny bunny, no more Richard."

Cassie's eyes darted to her plate, and she pushed her eggs around with her fork. "I'll miss everyone here, including Richard."

She thought she caught an exchange of looks between Debra and Millicent out of the corner of her eye, but when she glanced at one and then the other, there was no sign of it.

"I heard it's tango day again," Millicent announced. "Either of you two up for that?"

"I forgot all about it," Cassie admitted. "I'll have to pop in to the house and change my shoes."

"Mom, you can't go inside when an open house is in gear."

Cassie lifted her foot out from beneath the table and wiggled her toes. "I'm wearing open-toed sandals, Debra. I might need these toes at a later date, so trying to dance in them may not be the best idea. Besides, I'll just run in for a second, grab my shoes, and run out. They'll never know I was there."

"While seeing who's looking at the house," Debra pointed out.

"There's also that."

"Seems like the real danger," Millicent mumbled without looking up from her plate, "would be if I had to wear the open-toed shoes."

Cassie and Debra exchanged grins and then Millicent glanced up at them, seeming surprised that she'd spoken the words out loud. Debra snickered first, and then all three of them let out laughs that rolled over sniggers and snorts.

"Come on, then," Millicent said, drying her eyes with the corner of her napkin. "Let's go fetch those shoes."

They had to park at the corner for all the cars gathered for the open house. Millicent and Debra waited in the car while Cassie sauntered down the block and up the driveway.

An elderly couple nodded and greeted her as they exited the house, and Cassie found herself hoping they weren't about to become the new owners. With the pronounced limp she had, there was no way that particular blue-haired woman was going to be able to enjoy the garden tub in the master bath.

It would take her husband and several of the neighbors to get her on her feet again after one good soak.

A younger couple with a toddler stood in the kitchen. The husband inspected the cabinets while the wife allowed their young son to pull a large plastic truck on a string across the new stone floor.

No, Lord, not them either. Please.

She made her way down the hall and noticed a middle-aged couple in the guest room, and the woman was running her hand along the edge of the door.

"Hollow doors, Milton? Do you think these are hollow?"

Not as hollow as your— Cassie cut herself off. *Well, that wasn't nice.*

Just as she produced a pair of walking shoes from the closet and shut the door behind her, Cassie turned around and bumped into a tall man with a funny little pencil-thin mustache and a face like a boxing glove.

"Oh, I'm so sorry!" she exclaimed. "I didn't see you there."

"You're not stealing those, are you?" he asked her.

"Certainly not," she replied. "They're mine. I own this house."

"Yes, she does," Tameka interjected from the doorway. "And the owner *is not supposed to be here* during an open house."

"I know, Tameka, and I'm sorry. We decided to go over to the rec hall for a dance lesson." Cassie looked at the stranger standing much too close to her and added, "It's tango day at the senior's class."

"Certainly you're not a senior," he said in a slow, slithery voice that reminded Cassie of how a serpent would sound if it spoke.

"I'm well on my way to being a senior," she said, folding her body awkwardly in an effort to navigate around the immovable man. "I'm sorry, Tameka. Consider me gone."

"I'll walk you out," Tameka answered. She turned to the man and smiled. "Take your time looking around, and let me know if you have any questions."

Once they exited the house, Cassie stopped on the sidewalk and pinched her nose and lips at Tameka. "Don't sell my house to him. He's creepy."

"What do you care? Creepy money still spends."

"Have you gotten any other interested parties?"

"Half a dozen of them, Cassie. I can almost guarantee you there will be at least a couple of offers resulting from today. By the way, I had James take down the Christmas lights and store them in the garage."

Cassie glanced at the palm tree and noticed that the flamingos were gone, as well.

"Where are Mutt and Jeff?"

"Who?"

"The pink flamingos."

"Oh, they're stowed in the garage, too."

"You don't think they gave the place personality?"

"The kind of personality you avoid at parties," Tameka cracked. "You hate those things anyway."

Cassie knew she was stealing the argument from Zan, but she mumbled, "They're *kitschy*."

"Mm-hmm. Go dance the tango, and call me afterward so we can decide which offer you're going to take."

Cassie's heart fluttered a little, and she nodded and waved as she inched her way down the driveway.

"Oh, Cassie, by the way," Tameka called after her, "remember that young girl with the tattoo and the nose thingy down at the pizza place?"

"Vanessa?"

"I'm not sure. I ran into her over there yesterday, and I guess she remembered me having lunch with you in there. Anyway, she asked me to tell you that she's staying in Holiday for the summer. She said you'd know what that meant."

Cassie grinned and nodded. "Thanks, Tameka. Talk to you later."

Cassie recalled her conversation with Vanessa as she made her way up the street toward her car and swung her shoes by the laces. She was so pleased that something she'd said had encouraged Vanessa to follow her father's advice and stick around for the summer.

"So? What's the feeling like inside?" Debra asked her. The shift in subject took her right back downward. "Any takers?"

"We'll see."

Her spirits were dampened considerably toward dancing as well, but Cassie trailed behind Millicent and Debra as they walked in the door. The lesson was already in third gear, but Richard beamed when he saw them, and he immediately made his excuses to Maureen and headed straight for Debra, grabbing her by the hand.

"Baila conmigo, hermosa chica?" he asked with a gallant swagger.

"Mi placer, señor. Gracias."

And the two of them moved right into a tango, straight across the center of the floor. When they reeled around and headed back, Richard called to Cassie, "She's a fantastic dancer. Are you sure she's your daughter?"

Debra giggled, and they spun around and headed off again.

Millicent tugged on Cassie's arm. "Get your shoes on so we can dance!"

Cassie worked her way around the edge of the dance floor and sat down on one of the metal chairs along the wall. As she kicked off her sandal and stepped in to her other shoe, a sudden and overwhelming urge came upon her. Despite the fact that it was neither the time nor the place for some sort of religious experience, Cassie's heart was consumed with the need…to pray.

I know it's been a long time, Lord, she thought, looking around in a clumsy attempt to hide the fact that she was thinking straight up to God. *A really long time. And I'm sorry about that. But…please…I really need You right now. The sadness that's coming over me about giving up the house in Holiday—I just don't understand it. What's going on with me?*

Cassie clutched her shirt just over her heart and winced. Then she tossed the shoe she was holding to the floor and bowed her head.

I remember a time when I used to talk everything over with You, from what I was making for dinner to the pain in my right foot when I'd run. And I would feel You speaking to my heart. Remember that? Can You just take me back there, Lord? Just for a moment? Please talk to me the way You used to. Tell me how to rid myself of this awful pain in my heart at the idea of—

Richard plopped down in the chair beside her, completely unaware that he was interrupting a very private moment. "I thought Millicent deserved a decent partner for a couple of steps," he teased. Cassie looked up and caught a glimpse of Millicent and Debra tangoing their way across the room. "It's only fair."

Cassie tried to smile, but it didn't quite make it up and over her face.

"What's going on?" he asked her with a tenderness in his voice that gave her a pinch.

"I just came from the open house," she told him earnestly. "Tameka says there will be more than one offer."

"That's…good. Right?"

"Yes. It is."

Richard knelt in front of her and tightened the lace on her shoe. "Then what's that face about?"

"I don't know," she admitted. "It was the strangest thing."

"You don't want to leave." He said it with such confidence that Cassie didn't know how to reply. She just sat there for a moment, her mouth forming a lazy little O. "Am I right?"

"Kind of."

"So don't."

"It's just that I put so much work into making the house what I would like to live in. And now I have to hand it over to someone who is never going to appreciate it the way I do."

"So stay."

"There was this one woman with a bum knee, and another one that let her son scrape up the kitchen floors with his tow truck…"

"So keep the house, Cassie."

"And I just walked out of there feeling so…so…"

"Cassie," he stated. She jerked her attention toward him. "Keep the house."

"I can't do that, Richard."

"Why not?"

"I have to go home. I have a home there…and friends. And I have to work."

"You'll come to work for me," he said, and then he stood up and smiled at her. "I'll need someone to help me run the golf course."

She jumped to her feet and waited. "You… Did you… Is it a…"

"Done deal. I sign the paperwork this afternoon."

"The golf course is yours?"

"You'll never believe who helped push the deal through."

"Who?" she exclaimed.

"Stella Nesbitt. It turns out she's very close friends with Barney Lipton, the gentleman at the bank handling the foreclosure sale."

"You're joking."

"Nope. He called and asked me over to his office this morning."

"Oh, Richard," she said. Cassie slipped her arms around his neck. "I couldn't be happier for you."

"Then come to work for me."

"Richard."

"Cassie," he mimicked. Then he turned serious. "Don't leave."

She folded in half and sat on the edge of the aluminum chair. "Do you have any idea how tempting that is?"

"Good!"

"But I can't just pick up my whole life and move down here for someone I barely know." Cassie's heart was pounding so hard that it made her ears ache.

Richard sat down in the chair next to her and touched her hand. "I'm not proposing marriage to you," he said softly. "I'm proposing that we take the time to see what this means, and we can't do that if you sell your Holiday house and go hibernate in Boston."

She looked up at him, her eyes misted with emotion as she clutched the seat on either side of her.

"I know you feel it, too, Cassie. *I know you do.*"

Finally, she nodded. "I do feel it, Richard."

"Then don't walk away before we find out what it means."

Cassie rocked on the chair, still clutching the seat, her eyes closed for a long moment. And then she opened her eyes and one lone tear escaped and cascaded down her cheek.

Richard wiped it away with two fingers; then he lifted her chin with them and smiled at her.

"I can't stay here on the hope that something will develop with a person I hardly know, Richard."

"No, you can't," he said. "But I'm not asking you to stay here for me, Cassie. Stay in Holiday *for you.*"

Cassie bit her lip and stared into Richard's eyes. It had been a very long time since she'd done much of anything just for herself.

Stay in Holiday, just for me? she considered. *Leave Boston behind for tropical weather, pink flamingos, and the chance to run a golf course instead of a law firm?*

Cassie couldn't think of anything more absurd.

Epilogue

....

14 ACROSS: One who accompanies; helpmate

Richard clutched Cassie's hand in his, and he lifted it to his lips and planted a kiss on the center knuckle.

"You look so beautiful," he told her. Cassie beamed back at him. "Any regrets?"

"None. I'm really happy that I'm here," she admitted. "I'm not sure when I fell in love with Holiday and the people in it, but it happened."

"So you're in love with the people of Holiday," he said, mulling over the words. "Any *Holiday-ite* in particular that you love?"

Cassie chuckled and squeezed his hand. "All right, Richard, I love you. Okay? Are you happy now? I admit it. I love you."

"I *am* happy now," he confirmed.

"It doesn't change anything, though," she warned him. "Just because I love you, it doesn't mean that I'm going to be giving up anything for you. It's much too soon for that. I want to make sure you get that."

"Oh, I get it," he conceded. "You are an independent woman, with your own life."

"That's not to say I won't share that life with you, Richard, but I'm not going to hand it over to you completely. You get that, right?"

"Yes, Cassie. I get that."

"I mean, just because I love you…that doesn't necessarily point to a full surrender of my independence quite yet. Or maybe ever. You understand what I mean, don't you?"

"*I do*, Cassie."

"Not yet, Richard," Pastor Sullivan interjected. "Be patient. That comes later."

Richard and Cassie shared a smile and stepped up to the flower-draped altar before them.

"We are gathered here today, before God and the good people of Holiday, Florida, to join two of their own, this man and this woman, in the holy state of matrimony," he told the three dozen or so people in the pews behind them.

Cassie smoothed the slate blue taffeta skirt with her palm and then turned around and handed her bouquet to Rachel.

"If anyone here has good reason to object to a union between Richard and Cassandra, let them speak now or forever hold their peace."

Richard's hand jerked up toward Cassie's face, and he placed one finger over her lips.

"Not a word, my love. Not one single word."

25th Anniversary Cassie Puzzle

VIBRANT

ORDERLY

DYNAMIC

NATTY

STUTUT

RADIANT

MEMORABLE

EXCEEDS

COUNSELOR

FLAWLESS

AUTHENTIC

GLORIOUS

ONEOFKIND

SEDUCTIVE

COMPANION

PASSIONATE

BREATHTAKING

EXQUISITE

CLEVER

FIERY

PROFOUND

Want a peek into local American life—past and present?
The *Love Finds You*™ series published by Summerside Press
features real towns and combines travel, romance,
and faith in one irresistible package!

The novels in the series—uniquely titled after American towns with unusual but intriguing names—inspire romance and fun. Each fictional story draws on the compelling history or the unique character of a real place. Stories center on romances kindled in small towns, old loves lost and found again on the high plains, and new loves discovered at exciting vacation getaways. Summerside Press plans to publish at least one novel set in each of the 50 states. Be sure to catch them all!

Now Available in Stores

Love Finds You in Miracle, Kentucky by Andrea Boeshaar
ISBN: 978-1-934770-37-5

Love Finds You in Snowball, Arkansas by Sandra D. Bricker
ISBN: 978-1-934770-45-0

Love Finds You in Romeo, Colorado by Gwen Ford Faulkenberry
ISBN: 978-1-934770-46-7

Love Finds You in Valentine, Nebraska by Irene Brand
ISBN: 978-1-934770-38-2

Love Finds You in Humble, Texas by Anita Higman
ISBN: 978-1-934770-61-0

Love Finds You in Last Chance, California by Miralee Ferrell
ISBN: 978-1-934770-39-9

Love Finds You in Maiden, North Carolina by Tamela Hancock Murray
ISBN: 978-1-934770-65-8

Love Finds You in Paradise, Pennsylvania by Loree Lough
ISBN: 978-1-934770-66-5

Love Finds You in Treasure Island, Florida by Debby Mayne
ISBN: 978-1-934770-80-1

Love Finds You in Liberty, Indiana, by Melanie Dobson
ISBN: 978-1-934770-74-0

Love Finds You in Revenge, Ohio by Lisa Harris
ISBN: 978-1-934770-81-8

Love Finds You in Poetry, Texas by Janice Hanna
ISBN: 978-1-935416-16-6

Love Finds You in Sisters, Oregon by Melody Carlson
ISBN: 978-1-935416-18-0

Love Finds You in Charm, Ohio by Annalisa Daughety
ISBN: 978-1-935416-17-3

Love Finds You in Bethlehem, New Hampshire by Lauralee Bliss
ISBN: 978-1-935416-20-3

Love Finds You in North Pole, Alaska by Loree Lough
ISBN: 978-1-935416-19-7

Love Finds You in Lonesome Prairie, Montana
by Tricia Goyer and Ocieanna Fleiss
ISBN: 978-1-935416-29-6

Coming Soon

Love Finds You in Bridal Veil, Oregon by Miralee Ferrell
ISBN: 978-1-935416-63-0

Love Finds You in Hershey, Pennsylvania by Cerella Sechrist
ISBN: 978-1-935416-64-7

summerside
PRESS